I0724496

PROJECT CHARON 4: SWARM

PATTY JANSEN

GET FREE EBOOKS

Visit pattyjansen.com
or scan the QR code below with your phone to sign up for
Patty's mailing list. You get four series starter ebooks for free!

DID YOU KNOW?

Project Charon 4: Swarm is also available in audio. Click the
image or visit https://pattyjansen.com to find out more.

CHAPTER ONE

"EVERYONE READY?" Rae asked.

Tina looked around the group of people in the makeshift hospital room, Arkady, Yalinda and Jette and so many other regulars who had spent the days and many of the nights working on this project.

The light was low. The bluish glow from the cabinet in the middle of the group lit their faces. Under a cover of glass lay a man, or better said, a figure resembling a man. He was taller and broader than a regular person, with big, beefy shoulders. His skin was irregular, with little lumps all over, grey and mottled. His hair that used to be thick and black had fallen out in clumps and in its place grew a cover of elongated skin flaps. A row of the same flaps lined his jaw. They were all limp now, draped over each other like a curtain hanging sideways, but these flaps would later turn into moving tentacles. The further the transformation away from the human form progressed, the longer these flaps would grow.

Before he became infected, he had been a round-faced, moustachioed, friendly man when they rescued him from the pirate lab at Aurora Station. A bit goofy, a larrikin. At first, he recovered well from the ordeal. Then he murdered his girlfriend.

That was before the transformation took hold of his body. Before the sparse crew remaining on the Starfighter *Manila* had seen no option but to lock him up and keep him and the two other men locked up despite their pleading and their attempts to escape, and despite the fact that they still looked very human. But that would not remain like that for long, Tina had said.

And sadly, Tina's dire predictions had proven true. Over the months of travel, the men had transformed into the grey and monstrous creatures people called "pirates".

They'd seen it happen under their eyes. The pain, the discomfort, the degeneration of their minds that turned them into creatures that thrived on violence and possessed only limited abilities to communicate.

For the experiment they were about to carry out, the second trial of a treatment that would hopefully halt the infection, they had been forced to sedate him with a tranquilliser gun, then stuff him into a transport crate and drag him across the ship from the loading bay—where the Freeranger captain and crew had, after much pleading, allowed Tina and her group to house the men.

Now they were ready to try the treatment on him.

Vito. They should use his name. Becoming a monster wasn't his choice.

"I'm ready," Yalinda said.

She pulled her box of implements closer by the tether that tied it to the central bench. The tops of syringes stuck out of the holes in the foam that they used to stop the items floating away in zero gravity.

"Make sure the door is shut," Rae said.

One of the young lab assistants did that. Double-checking what they'd already checked.

Tina shuddered. Memories of the last attempt still haunted her nightmares.

That time they tried treating Gerry because he was the least affected. They'd wanted to run some tests on him.

They'd allowed him to wake up in the hospital to make sure he was all right, and he had become aggressive as soon as he regained consciousness.

This time, the preparation was a little more advanced.

No more fiddling around with asking how he was and letting him recover before returning him to his cage. Everything was set to complete this procedure as quickly as possible.

This time they were also locking the doors, for one, so Vito couldn't escape into the ship and disturb the Freeranger family and crew.

"Starting now," Yalinda said. She glanced at the camera in the ceiling that recorded the activity in the lab. "Experiment 3, treatment 1A."

One of the younger assistants opened the glass-fronted door to a cooling cabinet and took out a bottle with clear fluid. She placed this lid first into a machine to mix the fluid with a simple saline solution.

The machine hummed softly while it shook the bottle.

This treatment resulted from months of amazing hard work.

The infection caused a rogue strand of DNA to wrap itself around the regular DNA and resulted in mutations at the spots where the two engaged.

The treatment sought to break that bond so that the cells could expel the rogue DNA through the usual mechanisms.

They'd already achieved decent success with the cactuses and Rasa's geese, which had returned to their normal form, even if one animal still squawked like a parrot. Tina's cactuses had stopped mutating with every generation. They no longer grew leaves and no longer produced pink foamy globules.

Whether the treatment would work in people was a big question.

And they needed this to work, because the Freeranger patience and hospitality, already grudgingly given, were running out.

The Freerangers had not been happy to find out, soon after departure from Aurora Station, that the group of military women and their lame ship included this trio of damaged men.

Why didn't you say you carried these freaks on board?

Tina could still hear Clementine's voice. They had *not* been impressed.

You call us pirates, yet you bring some of those monstrosities on board our fleet?

It had been up to Tina to explain that these three men were former crew members who had been deliberately infected by the pirates.

Why? Clementine had wanted to know.

Yes, why would anyone want to look like a warty toad? Even if it could cure diseases and you might live a very long life, what was the point of such a life if it meant living with a diminished mental capability?

Tina had struggled to explain, because she wasn't sure herself.

Even after meeting Dexter, she wasn't sure she understood the point of transforming people. To create an army to fight for whatever aims Dexter supported these days, she guessed? Although that sounded like a cartoonish plot pulled from B-grade movies. Pirate soldiers weren't terribly loyal and often ended up fighting each other.

Her jumbled explanation hadn't convinced the Freerangers, a proud and independent people.

They had been even less impressed when, during the previous trial, Gerry escaped into the ship and caused havoc in the storage room. It had been hard enough to recapture him.

Clementine wanted all three men killed.

But if they did that, and it was easy to see where the Freerangers came from and to agree with their stance, they wouldn't have any subjects for medical trials.

And these men didn't deserve that. Their predicament was not their fault.

Tina couldn't afford any more mishaps.

Rae started the other preparations. She slid the glass off the cabinet and turned down the sedative that was being pumped into Vito's body. She detached the drip and attached the bottle of precious medicine that Yalinda handed her. Then she attached it to a clear tube and clipped the end of that onto the cannula in Vito's arm.

"It's done," Rae said, her voice soft.

The fluid in the bottle took a bit under half an hour to disappear.

Rae then detached the empty bottle and attached another one with plain saline fluid. She'd take the drip off once he was back in his cage in the cargo hold.

Now they needed to wait. So much hope rode on this attempt.

How long it would take before the success or otherwise became apparent was anyone's guess.

The geese had started behaving like proper geese again almost immediately, even if it took many weeks for the colourful feathers to fall out.

They would now need to transport Vito back to his prison, and one of the young assistants would observe him day and night.

Rae pulled the blanket back over him. She was pulling out the straps to restrain him when a small shudder went through Vito's body.

Yalinda said, "Watch out. He's waking up."

She quickly did up the straps around his wrists.

Rae dialled up the rate of sedative delivery.

But it was already too late.

His finger twitched. His eyelids quivered. Then his eyes opened.

"He's awake," Yalinda said.

"That's OK. He's safely tied up," Rae said without looking.

Tina looked at Vito's face.

In the time since they had been forced to keep him locked up, his eyes had turned dark with almost no whites remaining.

His eyes moved as he looked around. He flexed his fingers. He tried to lift his arm, but it was tied to the bed.

Then he lifted his head. His eyes met Tina's. They were dark and fathomless. A chill went over her.

"How are you feeling?" Rae said. She was preparing a syringe to knock him out again.

His face possessed a fleshy ridge where his eyebrows used to be. It sported a row of warty growths and those now bunched together.

"Can you hear us?"

All of a sudden, Vito sat up. The restraints that were meant to hold him down popped loose. Rivets flew across the room.

"Crap," someone said.

The junior lab workers retreated. All except Rae, who still held the syringe to deliver the sedative into the drip.

Vito tried to rip the cannula from his arm.

Rae batted his hand away. "Don't do that. We are trying to make you better."

He gave a rough laugh, grabbed her by the sleeve of her suit, and pulled her towards him. His feet also popped out of the restraints.

"Code Orange!" Tina called out.

They had rehearsed this.

Arkady and Rex came forward, grabbed Vito by the arms to

push him back into the crib. One of the young Freerangers held the sheet of glass, ready to close the lid.

But struggling with Vito in reality was not the same as their practice with a sack filled with nuts and bolts.

Vito was stronger than they expected. He pushed Arkady away. Rex still held onto him. The two floated through the room and slammed into the opposite wall. In Rex's case, this produced a heavy metallic thud. The impact might have winded someone else, but not Vito.

He swung around, causing Rex to lose his grip and fly in the other direction. His foot hit a storage rack with a clang. He slammed into the wall and used his feet to push off. Vito grabbed Rex's metal arm and twisted it. No, he was going to dislodge the metal rod from the attachment point on the harness.

Tina called out, "No, Rex, let him go."

They couldn't afford Rex's harness to get damaged.

Rae called out, "Evacuate."

Rex yanked himself from Vito's grip. Vito came after him. The two raced around the workbench holdfast area in the middle of the lab. With both of them possessing superhuman strength, everything happened at lightning speed. Rex swung himself around, with each movement making his arms zoom like giant springs. But Vito was almost as quick. The transformation made men stronger and faster.

"Come over here, Rex!" Tina called out.

"I can't!" His voice rose to a panicked squeal.

A young Freeranger man pulled open a storage cupboard. He rummaged through the contents, probably looking for something to use as a weapon. But they had removed everything before bringing Vito here.

Another man yelled for everyone to leave the room. People bunched together near the door while Yalinda fumbled with the lock.

Tina was about to help her when there came the soft but unmistakable pop of the tranquiliser gun's discharge.

Rae held the weapon in both hands.

The dart hung in Vito's shoulder. He stared at it, reached up, and pulled it out. He threw the syringe to the side. It bounced against the wall before ricocheting back into the central space, trailing drops of fluid.

He still stared at it, his expression transfixed.

Yalinda had opened the door. The junior lab assistants had already gone out, and now Tina and Rae also used Vito's confusion to slip out of the room, followed by Yalinda and Rex.

They slammed the door shut behind them.

The clack of the lock shook Vito out of his funk. He made for the door and pounded his fists on the little window.

It held.

Phew.

"Do you think you got enough sedative into him?" Tina asked.

"I hope so." Rae's expression looked haunted.

A young lab assistant said, "Well, that treatment obviously didn't work."

"We'll have to wait until the sedative takes effect," Rae said. "Most likely, the treatment won't have an effect until at least a few days from now."

A voice drifted from down the corridor. "What is going on?"

It was Clementine, the Freeranger family's elder.

Oh dear, that was trouble.

CHAPTER TWO

CLEMENTINE REACHED THE GROUP, her eyes blazing with anger.

Her gaze flitted from Tina to the door that Vito was still pounding, and then back to Tina.

"What is going on here?"

"We got him contained," Tina said, trying to school her voice into calm. It never paid to get flustered in Clementine's presence, because she knew how to take advantage of the slightest sign of hesitation.

"I see. Then why is he in there and are you all sheltering in the corridor?"

"He woke up too early," Yalinda said.

Well, thanks, that was helpful. That was Yalinda's typical innocent honesty speaking. Both Jette and Arkady glared at her. But, as usual, Yalinda was oblivious to those kinds of reactions. She was honest, and kind of innocent, too. In a good way. Usually.

Clementine snorted. "Woke up too early?"

"Yes, he obviously required more sedative than we—"

"Didn't I tell you I wanted these freaks to remain incapacitated for the rest of our journey until we could transfer them to your ship?"

Yalinda flinched.

Rae came to her rescue. "We also agreed we need to conduct our experiments, and we need the men here because how else are we going to test our work? We can't do it aboard the *Manila* because we'd need to fire up all the recycling plants, which will take at least a week, and we both agreed that there were more productive uses of our time and energy."

She glared at Clementine, and Clementine glared back. Clementine's blue robes were floating in all directions in the Zero-G environment, even though the elastic bands around her arms and legs were supposed to hold the fabric in place.

Rae was much more modern, dressed in the typical formfitting one-piece uniform that was typical for Force service personnel. She had collected this set from the stores at the *Manila*. It displayed no markings for rank, because those were usually purpose-printed and there was no one who knew how to operate the printer. But the material was sleek, dark grey and sat snugly around Rae's wiry body. She looked half the size of Clementine.

It would have been funny to see them each floating at a different angle because there was no up and down in Zero-G. But there was nothing funny about this situation.

The two women had come to disagreements before. They couldn't use any more disagreements. After months of travel and no results, the relationship between the Freerangers and the women from the Starfighter *Manila* was fragile.

Clementine snorted. "I don't care. Take a week if you want. I want these monstrosities off our ship. I have put up with this for long enough."

"Put up with what? He is safely contained," Rae repeated, saying the words clearly as if speaking to a child.

"You call that safe?"

Clementine glared at the door.

"Safe inside that room. There is nothing in the room that he can destroy. We set it up like that. He will go to sleep soon, because I shot some tranquilliser into him. We're waiting here for it to start working."

But that was going to take a while longer, judging by the pounding on the door.

Clementine snorted again and changed the subject.

"If he is still reacting like this, you're obviously not getting anywhere with those cures of yours, and you're endangering my family and our home. Maybe you have a house on a planet to go back to, but none of us do. People in the family are getting anxious about these freaks."

There was that argument again. Tina jumped in. "There is no need for anyone in the family to be anxious. These men are not going anywhere."

"You agreed to keep them in the cargo hold." Clementine's voice was icy.

"That was before we found potential treatments."

"Treatments that don't work."

"We can't test our treatments while they're in their lockup in the cargo hold. We need to take them here. I have asked for a lab closer to their lockup, but we agreed that this was the most suitable place." And in fact, most rooms in the Freeranger ship were not very suitable, too open, or without connections to water or other facilities. "And of course any treatment's effect will not be immediate. Medicine takes time to work. Weeks. Months. I've explained that many times already. We have him under control and now that he's been treated, we're going to return him to the cargo hold and then we need to wait and monitor him."

"As long as that monitoring doesn't involve opportunities for him to escape."

"He won't escape."

"That's what you said last time. It's time that we made some hard decisions about this hare-brained venture. Because our patience is running out."

Tina glanced at the door. By now, the pounding on the door was definitely slackening.

Good. They could prepare to move Vito back to the cargo hold, and hopefully Clementine would calm down.

Tina floated to the door and peeked through the little window.

Vito stared back at her through the glass, but his expression was unfocused. He blinked slowly. His hospital gown hung half off his shoulder.

"He's almost ready to be transported," Tina said.

Clementine crossed her arms over her chest.

Tina added, "Just a short wait until he is ready to be bundled up."

Clementine still didn't leave. She watched while the others waited. She was still watching when they entered the room after Vito had passed out. He floated through the room with his arms flailing. The exposed skin was grey and lumpy. At least it no longer oozed fluid. His head bumped into the wall with a soft thud.

The team sprang into action. Yalinda stripped off his gown and wrapped him in a blanket. Rae attached monitoring leads. The younger assistants prepared the stretcher. Some of those youngsters were Freerangers, and they kept looking at Clementine, even while Rae attempted to tell them what they needed to do.

These were good kids. Their names were Katya and Milo. They were smart and learned eagerly. Both of them were also friendly with Rex, Rasa and Jens, the teenagers in Tina's party. But their elder's presence distracted them.

Rae told Clementine that all was under control now. But she still watched.

The team was finished. Vito was tied up, knocked out, wrapped in blankets, ready to be transported.

The two Freeranger assistants each grabbed a corner, and two of Yalinda's lab assistants took the other two corners. They manoeuvred the stretcher out the door, past Clementine, who was still watching.

Rae followed them, and when she came past Clementine, she snapped.

"Why don't you get out of our way and stop distracting us? You're keeping us off our work."

"Because I never realised just how deluded you are. There is not going to be a cure. It's a smokescreen to get us to give you a free ride. And to subvert our youth."

Oh, no, no, no, they were *not* going to enter that argument.

"Stop it." Tina held up her hands and pushed herself in between Rae and Clementine. Both women glared at her. They wanted to argue. They'd been rubbing each other up the wrong way for months.

"We made an agreement. If you want to revisit the agreement, we need to do that with everyone involved."

Rae snorted. "You're kidding. You'll allow them to backslide on our agreement? We're already so far behind with our work that—"

Tina held up her hand to stop her.

"If there is a problem, we will discuss it with all involved."

Clementine nodded. "That's right. I am not willing to risk my ship and my family for this crazy plan of yours. You heard me right. I want you to take him and the other two freaks back to your own ship. We'll take you to inhabited space as we promised, but then we're done. This was a bad deal, and I should never have entered it."

Rae said, "Oh, so you would rather these dangerous men escape into a big warship? Because that is obviously not dangerous like they might get their hands on weapons?"

"You should have thought about that before allowing them onto that ship. Anyway, if that is how you feel about it, why don't we just execute them and be done with it. We Freerangers consider ourselves a fair community, but we have a three strike law, and these hideous abominations are well past their third strike. They should face the Shipworld Mara court, and they will deal with it."

And the Mara court consisted of the oldest and most conservative members of this rambling extended family, far more traditionally minded than Clementine. No, thanks.

It was time to intervene before the discussion went seriously off the rails.

Tina said, "If you want a meeting to discuss this, we'll having a meeting. Meanwhile, I will make sure that he doesn't get out. We will take him back to the cargo hold. He will remain sedated and restrained while we transport him. What I ask from you is that you stop harassing our workers, including those from your family. You wanted greater legitimacy for your family. Education is the way. We appreciate having the assistance of these young people. Don't put any pressure on them to choose either us or you. That's not fair to them."

Clementine breathed out. Over the past few months, she had also told Tina in late night discussions that she feared for the future of the family Shipworld Mara if they didn't engage with the rest of the settled worlds. Living as reclusive nomads had suited the Freerangers this far, but times were changing.

When she next spoke, her tone was softer.

"Look, it's not easy. The shipworld council demands I do something about the danger posed by these creatures. They worry that the children have been plagued by nightmares about them. I respect your work. Honestly, I do, and you know that, but there comes a point that we have to back out of a situation that doesn't benefit us. We're not scientists or whatever, like you lot. Give me something, a result I can use to convince the elders of the council that this is going to pay off. Because we've helped you for months, and I have nothing to show them."

"This is research, and you cannot hold it to ransom. You cannot produce the results you want when your work doesn't support it. We're working on it. Science is not quick. We're already making major strides, but we're not there yet. This is biological material, and it doesn't conform to human ultimatums."

But of course Tina's words obfuscated precisely what Clementine stated: there were no results.

After months of work, they had made frustratingly little progress.

Clementine shook her head.

"I'm still going to have a hard time arguing about this in the council, because we're merchants and we need to trade. You've had this long, because things were getting too uncomfortable for us at Aurora Station and we needed to get out of the sector. Now we need to return to our regular way of life. We're not a charity. We have to live. There's either going to be a way for us to benefit from your work, but I can't see that happening, so we might stop off somewhere safe for you to go your own way. It's becoming very hard for me to reject that option in the council."

CHAPTER THREE

GO THEIR OWN WAY.

Tina had feared for a while that things were headed in this direction. The collaboration between her group and the Freerangers had not been as successful as she hoped.

She'd thought that seeing the type of work that needed to be done would make the Freerangers understand why it was important, but these people were so different and had such different aims.

After Clementine left, everyone who had been in the treatment room hung around in the corridor, looking at each other.

"Well, that didn't go down too well," Arkady said.

"All we need to do is to make sure that they understand the importance of our work and be really clear about what they can expect," Yalinda said.

"Sure. We've tried that for months," Rae said. "They're too pig-headed to understand."

Arkady glanced sideways at Yalinda, and Yalinda adored Arkady, so she pulled in her head, even if she might not understand why, because she usually didn't.

"We need a promising result to show the Freerangers," Tina said.

"Yeah," Arkady said.

The problem was what.

"How long before we get results from Vito's treatment?"

Rae shrugged. "Could be today. Could be much later. Could be it doesn't work at all."

"The real problem is that we're stabbing in the dark," Arkady said. "The enzyme blocker worked perfectly in the geese and cactuses because we could trace the history of how the infection developed and could extrapolate how it would develop in the future. With humans, we only have the data from the three men and they display different sequences, so there are probably different sources for their infections, and we lack information about a common parent or about links between the variants."

"Yeah," Tina said. "I'm sure the Freerangers wouldn't be happy if we asked them to collect a few more pirates. We only have the three."

"We can ask them to drop us at a place where we can collect additional material," Yalinda said.

"Sure," Rae said.

Yalinda looked at her with wide eyes before realising that Rae meant it sarcastically.

Poor Yalinda. She was a genuinely good research lab manager, but her people skills left something to be desired.

No one could offer solutions to their predicament, so everyone continued with their work.

The four youngsters returned from taking Vito back to his cage a while ago and were already at work.

Katya and Milo sat at a row of computers with Rex and Rasa. The four of them, with Jens, who crouched in the hub, made a nice group.

Only a few days ago Rex had told her how much he appreciated that she had allowed Rasa to stay and Jens to come, because otherwise he would have been very bored.

"Allowed?" Tina had laughed. "Rasa came with us by accident because I couldn't leave her alone, and Jens came with his father. I should have separated them?"

But other people might, and she knew that. The Federacy Force delighted in taking in young recruits and keeping them away from their families so that the Force became home for those kids in every sense of the word. Not always a warm home, either.

She'd had a weird thought about a military unit that consisted entirely of parents and their children.

Yeah. Like that was ever going to happen.

Splitting up with the Freerangers destabilised everything about the safe haven they created.

The space they had been allocated in the Freeranger ship might not be ideal, but it was very much appreciated.

All the work currently going on in this cube-shaped box depended on the comfort of its relative safety. You couldn't do research while on the run.

The research team was working as a unit.

In the bottom right corner of the room, Jette and a few computer technicians ran auto-generated DNA combinations through a simulator to create many different versions of the single-strand infectious molecule. She ran simulations that wrapped the molecule around DNA in a living creature to initiate the infection. It generated potential bonding sites that the treatments could target.

In the middle, Rex, Jens, Rasa, Katya and Milo added computer-generated treatments based on existing substances and passed the best results through a battery of tests. Arkady evaluated the results and in the top layer of the room, Yalinda and her team tried to recreate the most promising candidates in the lab.

Rae had injected one of those candidates into Vito's arm.

Tina worked in her domain next door: the greenhouse, and tissue culture room. It was not as big as the other room, but it was quiet and warm.

Fans circulated humid air and the bright lights simulated sunlight. Tina remembered cursing the heat in Dickson's Creek, but now she'd do anything to feel the sun on her skin.

She missed her shop and her quiet life at Cayelle.

She liked having only cactuses and hundreds of jars with amorphous growth for company. She even got used to the racket made by the resident geese. The birds were cured and had returned to their previous form. Eggs were once again on the menu. So while they were annoying, the geese comforted her.

It was possible to halt or even reverse the infection. They just hadn't found how to do it in humans, and time was running out. Arkady was right about having too few data points. They had already tried swabbing every smooth surface of the *Alethia* in order to collect different versions of the material that had caused all this trouble: dust that had come from a rift in the fabric of the universe.

Collecting that material had been a major undertaking, because the *Alethia* still sat in the docking hall of the *Manila*, which was being towed by the Freeranger fleet by a couple of long and stretchable tethers. To get to the ship, they'd had to EVA in environment pressure suits and take a large team with extra air tanks.

All for nothing.

They'd found nothing of use.

What other avenues could produce a shred of hope that would keep the peace between them and the Freeranger family?

Tina was restless.

The greenhouse always provided an endless amount of

relaxing work, but Tina didn't have the patience to do any of it today.

She left the lab and entered the central space of the habitat module of the ship.

The official name of the Freeranger Mara shipworld vessel was *Endeavour of Deepest Night* if ever there was a more nonsensical name.

The Freeranger ship dated back at least a hundred years, when it served in the Federacy fleet.

Once upon a time, the squat cylinder that formed the habitat and sat atop the engine chamber would have rotated, providing the crew with artificial gravity. But no one in the Freeranger Shipworld Mara remembered that this feature had ever worked in their lifetimes.

The rotating habitat normally dictated that the rooms occupied the inside of the outer wall of the cylinder. People would walk on the walls.

Unconcerned with artificial gravity, the Freerangers had connected all the rooms with beams that cris-crossed the central space. Tina thought at first that these were support struts that fortified the structure, but the Freerangers had added these.

The ship never docked at stations and never took artificial gravity from a station. The Shipworld family owned shuttles for that purpose.

A good number of old shipping containers hung off the support struts. These formed the individual cabins where the inhabitants lived.

They were the sleeping and living quarters, and the original rooms of the ship that lay around the perimeter were used as storerooms and computer hubs.

The women from the Starfighter *Manila* had been allocated one such store room for monitoring their own ship.

The women from the *Manila* almost always hung around

somewhere in this area and the surrounding cabins where they slept.

They spent their days playing games with each other, because there wasn't that much to do. The *Manila* had been powered down, and the engine had been completely shut down.

When they first did this, Finn and Thor spent some time trying to fix it, but pretty quickly concluded that the problem required time in dock and needed more parts and people than were available.

Federacy Force flight crew were excellent at keeping themselves busy during long flights, but here, on the Freeranger ship, the women lacked the framework of artificial military business—and how Tina hated being reminded of this futile activity—and were scratching the barrel for things to do, especially since the Freerangers ran a highly efficient operation and distrusted strangers.

Some women took classes to teach themselves new skills, but even their resolve was limited, and spending four months with people who didn't really want you as company was starting to grate on everyone.

Tina entered the computer room. People turned to the door. Aliz sat in front of the monitoring screen that displayed a section of the outer hull of the *Manila*. A few lines of text scrolled lazily over another screen. A third screen displayed a navigation course plotted out through space.

Tina had long since given up asking the women whether there was any news. There never was.

Similarly, Aliz had also stopped ranting at Tina about why the Freerangers weren't sharing where they were going. Yonta was no longer asking to go to the *Manila* to check the ship. She had kept morale up by proving to be an excellent singer but she hadn't held any performances for a while. Even Margot no longer wanted to go to the stores to get extra supplies.

They were worn out, despondent.

The Freerangers were in charge and didn't want to tell the women where they were going.

Everyone was bored and getting annoyed with each other.

At least in the next room, the makeshift school still operated.

Several children from about eight to thirteen attended a class given by Finn's ex Zia Partlow. It looked like they were covering the Federacy's important but complicated administration system, which was something Zia, as officially appointed director of Aurora Station, knew a lot about.

Tina held onto the doorframe and watched Zia talk to the kids. The class held only seven children, all children who had come with Arkady and the scientists and lab workers and other hangers on from Aurora Station. Jette's son Aerin was there, a lanky, pale-skinned boy who could have been Jens from a few years ago.

Zia moved around the room, looking over each child's shoulder at something they were doing on the screen. She acted with confidence, and by the way the children spoke about her during meal times, "Mrs Zia" was very popular.

In fact, everyone liked Zia, except her ex-husband, who spent far more time sulking about it than the situation warranted.

The marriage had fallen apart before there were children, but Zia was excellent with children. Federacy admin was an insanely boring, if also necessary, subject, but she got the kids to listen, even follow along and laugh at her in-jokes.

Evelle was also in the room. Having ditched her military outfit had made her appear softer, and in the past few months, her hair had also grown, because she didn't trust anyone except a proper hairdresser to cut it, and the group didn't include one of those.

When Tina asked, Evelle had said that she opted not to

wear a uniform because she said that they were running low on her size and she didn't want to scare the children.

Yeah, sure.

To Tina, it looked very much like Evelle was contemplating a life outside the military.

Evelle now came to join her because the children were busy.

"How did you go with Vito? You were going to do a test on him, right?"

"We did."

Evelle raised her eyebrows, as if she wanted to say, "And?"

"It's too early to tell. He woke up early and tried to make threats. We had to activate our evacuation routine. Clementine dropped in when we had locked him in the lab."

"I bet she was unimpressed."

"Yup."

They didn't need to say more. They'd both been present when Gerry escaped and had been subjected to Clementine's anger.

Eventually, Tina said, "Something needs to change."

"You can't always control your path," Evelle said. That was a very military thing to say. New recruits were hit over the head with statements like this. *Space is big, you'll spend a lot of time travelling, and it isn't always to places where you want to be. Oftentimes, to travel somewhere is better than not to travel at all.*

If you were in the military, other people decided for you, and it was up to you to be patient enough to wait without making too much fuss.

Tina sighed. "Maybe, but people are getting very antsy, and it doesn't look like our research is going to deliver the results that Clementine wants to hear any time soon. Our people want to know where we are going, which is only natural. The Freerangers want to know when we are going to have a result, and we can't answer that question for them. They want to continue trading, and I don't think anyone at their home base is thrilled that we are coming."

"You know that they never promised that they would take us to their base," Evelle said. "They promised they would take us to safety, and they have, but I don't think they want to share too many secrets with us. Such as where the Freeranger home base is."

Tina also doubted that, for a society based in space, there was even such a locality. Shipworlds were independent, and they travelled in small groups of ships, all belonging to the same family.

One group of lessons had finished, and the group of younger kids came in. The first group rushed out to play games in the next room, and Evelle went to help Zia with the preparations, handing out pads and setting up the projection.

Sinolese. Maybe Tina should sit in on the lesson.

Urgh.

No.

Life on board this ship wasn't quite that bad.

CHAPTER FOUR

THE CARGO HOLD in the Freeranger ship was a compartment at the back of the habitat module. It lay at the end of the docking hall, where the Freerangers kept their small shuttles they used frequently, and the ones they rarely used. For example, a very old and dusty vehicle hung there that was capable of landing on a planet. It even had a smooth base that suggested that it could land on water. The thing was so old that Tina didn't recognise the model.

The Freerangers inherited it from a ship they had bought and sold. Evidently it had barely been used since, if at all.

Like the docking hall, the cargo hold was surrounded by a heavy wall with a thick door that could be closed hermetically and the compartment depressurised.

Tina entered the code in the panel next to the door, and when the light started blinking, heaved it open. Maybe it had once worked automatically, but the mechanism had long since broken.

She braced herself against the waft of fetid air that came from inside.

The place reeked of neglect, chemicals, mould, and piss.

Back when this was a military craft, the hold would have contained supplies for the crew, and military installations and weapons. The Freerangers occupied only as little as a third of the ship's capacity. They had plenty of space to store their things and only used this space for items they didn't need and that were non perishable.

Most of the time, the area probably *was* depressurised.

The semi-darkness made it hard to see, and the cloying humidity left Tina with a desire to keep the door open, but the smell would spread through the ship, and people would start complaining.

So she closed it again.

All the women from the *Manila* complained about the poor lighting in the Freeranger ships, but this area was even worse: shrouded in semidarkness that made it almost impossible to see the entire space.

Tina needed to wait until her eyes grew used to it.

In that time, *sound* filled the space: the creaking and clanging of the ship as the engines were still pushing it to higher speeds. The soft hum of the air and water filters. And grunts and snorts, as if a large animal lived here.

Three animals, in fact.

The three cages hung in the middle of the open space, attached to one of the support beams.

Finn and two Freeranger men had made them out of maximum strength transport webbing, the type that consisted of cris-crossed thick metal bars about a hand's width apart. The sheets had come from the *Manila* where they would be used to keep heavy items in place during high-g manoeuvres.

From her position near the door, Tina couldn't see all three of the men, but she could see Milo, who observed them from the monitoring station that hung off the next support beam.

He looked over his shoulder when she came in and greeted her.

Tina pushed off and drifted over.

Milo was a very diligent kid. He had the monitoring program displayed on the screen.

Some of the other kids, like his brother Corby and some of the lab workers' kids, would play games while sitting here. But not Milo. He was very aware of his task.

"How is it going?" she asked.

Implied in that question was a second question: whether there had been signs of improvement in the past few days since Vito's treatment.

He shrugged. "It may be too early for any signs."

He had also made distinct efforts to speak more clearly and drop some of the Freeranger dialect that crew from the *Manila* or the scientists from Aurora Station found so hard to understand.

Tina knew that his peers teased him about it.

"Has Mattias been in here to take his samples?" Tina asked.

"I haven't been here every day, so I haven't seen, but the days I've been in here, he has been here to take the samples."

"What about the other two days?"

"You will have to ask someone else. I can check."

"Do that. We are lacking some samples for the last two days. We've been very busy with other things."

In fact, Tina was annoyed that there had been so much discussion about Clementine's reaction and what they should do now that the lab workers had neglected to tell her that there had been no samples from Vito for the past two days.

Tina went up to the cage but made sure not to touch the bars. She wasn't wearing gloves, and she had witnessed the men smear faeces on them.

Vito sulked in the corner.

He'd ripped off the shirt he'd worn when he was in the hospital. It was probably the rag he'd tied around the bars in the corner and that he may or may not have used to wipe his backside, or to collect poop and use it as a slingshot to launch the poop across the room.

Like a monkey.

He glared at her from under his heavy brow, two featureless black eyes that chilled her.

His grey-skinned chest heaved with his breaths, and the tentacles that lined his jaw and his arms moved like worms.

She so much wanted to see signs of improvement due to his treatment, but could see none. It might well be that in humans, improvement didn't show until much later.

She still remembered how elated she had been when the geese started shedding their coloured feathers. But their initial giddy-making successful progress had stalled.

Vito looked exactly the same to her as he had looked a few days ago.

And he seemed to be getting agitated by her attention.

He turned around, but then he faced Stan in the next cage, and Stan growled at him.

Stan was further along the path of transformation. His shoulders were broader, and the wart-like growths had spread all over his chest. His face no longer looked human—and how were these men ever going to return to something that resembled a human being?

Vito grumbled and lowered his head.

Stan pushed himself off the side of the cage, sailed through the air, and bashed into the side of his cage close to Vito.

The tentacles on his jaw and arms swung through the partition.

Vito reacted fast as lightning.

He grabbed a handful of the tentacles and pulled.

Stan yelled out, a rough scream akin to the bellow of a cow.

He hit Vito's hand so hard that several tentacles snapped off.

Stan howled again.

Globules of dark red blood floated in the air.

"Stop that," Tina called.

Stan laughed, making for her side of the cage, landing with a heavy thud against the metal bars that made the entire cage structure rattle, then shoved his hand through the bars, still holding Vito's tentacles like a bunch of live worms.

The disgusting, slimy things looked like entrails.

"Stop it," Tina said again. "Behave yourself, or there will be no food."

Stan retreated.

No one was sure if the men still understood speech, but maybe it was only the tone of voice that made them listen.

But now Stan drifted back so far that he came to the other side of his cage, within reach of Gerry.

And Gerry was something different altogether.

His skin had started to darken. It was much smoother than that of the others, without the warts. The tentacles on his jawline and the tops of his hands were longer and thicker than those of the other two men.

With time, he'd become like Artan.

And right now, he was clearly irritated.

He reached through the bars, grabbed Stan by the shoulder, and pulled him into the side of the cage with a thud.

He snaked an arm around Stan's neck and jammed him up against the bars.

Stan made a gurgling noise and tried to wrench Gerry's arm off.

"Stop it, stop it," Tina called out.

He produced a bellowing laughter.

"Let him go, right now!" a male voice called.

The noise had drawn the other monitoring person from the computer station.

This shift, it was Mattias, Jette's husband.

He drifted through the space, pointing the tranquiliser gun at Gerry.

"Let him go immediately, or you will get a dose of this medicine."

Gerry hesitated, but let go of Stan.

Mattias kept the gun trained on him until he returned to his hammock in the corner and all was quiet

Tina looked at the spot where he had held Gerry against the bars.

Two of the metal bars were bent.

"Come," Mattias said.

He tucked the gun away.

Tina floated with him across the open space to a little cubicle he used as his office. All the computers were in here.

"Has this happened before?" Tina asked.

"This is the third time in two days," Mattias said.

It was hard to remember days inside the ship because they didn't maintain a diurnal cycle, but Mattias was one of the people who kept meticulously to their time schedule.

"Is this why we haven't been getting any blood samples?"

"One of the reasons, yes, although I do have Vito's samples for you. I've just forgotten to take them to the lab, and I figured that if people really wanted them, they would come to collect them."

Why would anyone not want the samples? "Have you had a disagreement with Rae?"

"No. It's just that I can't make results appear where there are none. She can ask me again and again, but the answer won't change. I'm not seeing results. I'm not going to lie to her."

In other words: there *had* been a disagreement.

And Rae, being Rae, had said nothing about it because she knew it wasn't right, but also because she could be so secretive about the most ridiculous things.

There were signs all over that the team was starting to disintegrate, that people were losing heart, that people were too preoccupied with survival to worry about trying to find a cure for the men.

"Have you seen no signs of improvement at all?"

But before he replied, she saw the truth in his eyes. There had been no change.

He sighed, and then they were both silent for a while.

"Did you notice how he almost broke the bars of the cage?" she asked.

"Yes. We've already made a few fixes. We are going to have to sedate them in order to keep them inside."

And they didn't have the facilities to do this long-term, so basically the window in which they could find a cure was narrowing all the time. They were not going to make it.

"We're going to have to sedate them, anyway. Before they get out and start killing people."

Mattias nodded. "I'll talk to Rae about it and discuss the best way of doing it."

There was a sense of defeat in his voice.

CHAPTER FIVE

AFTER THAT EPISODE, Tina went and talk to Rae herself.

But when she got to the hospital, Yalinda informed Tina that Rae had gone to bed. Tina raced back to the cabin she and Rae shared.

Fortunately, she found Rae still awake. She had actually bothered to get changed into nightclothes. She looked tired. "You wanted to talk to me?"

"I'll be quick," Tina said. Now she felt guilty.

"Is it important?"

"I think so. I've just been to see Mattias in the hold. There was an incident, two actually. Fights between the men. Gerry bent the bars to the cage. I think we're going to need to subdue the men. I don't think there is another viable option that we can employ to keep them quiet in the long run."

"You mean sedate them?"

"Yes."

"But I don't want to sedate them, because it might further damage their bodies, and we won't be able to use them to test our treatments any more. If we have to wake them up each time we want to test something, that's going to be unhealthy for them in the long run, and won't make them suitable test subjects. We already have too few live samples."

"I don't know what the alternative is," Tina said. "They're getting dangerous."

"We should try to build stronger cages."

That was something to try, even if it would only be a temporary solution.

Tina discussed this with Finn and Thor while she let Rae catch up on much-needed sleep.

Rex and Jens were also in the cabin, although they shared a larger room with a group of younger teenagers from Aurora Station.

Thor said they should build a second wall around the cages, and he knew where to find additional sheets of webbing.

The five of them then collected this material from a storeroom and returned to the cargo hold with it.

Milo had gone to bed, and Mattias had slotted into the monitoring station.

The men were dozing, but woke up as soon as Thor took out his tools.

Stan extended his tentacles out of the cage, trying to grab anything that came within reach. He once got hold of Thor's screwdriver, but Rex slammed down hard on the tentacle and retrieved the tool.

The exchange chilled Tina.

If any of the men got out, no one in this room except Rex would have the faintest chance of survival.

And there might not be a lot of time before that happened.

Rae was also right that keeping the men sedated would severely hamper their ability to test new treatments.

Ideally, they should have more victims and have a wider range of genetic variability in the infection.

After they finished fortifying the cage, Tina had duty in the hub.

The *Manila* might not be pressurised any more, but Aliz had sent some cleaning robots into the engines to perform tasks that would be too dangerous for humans.

Someone needed to be at the controls and monitor these to make sure everything was going all right.

Monitoring the bots was insanely boring work, because the little carts moved slowly, but they usually asked a few times about whether a particular operation needed to be performed.

If there was no response, the robot would just wait.

Tina sat thinking in silence while someone else came into the room.

She had expected Finn or Thor, because they would sometimes come to talk about technical things, but it was not.

It was Zia Partlow.

Without her stiff station suit and her accompanying guards, as when Tina had first seen her, she looked much friendlier and younger than Tina had thought her to be.

"I'm glad I find you here," she said.

Tina chuckled. "I'm not going anywhere. I'm babysitting the bots."

"No, but usually he is with you or somewhere close."

He was Finn, her ex-husband.

Tina sighed. "It's not very helpful to maintain this stand-off inside the group. Our group is small enough as it is."

"I know, but that's just the way it is. And the way he wants to play it. Trust me, I know him."

Tina never had much of an opportunity to ask Finn about his previous marriage. He preferred not to talk about it, which was understandable, and she respected that. Tina didn't want to air the dirty laundry about Dexter, either.

Zia floated into the control centre.

"Anyway, I would like to talk to you about some information you would find interesting."

Tina raised her eyebrows.

Zia pulled out her screen and showed Tina an image.

"Do you recognise this?"

Tina squinted at the picture. It was a poor, pixilated image, enlarged to the point of uselessness. It showed a grey ring on a dark background. Spokes cris-crossed the ring attached to a central post.

"It is a space station," she said. "Where is it?"

"Do you recognise the station?"

"There were hundreds built according to this design," she said. "It's a typical design that gets used by the Federacy Force. This type of station houses up to three thousand people. I've lived on stations like this."

She was wondering where Zia was going with this line of discussion.

"They say once a soldier, always a soldier, right?"

"Er, yes? Maybe?" What was this about?

"Well, once a station director, always a station director. If you leave your job, certainly in the manner I did, your retain access to the systems station directors can access. One of them is the large assets market."

"Isn't that a euphemism for the place where the junkyard operators collect vast amounts of scrap metal in the form of depreciated hardware, hoping that someone will buy it?"

"That's it. It's a bit of a sleazy place to be sure, but there isn't one manager who has never bought anything there. Anyway, I was bored—as we all are... I looked at the catalogue." She chuckled. "And I saw this. This is an item that came into the database. Ex-military. A space station for sale."

Tina was getting an ominous feeling about this.

"Wait. You're not saying this is the station at Project Charon?"

"It matches, but I don't have access to the list of military database item numbers. They rarely change those when they put in the original sale notice."

And because the *Manila* was a military ship, and they controlled the ship from here, they could access some of those databases.

Tina looked. It was indeed the station.

Well, that was interesting.

The project had been decommissioned, but she had expected at least the hardware to be used elsewhere in the Force.

"Does that mean they've completely decommissioned the station? Why? It isn't that old. They could easily reuse it elsewhere."

Zia shrugged. "I don't know. At a higher level of management, strange decisions get made now and then."

That was definitely true. "Maybe we can do something with it."

Zia laughed. "Buy it?"

"I doubt our funds extend that far. But we can pretend."

Because this opened options. She had been wondering how to get additional samples of infectious material. Here was her opportunity. This discovery meant that she could retrieve the original rift dust. The Force would have emptied the station, but the dust was everywhere. Tina had even done experiments to prove that to station management.

"Thank you," she said.

"I thought it might be useful," Zia said.

"How long ago did you find out about this?"

"A few days ago."

"Why didn't you say so before? I'm sure you've heard Clementine got stuck into us."

"I did, but what would you have done with the information? We're nowhere near the junkyards. They're on the outskirts of the Olympus system. I didn't think there was any hurry."

True. But... Project Charon. She could "request" the station in the name of the Federacy Force, as she had done with the

Fireseed in the pawn shop. And then it could be their research base, and they wouldn't need the Freerangers anymore.

"Also, because he has been trying to keep me from talking to you."

Tina met Zia's eyes.

"What do you mean?"

"You know, Finn. He is always with you when you are out in public. He does that on purpose."

"That's not true, and he's been friendly and useful to me. He's a good mechanic. Look, I accept things didn't work out between you, but I'm not interested in other people's petty grievances. I have enough of those of my own. Finn is a competent worker and you are a competent worker. Your personalities don't match. None of us are perfect. Let's leave it at that."

Zia breathed out through her nostrils. It was clear to Tina that she was here partially to complain, or "warn" Tina about Finn, but she didn't want to hear it.

"How did you two even end up getting married?"

Zia pushed herself into one of the holdfast stations and strapped in, ready for the story.

Tina glanced at the clock. Her shift lasted another hour and a half before Cally would take over. She hovered in between hoping Zia wasn't going to be that long and knowing she should have spoken to her earlier.

Right now, she had no mental space for other people's personal problems. She had sorted out her own shit after her failed marriage. No one had helped her with raising Rex.

Why couldn't other people do the same?

Of course, things weren't as simple as that. And she was being a horrible, prickly, grumpy old bat.

But at the same time couldn't help being like that.

Zia started. "It's quite a long story. My parents were stationed at Olympus, and Finn and I went to the same school. I used to lead the sports teams and debating teams, and the teachers and other students wanted him on our teams, but he was never interested. He didn't enjoy the attention he was getting because of his uncle's antics. I asked him why and he said he wanted to be asked because he was good enough in sport and debating, not because of his family. And then I said with my big mouth that he would never make the teams because he really wasn't good at either sport or debating. He was very shy and didn't want to stand out and his sport skills were lousy."

That was one thing Tina had also noticed about Finn. He desperately didn't want to stand out.

"I wanted him to go away, but he didn't mind that I was rude. He tried to get better at sports. Finn and I were both at the age where boys and girls get interested in each other, and he was trying to impress me. When my parents heard about it, they encouraged me. My father was my god, so I did as he wanted me to. Finn can actually be really nice."

"I'm glad you acknowledge it. He's been extremely helpful to me."

"It was okay while we were still kids and goofing around. But when we officially announced the relationship, everyone who is anything in the world of Olympus tried to get our favour. Finn hated the attention, and I could do nothing but try to entertain guests as much as possible without upsetting anyone. I did it but hated it. I hated how he got away without doing it. I like organising big projects but would never be a society wife. I think Finn was kind of jealous of my ability to entertain these people. He is uneasy with his family. He hates all that stuff. He got involved in projects just because they made him get involved. He would rather just be an engineer. But with us together, that was never going to happen."

"I assume your family also moves in leadership circles?" Tina said.

"Not like the Kasparis. My parents' friends are the people

who get elected and appointed. Not the ones who are born into money. That's a different group of people altogether. Our relationship became extremely awkward, because I wouldn't give any of my father's lobbyists access to Finn, and Finn wouldn't acknowledge that I did all his networking for him. And I realised I disliked his immediate family. It was never going to work."

"I don't think he knows what he wants with his life. He doesn't want to assert influence over his family, and he doesn't want to be completely away from them either. He has not once used his family as a way of getting something. I'm sure he can access money, but he has not once offered me the money."

They could have paid fairly for ship supplies and docking fees that Tina had put on credit. Life would have been a lot easier and they might not even have been in the current mess.

"Finn doesn't want to take his family's money. His family bailed him out once and he swore it would never happen again."

Tina frowned at her.

"I'm sure he's never spoken about it. Don't ask, because it's an extremely sore subject. I don't even know all the details. It was about a company venture that failed."

Hmm, Tina could see how Finn was reluctant to ask for money if his track record was poor.

"All right, it's probably best this way. Money is never free. Life is not free either, and it would be great to have a sponsor for our work, but I bet the Kaspari family would want to own all the results. I'd only imagine asking them once we have a product that puts us in a strong position to negotiate. Never negotiate when you're desperate, my grandfather used to say."

No, Tina realised, it was Dexter who used to say that. Dang it.

CHAPTER SIX

EVERY TIME SOMEONE came to gossip to her, Tina realised how much she hated gossip.

She couldn't work out what Zia wanted to hear about Finn.

Was she supposed to agree with her that he was hopeless?

Finn was hopeless, in a way, but so was everyone else, each in their own way. Tina had no need to dig into and endlessly spin out other people's failures.

She spent most of the rest of her shift making wild plans, now that she knew where Project Charon was.

They could check the station for any material to use in their research.

They could buy the station and use it as a research base, seeing as it was already kitted out for that purpose.

They could ask the Freerangers to tow it to a safe place, and set up a research hub.

Yeah, like any of that was going to happen.

Perhaps the first one was most realistic, but she wasn't sure how close they would come to Olympus on their current trajectory. She had earlier decided she preferred not to go anywhere near the Federacy Assembly unless she had something to show them. The Federacy hadn't been interested in her data for fifteen years. They could do without it for a couple more years.

It didn't look like they had been interested in the rest of the research done at Project Charon, either.

So in the fifteen years since she left, the station had been returned to the Federacy Force headquarters who had subsequently decided they no longer wanted it and passed it off to a junkyard seller.

The whole thing seemed really odd to Tina, even if only that the time frame was impressive. It was a long way from the rift to Olympus.

The Federacy were not just disinterested. They had processed all those steps so quickly, one might be forgiven to think they were trying to get rid of the station.

What would have happened to all the material the project had collected over the many years of its operation?

Samples packed away in the storerooms that had been full to bursting even when she joined.

She was quite tired when her shift ended, but she knew that unless she did something about this new information, she would not be able to sleep.

So she made her way to the research lab, where people were occupied on a continuous roster.

She found Arkady at work in his cubicle, lit only by the glow from his screen. He was so deep in concentration that he didn't hear her, until she was at the door. Then he turned his head and frowned at her.

"What are you still doing here?"

"Do you have some time?" she asked.

He gestured for her to come in.

She told him about Zia's discovery. After having asked the same question she had also asked—why hadn't Zia said anything earlier—he said this was their opportunity to get the greater variety of samples they needed.

"We don't know what happened to those samples when they passed the station onto the junkyard seller," Tina said. "Surely, they wouldn't be so stupid as to leave anything sensitive on board the station?"

"You'd be surprised," Arkady said. "But even if they've removed the samples, they are unlikely to have deep-cleaned the storage rooms, and there will be dust we can collect."

"If we can convince the Freerangers to take us there," Tina said.

"Yes." Arkady breathed out deeply through his nose.

"The problem is that we have no idea where we're going. From talking to Aliz, I'm pretty sure we can still diverge from our course to go to the Olympus system, but I'm also pretty sure the Freerangers won't be too keen to go anywhere near it."

"They will go anywhere there is money to be made," Arkady said.

"Yes, but is there any money to be made in Olympus? The Federacy is pretty clear with their rules about ID and legal goods, and they have no love for the Freerangers. The Freerangers spend most of their time supplying smaller stations and semi-legal settlements. When they enter the vicinity of Olympus, someone is sure to start asking questions. So they prefer to stay away, especially when towing a Federacy warship that has not been officially decommissioned."

"Wouldn't the Freerangers want to buy hardware from these junkyards like the one where the station is?" Arkady asked. "I mean—they probably bought this ship at one."

That was a thought. If the Freerangers bought old Federacy equipment, they would have to buy it at places like the junkyards that bought and sold decommissioned hardware.

She said, "I guess we can ask them if they can take us. I just wouldn't be surprised if they said no."

She also wouldn't be surprised if the time had come for both groups to go their own way.

She and Arkady agreed that they needed to ask the others.

Tina went to sleep and still spent most of the night thinking about all the different options. She wanted the dust still hiding in the corners of the decommissioned station. The research needed it. They were not getting anywhere with just the three men.

But they still had no money to pay the Freerangers for their help. They had no product to sell, so the Freerangers might not be willing to let them go.

If the Freerangers did agree to let them go, then they'd be stuck at Olympus with a lame ship that would probably be pulled into dock at the Federacy headquarters, so they'd lose their independent research space. There would also be questions about what the *Alethia* was doing in the system.

Finn could argue that he wanted to go back home, but the *Alethia* was not his ship, and the ship was too small to have carried the group of scientists from Aurora Station. They would need to explain to authorities why they'd hitched a ride with Freerangers in a super-secret war ship.

If they did make it to Olympus, the current group of scientists would probably split up because, no matter how much they believed in Tina's project, they needed jobs to pay for accommodation, to rebuild their shattered lives and to buy tickets to wherever their families were.

It was time for some tough decisions.

Contrary to their own ship the *Manila*, the Freeranger ship had no central area where people ate their meals. The Freerangers had also given up on the concept of night and day. People kept their own times. The ship time did not correspond with any of the widely used time measuring schedules in the Federacy, and Tina and her crew had been on board for quite a while before they even figured out that the Freerangers kept a regular schedule.

The women from the *Manila* liked to keep those military

timetables, including for meals, so she met the others in one of the larger cabins at the time they had decreed to be breakfast. Just so that they could keep the cohesion in the group.

The group from the *Manila* had been allocated two large adjacent cabins for female members, and the crew had put up extensions to make a space to share meals, which Margot would prepare in the food storage area which the Freerangers called "The Store" and which held a mixture of storage cabinets and cooling units, ovens and preparation areas, all adapted to Zero-G.

Like at the *Manila*, the improvised dining area consisted of a holdfast bar with positions where people could sit. The structure—also retrieved from the stores—likely came out of a military ship. Finn and Rex had found it, and they had put it up with the help of a couple of family members of the scientists.

The seats were all occupied at the moment, as people hung in the space between the cabins, chatting and eating.

Whatever Margot had made, it smelled good.

Almost everyone was there, at least the adults, and these days Rex, Rasa and Jens were considered adults, too.

She explained that they had an option to collect much-needed additional samples from the station, and that they needed to discuss how badly they wanted to do this because it was likely to mean separation from the Freeranger fleet.

"Why can't they take us to Olympus?" Margot said.

"They probably won't," Tina said. "There is too much risk for them."

"How do you know? The Freerangers haven't been clear about where we are going at any point since we left," Yonta said.

"For what it's worth, I think we should stay as far away from Olympus as possible," Lisette said.

Yonta snorted. "Why? It would be one of the few places to get our ship properly fixed and checked out and re-join the fleet so that we can help..."

And there she stopped, because if there was one thing everyone had realised during these last four months, it was that the pirates were not some nebulous evil enemy but former friends, family and colleagues turned into grey-skinned monsters. That feeling that the *Manila*'s crew still wanted to return to Aurora Station to save the many crew members who were left behind, that was a feeling shared by everyone who had lost a family member to the pirates. It was not a simple matter of fighting the bad guys with guns and warships.

"That's it," Tina said, finishing the sentence Yonta had left open. "So we can help. We are already helping, but our working circumstances are poor, and we really need more resources and people, because we've just about reached the end of what we can do with what we have available to us."

"Okay then, I'll try to explain again," Lisette said. "These evil pirates aren't our enemies. The three men can do a lot of damage, but I very much doubt they choose to inflict it on us. If they were in their right minds, they wouldn't choose to do so."

There was no disagreeing with that.

Lisette continued, "Someone else is our enemy. These poor men are not our enemy. I have seen who the enemy is."

"Just tell us where you're going with this," Yonta said, blunt as ever. "Because if it's another one of those conspiracy theories, I don't want to hear about it."

"Yonta!" several women called at once.

Yonta glared at them.

"Well, it's true, isn't it? And I am the only person who dares to say it."

"And you are the fount of all wisdom?" Lisette said. Red spots had appeared on her cheeks.

"Lisette," Tina said, her voice soft.

"No, don't shush me, because I'm Lisette from admin and because I don't know how to handle a gun and all the ridiculous stuff I've heard people say about me."

"Lisette, it's not worth it," Cally said.

"Isn't it? Would I want to have it on my conscience that I could have warned you, but I didn't? If I warn you but you ignore me, you get to see I'm right, eventually, but I don't have to live with the fact that I could have saved you."

An uneasy silence fell.

"I think Tina's plan is excellent. I am getting sick of these lame merchants," Yonta said after a while.

Fancy getting Yonta as a supporter.

"I agree," Arkady said. "I harbour no special love for the Federacy Force, but all the best scientists and facilities are near Olympus. What is more, the people who make the decisions about the distribution of supplies, including medical supplies, are also in Olympus. The collaboration with the Freerangers was handy for us, but we're not getting anywhere with them so I vote that we go."

"And I vote against," Lisette said. "I don't want to go anywhere near Olympus. It would be suicide."

Aliz said, "I really can't see that. We will be stopped at one of the outer stations, we may be put into quarantine, and then we will be taken to headquarters for an extensive debriefing, after which they will split us up and re-deploy us elsewhere. I don't think you have anything to fear. I, however, lost a ship, and I will have to face some discipline. They will also have seen our logs and will know that we couldn't have done anything to stop being ambushed, but there will still be some unpleasant questions for me."

"I don't understand that. We are bringing the ship back, aren't we?" Jens said.

"To bring back the hardware is one thing," Aliz explained to him. "But the hardware is only one part of the ship. Sure, it's expensive, but it's only hardware. If anything has broken, it can be fixed. But if the pirates also got into the computers, which they sure would have, a lot more damage can be done. That ship contained a treasure trove of information about the Force, about the fleet, and about any planned movements."

Yes, they had discussed this before.

"However, unless we want to hide out forever, and I would very much like to see my family again one day, we will have to face the music, eventually. I vote we do it now. As I already said, the risk to most of you will not be that great."

"And I still think you're mad," Lisette said.

Aliz looked at her. "Can you suggest a better option?"

Lisette's cheeks coloured red. She said nothing.

But a small majority of people were in favour of going to Olympus, and those who were against didn't offer viable alternatives. If the ship was in better condition, yes maybe, but it was not, and it was unsafe to take it anywhere out of civilised space.

"Then that leaves us with one difficulty," Tina said. "And that is convincing Clementine to let us go without payment."

"Maybe the Federacy would like to pay them something," Gisele said.

"Dream on. The Federacy will never pay these people," Yonta said. "For one, according to the Federacy command, the Freerangers don't exist, and if they do exist, they are the same as the evil enemy pirates."

Tina and Aliz went to speak to Clementine later, who, as predicted, asked how she was going to get her money.

"If we are going to do this, we can only drop you at the edge of the system, because we're not going anywhere near that rat's nest. As soon as we put into a station anywhere in that area, they will find a way to keep the fleet in dock, and then we will be there for the next twenty years."

Tina liked to say surely she was joking, but Clementine probably knew this from bitter experience. The Freerangers had no legal status, so keeping them without arrest warrants for arbitrary reasons was perfectly possible.

Clementine didn't outright reject the proposal that she be be paid once the group got their hands on money, but it was clear that Clementine didn't hold high hopes that this would happen.

Tina suspected she rather be rid of the strangers and continue their trading than continue with their fleet hampered by a ship that shouldn't be there, en route to a locality where, if a Freeranger hideout even existed, they weren't wanted, and do all those things while waiting for payment that might never come.

They got the nod to contact the junkyard seller about the station and would then transfer to the *Manila* to be given a push into the system before the Freerangers would retreat.

That was the plan.

CHAPTER SEVEN

THE JUNKYARD MERCHANT must be doing well, because he used a system to communicate with his clients via a video link. Those weren't cheap.

Tina was with Clementine in the control centre of the Freeranger ship. It was a place where she didn't come very often. Like most other areas of the ship, it had been extensively modified. In the *Manila*, the bridge was tucked away at the top floor of the habitat module in an area closed off to most of the crew. The Freerangers had moved it to one of the container cubicles in the centre of the habitat module, close to the habitat's central axis that held the communication cables.

The cabin's walls were made of see-through material, in the places where those walls were not covered in equipment. Thick transparent tubes full of wires cris-crossed the space.

Tina hadn't been inside this cubicle often. The Freerangers were hesitant about allowing strangers in here. But in the semi-darkness of the open space within the habitat, you could see Clementine or any of the other family elders on duty here in the blue glow of the displays, as if they sat in a light-filled aquarium.

So now Clementine had allowed her to come into the ship's inner sanctum and had provided Tina with her own workstation. Over the top of the screen, she could look out of the cubicle into the habitat space of the ship where the other cabins lazily hung on their attachment points, and people floated from one to the other, sometimes looking in her direction.

She was also disturbed to find that all communication that originated in the ship scrolled over a box in the corner of the screen. There really were no secrets in space, huh?

She should tell Rex and Jens that everything they messaged to each other became visible in the control centre.

Right now, Clementine had opened a communication port, and the junkyard merchant's face appeared on Tina's screen.

His name was Paulo, or at least that was the name everyone knew him by. No one used a last name.

He was an unusual-looking man, with long straight hair and dark skin. The many piercings in his ears and his nose held bits of equipment that wouldn't normally be considered jewellery, like bits of wire and control chips. His mouth was wide and his teeth stuck out at strange angles when he smiled.

"Ah, good old Clementine. I was wondering when you would grace us with your presence again." His voice was annoyingly whiny.

What was that about never going to Olympus?

"You can't schmooze me."

"I know, but that doesn't stop me from trying. What else am I supposed to do when a pretty woman comes to my business."

"You're insufferable."

He laughed too loudly and too obviously fake.

Clementine glared at him. Her mouth twitched.

In a tone as dry as the desert at Gandama, she told him what they were after.

"We noticed you offered this station for sale. We're only

interested in the hardware and none of the usual garbage furniture the Force dumps in these structures. It says in the catalogue it's only forty years old, but come on, tell me the story, because the Force doesn't get rid of infrastructure of that age, or if they do, they'll lie about it."

While Clementine spoke to him, the conversation between Jens and Rex scrolled over the screen.

Do you notice he's wearing a control chip in his ear?

Yes, do you see you the light he is wearing in his nose?

And so on.

The scrolling text was quite distracting, even if also funny. Tina should tell the boys that whatever they said to each other would show up here, visible to anyone.

That would embarrass them.

Paulo said, "I don't understand. What, out of all people, do you want with an old space station? Have you grown soft in old age and want gravity?"

"It's none of your business, but it's not for us. I would rather die than come to your nest of conspiracy. Our companions here are looking for a place to live. The station seems ideal."

"How many extra people are you looking to house? That fleet of yours is not that big."

"You're being nosy. Tell us whether it's still available and how much or we'll find another place."

"You are really friendly today."

"There is no reason for me to be friendly. Tell me if my friends can inspect it."

"Oh, I don't know. We may need to clean it up first. We only got it recently, and it's not presentable yet."

"Paulo, presentable and you don't go in the same sentence. What are you bullshitting on about? Do you have it or not? Has there been interest from others?"

"No, no. It's just that... we got it recently and I'm surprised people are interested."

"Did it come directly from Pegasus?" Tina asked.

He frowned, as the screen's focus would have changed from Clementine to her. Maybe he'd been thinking that he was speaking to Clementine alone.

"You don't look like one of the Mara family."

"I'm not. We made an agreement with the family. We are interested in this space station, because we're looking for a place to live and settle. The Mara family suggested this might be a suitable candidate, if the price is right."

"Well, if you don't mind mess, you can inspect it. As I said, it's only come into our possession recently, and I'm not sure what state it is in. Normally, I would get my people to clean it, but if you don't mind…"

"I don't mind."

Tina was beginning to suspect that he might want to check if there was anything on board that he could sell separately, and that he didn't have the hardware or personnel to do this before the Freerangers arrived.

She asked, "My records say that the station was abandoned by the Federacy Force over ten years ago. Who brought it to you, and where has it been in the meantime?"

"The Federacy Force takes a long time to decommission their things. They need to take all the secret stuff out of the ships, and they always leave lots of it." He laughed.

Tina gave a forced chuckle. She couldn't imagine that the Federacy Force would be so sloppy, but on the other hand it wouldn't surprise her.

"There are other people who have expressed interest in the station. I suspect they think the Force may have left secrets. I think it's just a very nice medium-sized station for a group of people to live independently. Like merchants. You said you were merchants? I can also arrange a towing service."

"We'll talk about that with the next step. We want to see it first. We'll be bringing engineers to check out the structures.

According to my records, this station has been abandoned for close to ten years."

He gave her a sharp glance. She might just have warned him she had been in the military and that he better watch his words. His eyebrows rose. He looked like he was in the communication room of a ship without artificial gravity. His hair was flying at strange angles. She would have thought that he'd have his base on a nearby asteroid.

"So. Can we arrange an inspection?"

"Sure. I would need your details, a bond or guarantee and I can give you a passcode."

Reluctantly, Tina had to settle on a share of the *Alethia* as a bond, because they had no money and a large secret warship would not make a good exchange, because Freerangers weren't supposed to have a ship like that.

Now all they needed to do was get in and out, collect the samples, and make sure everyone went across to the *Manila* safely, so that the Freerangers could cut the ship loose and they could limp into one of the system's space stations. Easy.

CHAPTER EIGHT

"IS THAT IT?" Finn asked.

Tina peered at the murky projection on the screen. It was hard to make out recognisable shapes in the darkness of space, and the beam of light that came from their small shuttle cast only a small puddle of light on the enormous structure outside.

A tangle of metal tubes and support struts filled the entire front view screen. It would fill the screens on the sides as well, if it wasn't for the intense darkness. Big metal tubes and connecting structures all corroded with the black stuff that stuck to any surface exposed to deep space for any length of time.

"Yeah. The map says that it's it," Tina said.

She again checked the plain three-dimensional map given to her by "Paulo", the merchant who owned this giant junk yard. There it was, "Item P31: complete functional space habitat. Price to be negotiated".

Nothing about the listing mentioned the exact nature of the stock item. The merchant's catalogue even mentioned that there were "many other items included in this deal".

She hesitated to say too much about their discovery while within earshot of the junkyard merchant.

Either he or his people were sure to be listening in on their conversation.

She didn't trust Paulo. Even through the vid link, he looked sleazy, acted sleazy, kept winking at her, and she didn't like his smooth talk and unsubstantiated claims. He called himself "the biggest second-hand hardware seller in all of settled space" and he dealt with superseded military hardware "all the time".

The funny thing was that Tina hadn't mentioned they were looking for old military items, and the catalogue, sparse with information, said nothing about it.

Oh, he knew.

And he sure as hell didn't sell an entire space station every day, especially not to private people.

The story she had fed him—that the group planned to break away from the Freerangers and wanted their own place to live—only went so far. Everyone knew Freeranger families lived in tight-knit groups in ships. They didn't know how to live in stations. They weren't the type to settle. Tina and her small group hadn't even declared a craft big enough to tow the station to another place.

The merchant was suspicious, but hopefully he wouldn't figure out why they were here. Hopefully, he wouldn't ask questions about the giant war ship that shadowed the fleet like a silent ghost. Hopefully, no one else would find out about it, either.

"Are there any reports on the condition of the interior?" she asked the shuttle's pilot.

"Not yet," the young man said. His name was Ricardo, and over the past months, she'd come to know him as a competent operator of machinery, even if he was also very shy.

"Regardless of reports, I'd use nothing less than a full environment suit to go in," Finn said. "There won't be any useful atmosphere left this many years after decommissioning."

"I was worried about corrosive materials and other poisons that might have escaped the lab," Tina said.

Back when she worked there, the chemicals store used to be full to bursting with all kinds of nasty and interesting chemicals.

The shuttle made its way past the side of the station.

The merchant's used items catalogue stated the station had come to this enormous junkyard recently. Most of the other items in adjacent lots—mostly mining vehicles—they had passed while looking for it, appeared to have been here for many years. Those items were much smaller and hung as dark ghostly shapes, occasionally lighting up in the glow from the craft's floodlights.

Light from the distant sun barely cast a faint glow in this area in the asteroid field. It was extremely dark in here.

Paulo had sent them a schematic of the station, and it matched with Tina's data from Project Charon. She still couldn't quite believe that the station formerly belonging to the military had ended up here, but apparently that was what happened.

The shuttle drifted past the structures of the station. The pilot knew where they were going.

Tina spotted the docking hatch before he said anything about it. The craft engaged its engines to match speed with the slow rotation of the station.

The shuttle didn't have the right hardware to connect with the station, but the Freerangers didn't need matching hardware to board other ships. It was why the term pirates was used to describe them.

But Freerangers weren't pirates. They were opportunistic, commercially minded, highly adaptable and independent people. They didn't attack ships that were in use. Space junk was another matter.

The assistant crew members got ready.

Time to get into her uncomfortable suit. Tina wriggled her legs into the bottom, fished up the top, tied the strap between the legs and around the waist, and took the helmet and tanks out of storage.

Next to her, Finn was doing the same.

They were also no longer clumsy in the zero gravity environment. She still hated it, but they had spent so much time floating around that she had become used to it.

The shuttle's crew, four young Freerangers, prepared to send out the boarding line. They shot the projectile to the side of the station, where it stuck with a pad.

Then Tina and Finn cycled out the airlock. They had done this plenty of times recently, too, while doing maintenance and repairs on the Starfighter *Manila*, so she could almost go through the procedure with her eyes closed.

According to the schematics, the station possessed an emergency battery charger, but they didn't want to drain it, just in case. The Freeranger ship carried their own battery that provided power to open the doors on the station.

Finn attached the device to the outside of the airlock, and cycled through the menus to open it, while Tina hung back on the rope that connected the shuttle to the station.

If ever someone would have told her, back in the day she used to work here, that she would hang onto the outside of the station about to break in with a bunch of Freerangers in a distant asteroid field that belonged to a shady merchant, then she would have laughed. Back then, the only thing she envisaged for herself was a career as a leading scientist. She walked that path now, in a way, but her team consisted of civilians and not military officers and their task was not sanctioned by any authority. But finding a cure to the infection that turned people into mindless slaves with warty grey skin was more important than any research she could have imagined herself doing.

Finn opened the door, and she joined him in the airlock, in the golden glow of the light on his helmet.

He held up his thumb. *Are you OK?*

She signalled that she was.

Just a bit nervous. She hadn't been here for fifteen years.

Aboard the *Manila*, Evelle watched. She'd confided in Tina that she considered the station her birth home. Evelle had not been born here, because the station never provided much in the way of medical services, but she'd grown up and gone to school here.

Did she want to go back to the abandoned station, Tina had asked, but Evelle said she didn't. She'd been back once, and she felt no desire to return a second time. The place breathed unhappy memories.

The prospect of coming here didn't bring happy memories to Tina either. She thought back to all those times she'd paced around the apartment, clawing at the walls, not knowing who to speak to about her problems with Dexter.

He'd tried to pressure her for money.

For a great investment, he said.

It was *her* money, from her family, resulting from the sale of her grandparents' farm.

He pretended it was his, and then, when she wouldn't sign for his expenses, he'd make subtle threats. She'd be dishonourably discharged from the Force. What for, she didn't know. She had been so disturbingly trusting of him.

Why had she ever even half-believed his bullshit?

Yes, he was a superior, but he didn't have the authority to hire or sack people. She should have known that.

It was just that he *acted* like he knew people in high places who would dance to his tune.

The extent of his deception had not dawned on her until

much later. Dexter could be so utterly and disarmingly charming if he needed to.

Even two nights before she finally picked up the courage and left, he had sweet-talked her into dinner—and raped her afterwards. But that was sadly also a normal occurrence. She'd thought maybe life wasn't so bad after all. She'd *almost* stayed.

The thought chilled her. Thousands of bad memories associated with this place pulled at her while she waited with Finn in the airlock until the outer door closed, before he engaged the inner mechanism that opened the inner door.

They came out in a grey-walled, low-ceilinged corridor. A sliding glass door to the left led to a stairwell. To the right, the passage curved upwards and out of sight.

A feeling of familiarity washed over her. Part of her had been afraid she wouldn't recognise this place anymore, but she did, down to the ugly light fittings and the scuffed doors.

More bad memories. Why had she accepted this oppressive place as her home for so long? *Because the alternative was scary.*

Tina and Finn went through the corridors, deserted and cloaked in a haze of dust. The station's low rotation gave it some gravity, but it was less than half standard. Dust collected in weird clouds at the parts of the floor where air disturbance was lowest. That was a sure sign that no one had been here for a long time. She wondered if the sleazy merchant had paid anything for this station, or whether he would have taken it for free in return for not charging a fee to dispose of it. She imagined it would be quite hard to sell a station, and that he was really glad that they were showing interest in it right now.

He'd be watching them. He'd be asking questions.

And they weren't here to buy.

She didn't remember the place feeling so cramped and depressing. In the past months that they had spent together, she and Evelle had many discussions with each other about the time that they used to live there, and inevitably the subject came up of why Evelle was so keen to leave from the moment she realised there were other worlds and places.

There was nothing to do, she said. The walls were coming at you, she said. There were a few other children at the station, and there was a small school, but the children were the wrong ages and Evelle never felt she fitted in.

Tina had been quite happy with the project and hadn't understood. Looking at these narrow and dusty passages, she did understand now.

The station was only small and soon they came to the lab area at the end of the curved passage, where there was another glass sliding door.

The research lab sprawled over several compartments separated from each other with part-walls and wide doorways.

Tina remembered a visit by a safety team who had been astonished by the lack of properly sealed compartments in this area. They insisted the science lab inserted compartments in the form of ugly recesses in the wall where, as atmosphere pressure decreased, a metal barrier would roll across.

Tina remembered the safety drills that involved the closing of these barriers.

Most of the lab equipment had been removed, but Tina still recognised the areas where she used to work. Her old office now contained benches and connections for equipment and three workstations, as Evelle had already said. Evelle had also mentioned that Dexter's office was changed completely.

It looked like the decommissioning had been done with little care, or in a hurry. No one had removed the tables and cupboards, and when Tina opened one of the storage compartments, there were still various items in there that she recognised. The white plastic containers she'd use for samples. She slid one out. It was still full.

She opened the lid to find all the little sample containers still inside.

Well, that was an unexpected boon.

Maybe that meant the older important samples hadn't been removed either.

And indeed, they were still in the large storage room that looked like it had not been touched in all that time. Even the little handwritten labels she had affixed to the shelves when the cataloguing system crashed and wasn't fixed for months were still there.

Damn, she had forgotten about that.

And about Grace, who handled the system and who got flustered and frustrated when people asked her when it would be fixed and she didn't have the answer.

Tina pulled the sample file up on her pad. She checked her notes about when samples were taken and in which location. Thank the heavens that she had kept all this stuff.

She and Finn grabbed the important samples, some in tubes that dated back long before she started at the project. There was a lot more than she and Finn could carry, even if the size of his sack attracted jokes from the Freeranger youth. It might be an idea to negotiate with the Freerangers to tow this structure to another place. That was if they could negotiate with the merchant on a price, and if he wasn't going to be too suspicious to notify people who shouldn't know.

They were about to go into the corridor when a noise came from elsewhere in the station.

"What was that?" Finn said.

CHAPTER NINE

TINA TURNED AROUND and met Finn's eyes through the visor on his helmet.

"Maybe the shuttle crew is shifting the ship's position," he said.

She asked the shuttle crew if they were moving attachment pads to the hull and they replied they weren't.

"Have you seen a rock approach that might have hit the station?" Tina asked.

They hadn't, but it was dark. They also hadn't seen anyone else approach the station.

Finn said, "Most likely, it's just the metal expanding."

"We're not close enough to the star that the light would heat the metal," Tina said.

He grimaced at her. That was true, of course.

The junkyard was one of many in the outer reaches of the Olympus system. It was here precisely for the same reason the Freerangers didn't want to come to the planet: to avoid the scrutiny by authorities. The people who bought superseded equipment from Federacy agencies at these places moved in the shadows.

"Do we need to worry about an unidentified sound?" Finn asked. "We're not here to buy the place. I don't care about its structural integrity."

"I guess not."

Tina breathed out.

It was just that... this had been her home for so long.

They made their way down the corridor. Finn spoke to the pilot of the shuttle to tell him they were on the way back.

Following Finn, Tina struggled with her ambivalent feelings towards this place. Unless she did anything now, like starting negotiations with the merchant, this would truly be the last time she came here. Did she even care? Her time here had not been happy.

Then a new sound reached her through her helmet comm: the sharp intake of a breath.

"Was that you, Finn?"

He turned around. "No. I was just going to ask you the same."

They stopped and waited.

Since the sound had come over the radio, there was no way of telling where it originated.

Finn typed on his comm. To the shuttle, Tina was sure of that. Text scrolled over his screen.

He looked up and shook his head. The sound had nothing to do with the shuttle either.

They listened.

They didn't speak.

Whoever this was, if indeed a person hid in the station, was listening in on the airwaves.

Tina pulled herself past Finn and pointed towards the station's control centre. It wouldn't be possible that anyone still lived here, right?

Tina had been quite adamant that she didn't need to bring weapons. This was the way they were trained when she worked at the project: do not bring any weapons going into tight spaces, because the chance that a weapon accidentally went off was much greater than that of encountering hostiles and being able to put the weapon to good use inside a confined space.

Finn, however, had not been trained that way. He said that in his training, if they went into the engines, they were warned to always be armed, because sabotage from within was the biggest problem military craft faced. Crews of thousands often included at least one disenfranchised soul. It wasn't uncommon to have a stowaway on board either. It wasn't always easy to check the movements of a crew in the thousands. There were many checks for those people who had to go stationside when a ship put into a station, but if someone really wanted to bring a stray on board... well, that happened all the time.

He now produced his weapon that he had been carrying in a satchel on his side, a modern Fireseed from the stores of the *Manila*.

Finn went first. They slowly proceeded through the passage and up the steps to the control centre. It was hard to be silent in the awkward suit. For one, the air supply made a loud hissing noise each time she breathed. This was the sound they heard from the other person, who didn't realise that a channel was open. Who might not be aware that he wasn't alone in the station.

The control centre wasn't very big in a station of this size, just a square room with four workstations and four seats facing them. Large screens lined the walls, all of them off.

In Tina's days, there would be at least one person here, usually two or three during the day shift. They would each sit in front of banks of controls, monitoring ships that came and left, habitat operations and matters of military nature.

Most of those screens and computers had been removed, but the benches that used to house them were still there, including the seats, which were bolted to the floor.

A thick layer of dust had settled on the carpet. It kind of hovered low over the ground in places, swirling in eddies in the low gravity.

Finn pointed.

Yes, there were footprints from large boots, most likely belonging to an environment suit. The person or persons appeared to have walked around quite a bit, with tracks doubling up and going in different directions. They looked fresh, but "fresh" was a fluid concept in space. How long it took for tracks in dust to fade depended on so many things.

"Anyone here?" Finn said.

They listened.

There was no reply.

Had she been crazy to hear someone breathing? But Finn had heard it, too.

Still, those footsteps... Those looked so recent, with the edges still crisp.

They could have been made by the merchant inspecting the station.

But Paulo had said he hadn't inspected the station yet.

One of his staff would have, certainly.

Tina and Finn checked every cabinet and work bench, starting from the back of the room. While Finn checked out the hiding places, opening cabinets with his weapon in one hand, Tina made a video recording. The cupboards at the back of the room, that used to contain environment suits for the station admin staff, were all empty. Tina suspected that the military had removed those items.

The small cubicle containing the station's power board was empty and the lights on the wall panels were all off, and every surface was caked with dust.

Like the *Manila*, the station's control room had its own access tunnel to an emergency airlock which, from Tina's memory, came out at one of the emergency escape pods, rather than the station's docking area.

The principle was the same, however, to allow highly trained crew fast access to an escape route if that was necessary, and to allow rescue crew from outside an easy way to reach the control centre.

Finn opened the door and looked inside the dark maw—

A figure jumped from behind the nearest control module. He gave Finn a hard shove that toppled him sideways.

Finn called out, "Hey!"

He stumbled in the low gravity.

The suited figure ran in between Tina and Finn and jumped into the emergency chute. The hoses and other protrusions of the suit hit the rungs of the ladder on the way down.

Finn had hit the floor in a puff of dust, bounced and scrambled back to his feet. The bag of samples had rolled over the floor.

Tina had been filming Finn's activities and got a fright when the man ran through her recording in a blur. She offered Finn her hand, pulled him up and gathered up the bag of samples he'd dropped.

Finn jumped into the dark hole, slid down the ladder with a *ker-thunk-ker-thunk-ker-thunk*, and landed on the floor below with a thump.

Tina followed him into the chute. She half-slid, half-fell down the ladder, made more awkward by the large bag she carried.

"What's going on?" Ricardo asked inside her helmet.

"We got an intruder."

The man ran into the airlock opposite the chute, opened the door and slammed and locked the inner airlock seal from the inside. A sign on the door said *Careful: air lock. Emergency Escape Pod.*

"Shit, he's gone," she said.

Finn was speaking to Ricardo in the shuttle. "Beware, there's someone else here. He may come in your direction."

Ricardo called out, "Whoa! The pod just shot out from the launcher."

"Keep an eye on where he's going," Tina said.

"Can you follow him?" Finn asked.

"Not us. Unless you want to be abandoned here."

True. "What about someone else in the fleet?"

"Too far away."

"Try to monitor where he is going," Tina said.

But she already knew that it was next to impossible to trace such a small ship that had no engine. Tina had trained with these pods. They were designed to shoot occupants to safety and then wait for a larger ship to collect them. They only had enough air for a couple of hours. But out here, it was so dark that they'd hidden the Freeranger fleet, including the *Manila*, in the asteroid field. A tiny pod could hide with no effort at all. Maybe even a bigger ship that was here to pick the pod up, as long as the ship didn't move.

Finn blew out a breath.

He stuck the weapon in his belt. "We were too late. I didn't see him at all."

"No, I didn't see him either. Was he a pirate?"

"I have no idea. Probably someone sent by that sleazy merchant to spy on us."

"At least I have a recording," Tina said, holding up the camera.

CHAPTER TEN

TINA DIDN'T REALISE how shaken she was until they were safely back in the main ship. On the way back, while getting onto the shuttle, taking off her suit and strapping into the seat, she acted on autopilot.

Yalinda and Arkady waited for them in the shuttle bay of the Freeranger ship.

They were keen to hear whether Finn and Tina had secured the samples. Tina said that they had. She passed them the ridiculously big sack Finn had filled and explained that all the old samples had still been in the storeroom.

Arkady's face beamed.

"This is going to be extremely useful."

Elder Clementine informed the group through their comm pieces that it was time to move back to the fleet who were waiting.

The Freerangers were on edge. They didn't want to be here.

Tina had argued hard to make sure that they could come here at a meeting of the shipworld council. Clementine had wanted to keep the fleet out of the system. There were strange things afoot, she said, and none of the other elders spoke to disagree with her.

They'd been in this section of space plenty of times, and there were usually plenty of ships around. Usually Freerangers from other families, and independent bounty hunters, but the market for superseded space junk had collapsed, and the war prevented the acquisition of new stock. The Force was hanging onto their hardware, the pirates had snapped up a lot of stuff, and then the fighting had come closer and the junkyards went from not having enough to not knowing what to do with all the stuff.

No one was buying, and anyone who showed an interest in the hardware was viewed with suspicion.

While the ship ramped up the engines to rejoin the fleet, Tina went to see Clementine in her glass-walled command cubicle.

The screens gave off a blue glow which coloured Clementine's face. With the light coming from the side, she looked terribly wrinkled and old. Tina had learned that she was one of the oldest women in the shipworld family Mara.

As Tina came to the entrance of the cubicle, Clementine glanced aside but said nothing. She was listening to something on the comm. Something that came from outside, likely one of the other ships in the fleet, those displayed as dots on the screen facing Clementine.

How come there were so many ships in the fleet all of a sudden?

They'd started off at Aurora Station with just five ships, but now there were more than twenty, including the lame duck Starfighter *Manila*. Other ships had joined while they travelled. Tina had no idea who they were or why they had come.

This was the point where the Freerangers would go on to Freeranger hideouts—wherever they were—and the crew of the *Manila* would restart their damaged engines and slowly make their way to Olympus.

Clementine gestured at the holdfast station on the other side of her bank of controls. Tina made her way over there.

"Are we getting ready to decouple everything?" Tina asked.

"I didn't ask you to come for that reason. The merchant is demanding payment," Clementine began.

"We aren't buying anything," Tina said.

"No, he wants to keep part of the bond, because he said you removed something from the station."

An ominous feeling came over Tina. This wasn't all set up as a trick, wasn't it?

"We took the samples, but that was all. They're not worth anything, and if he wants some token payment for that, I am annoyed with that, but we can just pay him and be done with it."

"No, he says you took the station's control module."

"We most definitely did not."

But then Tina got a cold feeling. That was what the mysterious man had been doing.

"We did nothing of the sort. We encountered someone else inside the station. He probably removed this thing, if it wasn't a trick."

"Paulo will have posted his own guards, especially for a big ticket item like this. You might have seen them."

"No, it was someone sneaking around inside the station. We disturbed him, and he took off in another craft. Did you see him leave?"

Clementine raised her eyebrows. "We were not monitoring you. A fleet of ships joined us from Shipworld Vesa. They're an allied family. We were talking to them about things unrelated to you. But I can check the log."

"The shuttle saw the pod," Tina said. "Ricardo definitely saw it."

Clementine checked and found the emergency pod's departure from the station.

The large Freeranger ship had been at a far enough distance that the small ship was quite blurred in the visual scan.

"That's quite interesting," Clementine said. "I wonder where they were going, because a pod that size will not go far."

They watched the projection, and eventually the dot representing the pod disappeared into space because the signal scattered too much in the asteroid field for the equipment to register.

Clementine swapped to a different frequency, and they could follow the ship further, but eventually it disappeared there, too.

"Hmmm," Clementine said, and then she said nothing for a while.

"Where do you think they were going?" Tina asked.

Clementine shrugged. "There are a lot of asteroids in this area. A lot of places to hide. It's likely that a larger ship is hanging around in this area. It's one of the reasons I don't like being here. You never know who is watching you." Then she met Tina's eyes. "Are sure that this person took the control module?"

"Well, no, because I wasn't looking for that." Had the man been carrying anything? She didn't remember. Nothing that was big enough to be noticeable. "We can show Paulo this when he asks for proof that we didn't take anything."

Clementine blew out a breath. "Paulo is a sneaky, deceptive, distrustful character. He won't believe that this is real. He will say we fabricated this material in order to avoid losing part of our bond. He will say that we came here intending to defraud him. These people are very good at that sort of thing."

"But we didn't do any of those things."

"I know, but there is little you can do. You agreed to the

contract. I told you it was dangerous, but you wanted it so badly."

Tina cringed. Clementine had indeed warned her.

Clementine continued, "Whatever you say, to him, it will look like an extreme coincidence that we asked for the station and that someone else was there at the same time. He will say, not without reasonable assumption, that we set this up so that we could give this other person whatever it is they wanted."

Whatever it was they wanted with the control module of the station that was over fifteen years old and had been floating in space for the best part of ten years, anyway.

Tina could think of lots of things they might want, depending on who these people were. Maybe they had been alerted to the existence of the station by the presence of a ragtag fleet that contained a whopping great big Federacy warship that had been missing for the best part of a year.

She sighed. "The merchant can say what he wants, but I don't have money."

"You signed that agreement. He is unlikely to let you go," Clementine said.

"He's going to keep the whole fleet?"

"No, just you and the ship you put up as bond."

"What about you?"

"We need to look after our family. We can't stay here." She met Tina's eyes. "We have children in our fleet, and we need to think of our safety. I spoke to the family council. We have no choice but to part ways right now."

"And they will let you go?"

"Our family didn't put up a bond."

True.

And while leaving the *Manila* stranded here was a harsh solution, space was a harsh place, and she understood the Freerangers' motives.

It was time to talk this over with the others.

Tina found everyone from the *Manila* except Zia, Rex, Rasa and Jens in the cubicle that Lisette and Clodine occupied.

School was still going and apparently, after Zia had taught the older kids how to get into the Federacy's systems legally, Jens was demonstrating how to get in illegally.

They sat around a projector that showed the planet Olympus in bright yellow, and were pointing at little specks, presumably space stations, that orbited the planet.

"Did you get the stuff?" Evelle asked when she saw Tina come in.

"We did, but we also seem to have struck trouble. We interrupted someone who the merchant now says stole something from the station, and he seems to think that we did it and we arranged this person to be here. He wants payment, but we don't have any. The Freerangers want to back away from us right now."

"What's going on?" Aliz asked, coming into the cubicle.

"There was someone inside the station," Tina began. "We interrupted him and he fled in a small ship. The merchant thinks we organised for this person to be there. He says the man stole the station's central command module and that he wants to retain part of our bond."

"That's rubbish," Sarina said. "The Federacy doesn't leave any control modules intact when they decommission an asset."

"I agree," Aliz said. "Removing that sort of stuff is standard procedure. There is no control module in that station. He just wants money from us."

"There was quite a bit of stuff left in the station that I hadn't expected to be there," Tina said.

"Never the control module," Sarina said.

"Are you sure?"

"Absolutely sure."

Evelle asked, "So who was the guy you saw? One of the

merchant's employees or was he just a random thief with back luck?"

"I got a picture of him," Tina said.

Tina produced the vid she had taken of the man's face. Most of the relevant part of the recording, where Finn opened the emergency exit door and the guy came out from behind the console and pushed Finn out of the way before diving down the chute, was very blurry and there were sections where only the floor came into focus.

But when he ran past Tina, there was a stretch of a few seconds where the vid showed his face.

The blurring of movement made it hard to make out any distinctive features, but Sarina tidied the image up a bit.

He looked fairly young, had reddish hair and a short beard, and looked into the camera with startled grey eyes.

The women all gathered around Tina's screen, staring at him.

Aliz shrugged. "I've never seen this character before. Have you tried the recognition database?"

Tina said she hadn't, so Sarina pulled it up and fed the image through. It didn't give a match.

"Huh," Sarina said, and looked at the blurred photo. "He doesn't look like a pirate."

"No." Tina thought about Dexter, who also didn't look like a pirate, but was still aligned with them.

Evelle said, "He doesn't look like a Freeranger. He looks like he's from a rich family."

"How can you tell?"

"Look at his teeth."

Yes, they were white, in contrast to the teeth of the older Freerangers.

She pointed to a darker spot on his earlobe. "That's a chip. Not many people have those."

"Then what? Is he a spy?"

That question hung in the group, unanswered. No one knew. Tina and Finn hadn't seen evidence the man had collected anything.

A small alarm beeped in the intense silence. Aliz took her comm from her belt. Tina recognised the sound as coming from the *Manila*. It probably had something to do with a cleaner bot getting stuck in a corner.

Although wouldn't all those bots have been removed now that they were about to restart the engines?

"Huh," Aliz said after checking her screen. "He's posted sentries."

"The merchant?" Tina asked. "You mean, he's not going to let us leave until we give him the control module that we don't have?"

"Yes, he is," Aliz said. "We're going to board the *Manila* right now. Then cut the ties with the Freeranger fleet. They can leave. Then we'll turn on all the lights and weapons systems. Then we'll see how he peeps when he realises he's dealing with a Federacy war ship."

"Little of that stuff is operational."

"He doesn't know that."

CHAPTER ELEVEN

TINA WENT AROUND GATHERING everyone else in their group who were not Freerangers.

These were mostly the research staff, and those who had not been looking after the processes at the *Manila*.

Some people had been asleep and were quite grumpy.

Jette's husband Mattias said, "What? We need to go now? We've been preparing this for weeks. Why is there such a hurry?"

Tina explained about the merchant and also explained that the Freerangers were not part of the deal anymore.

"But why now?"

"Because he's threatening us, and we need to get out of here quickly. We have nothing to pay anyone with. We'd banked on having more success with treatments—"

"Well, I'm sorry to disappoint you. That's just science."

"I know and I understand, believe me. But we had nothing else to trade. The Freerangers are very impatient, and I understand where they're coming from. I'd hoped to change that, but I failed and at this point it's best that we each go our own way. And we need to hurry."

So he started packing, while his wife was still in the lab.

She also interrupted the school's lessons.

Jens and Rex were explaining something to a bunch of eager students, which included a couple of Freeranger kids.

Rasa occupied a workstation in the corner. Her face lit up when she saw Tina, and she pushed off from the seat.

"I have to interrupt the lesson. We need to return to the *Manila* right now," Tina said.

"I wanted to talk to you about something," Rasa said.

Tina frowned at her. A dozen different scenarios played through her mind. She'd decided to move in with Rex? Heaven forbid, they were only sixteen.

"Is it important right now?" Tina asked.

"I guess not that important. It can wait."

"All right. Later, then, when we're on our way to Olympus."

When she had the energy to deal with two love-struck teenagers. And patience. Should she ask Evelle to be part of this as well?

They collected the last items out of the cubicles they'd occupied in the past few months and made their way to the shuttle bay.

All the Freerangers came to watch. Apart from the Freeranger kids, who looked on with wide eyes, Tina didn't think there were many tears shed over this separation.

Those kids had enjoyed the lessons. Not all of them, and their parents hadn't allowed every kid to attend, but ones like Milo and his brother Corby would be worse off. Katya would be all right. There were usually more senior positions for women in the Freeranger shipworlds. But she had struck up a friendship with Yalinda's daughters, possibly the first friendship outside the family she'd ever had, or would ever have in the future.

All three youngsters looked on, sad-eyed. Corby waved to

Jens. Jens returned a hand signal. Tina had no idea what it meant.

An air of sadness hung in the docking bay.

The collaboration between the scientists, military women and the Freerangers had failed.

Maybe she'd been too naïve to think that people from such different groups could successfully work together. Maybe the project just needed more time. Maybe it was never going to work, anyway.

Maybe cooperation would come from the next generation. Rex, Jens, Rasa, Katya, Corby and Milo.

Clementine had given the word for a pilot to get ready. Ricardo would take them across. Good old Ricardo.

In the space between the ships, he turned on the outside screen.

The scarred hull of the Freeranger ship slid from view, followed by the view of the connecting umbilical, a thick structure made from multiple metal cables and a flexible tube for the power and data cables. It looked small but was as wide as an average person was tall. The Freerangers stored these cables on giant rolls. Once the flexible centre was removed, the metal structures folded up like a concertina.

Then they got a brief view of the distant sun in between the hulls of both ships. The merchant ships showed up as tiny black dots, back-lit by the feeble light.

They were still holding their position.

Tina had sent across the information she had about the thief, but as Clementine had already predicted, the merchant Paulo wouldn't have a bar of it.

"You've fabricated this so-called 'evidence' so that you don't have to pay," he had said.

They arrived at the *Manila* and used the regular air lock that would normally be attached to station umbilicals. It was where Tina had first entered the ship.

Now that they had turned the power back on, the ship didn't look half as depressing as it had when Tina had last come in here. The lights were on, the air was fresh and the familiar low hiss of air out of the vents made that it was never completely silent.

"Right. Situation Yellow. To your stations," Aliz said as soon as the door had closed and they were no longer connected to the Freeranger shuttle.

Everyone had been given a station.

For most, Yellow meant that they needed to return to their cabins, shut the door and keep survival gear handy. The scientists had never spent much time on board this ship, so Rae, who was in charge of passenger health, showed them where to go.

For Tina, it meant she had to be on the bridge.

Clodine declared she needed additional people to occupy the weapons stations, so she took Yonta, Rex, Jens and Rasa, the latter three because they had played with the simulation training over the past few idle months.

Rex had enjoyed that immensely. *Just like playing a game* he had said, and Tina continued to remind him to never forget it was *not* a game.

When this was over, he was going to sign up. She was sure of that. She didn't want him to, but she no longer had a say over what he did.

Her boy had become a man. He'd gone from an awkward teenager in an awkward old-fashioned harness into a modern machine of steel.

Finn and Thor went to man the maintenance control centre that was normally Yonta's, so that they could advise Aliz on any issues with the engines.

Everyone went about the operation in military efficiency. Tina noticed how the crew was determined, almost *happy* to finally be doing something that didn't require passing it through the shipworld council for approval.

The scientific party was not quite as organised. Aliz had told them to go to their allocated cabins, take food and other provisions, and not come out unless Aliz told them it was safe to do so. She passed the responsibility for the "civilian crew" onto Arkady, Jette and Yalinda, and they coordinated with Margot to get them rations and emergency pressure suits.

They were also responsible for the three men who had been moved back into the laundry, now each in their individual cages.

When Tina came to the bridge, Aliz, Evelle and Finn—remotely—were going through the pre-flight engine checks.

The engine idled at ten percent readiness, to allow the batteries to power up and the habitat control to be turned on.

After Aliz took the controls, it went to fifteen, twenty, twenty-five, thirty, and thirty-three percent. That was it. More was not safe.

While this was going on, the atmosphere on the bridge remained calm.

Tina was in charge of navigation and communication. She spoke to Arkady to make sure the scientists and families were safe. She spoke to Clodine who was happy with the functionality of the weapons. What that meant precisely, she left in the air. Tina also spoke to Finn and Thor, who informed her that there was no sign of too much stress on the engine. She listened to the voices of the small ships surrounding the *Manila*.

The Freeranger fleet was retreating. Tina could hear Clementine's voice talking to the merchant, assuring him that she had nothing to do with the station or with the occupants of the ship. The merchant called her names, and she said they'd just buy their stuff somewhere else next time, because the Mara family had no time for people who didn't believe what they said.

It was such a hard, unforgiving world out here, and yet, the Freerangers didn't seem to be overly interested in changing it.

"We're ready," Evelle said.

She sat in the second pilot seat, no longer flustered or bewildered by the controls. Evelle had spent a lot of her spare time reading piloting manuals and doing simulations. Tina was proud of her.

"Right. Moving now," Aliz said.

She pulled the microphone down from her headset and a moment later, her voice boomed through the ship's announcement system. "Ship move imminent. Please go to your holdfast stations."

Evelle gave her the thumbs up. "I haven't heard that for so long."

The *Manila* had returned to civilisation. It was a limp, weakened return, but no one needed to know that.

Aliz moved up the main engine lever on the controls. Lights started flashing. With a tiny jolt, the ship moved forward. Someone elsewhere in the ship cheered. Tina wasn't sure if the sound came from the loudspeakers or through the passage that led to the docks.

She was the ship comm and her job got busy. A burst of chatter broke out on the airways. People spoke in panicked voices. A lot of them in Sinolese, which Tina still didn't understand. Damn.

They would see the sudden appearance of a serious warship out of the shadows of the Freeranger fleet. Aliz turned on the exterior lights for extra effect.

Oh, she was enjoying this.

Finally Paulo called in.

"What is the meaning of this?"

Tina said, "We are the Starfighter *Manila* on our way to the Federacy Force headquarters. We did not steal anything from the station. It is an ex-Federacy Force structure. We checked the station for the presence on board of Federacy-owned items that have become of interest to us recently. We demand to be let go."

"I don't care who you are. You agreed to pay a bond. The station's control module is missing. I demand compensation."

"The station is Federacy property until you sell it. Control modules are removed prior to decommissioning so the station's control module cannot have been on board for us to steal it. Even if the module was on board, and we did remove it, and it wasn't, and we didn't, the Force has the right to demand it back."

"Fuck you. My fleet is watching you. They're armed."

"So are we. If you want to play that game. But I suggest that if you allow an armed conflict to happen, it will end badly for your ships."

He didn't reply.

Tina waited, but he said nothing more.

She signalled to Aliz.

The merchant ships didn't move when Aliz slowly increased the ship's engine output, leading to forward motion. They didn't retreat from their positions either, but there was just enough room in between them for the ship to pass through.

Tina held her breath, thinking of Rex in the rocket station. He was too young for this. He'd be scarred forever if an armed conflict broke out and he ended up killing people.

The Freeranger fleet had retreated and was only still visible on the radar. The merchant's ships hid them from view.

Very slowly, the *Manila* slid between the ships of the merchant fleet. No one said anything. No one else moved.

When the ship came out of the asteroid field, the sound of cheers drifted through the ship. Evelle and Aliz clasped hands.

But the merchant's voice sounded in Tina's ears. "You may have won this game, but I don't forget. I'll get what I want, legally or illegally, mark my words."

CHAPTER TWELVE

ALIZ MADE the official announcement that it was safe for the non-military crew to leave their cabins now, and Tina first met the scientists in the mess when they came in for a meal. They entered in a group, with the adults leading the children.

Jette said, "This ship is so huge. It's easy to get lost."

"Not that huge," Margot said, while bringing trays from the kitchen. Through the doorway, Tina spotted Gisele opening the oven. The two seemed very much in their element now that they could once again work in the kitchen.

"The *Manila* is smaller than the Freeranger ship," Lisette said. "It's just a lot more efficient with space."

"It's a warren," Jette said.

Tina had almost forgotten that the people from Aurora Station had spent little time aboard this ship.

It was strange to have another extra fifty people on board.

Arkady came into the mess with Benjamin, Mattias, Rex and Finn.

"All safe?" Yonta asked.

"For now," Arkady said. "We separated the cages so they can't reach each other. We double-locked the door in case one of them gets out. Although I wonder how much longer we can keep them in these cages, because they will damage themselves too much."

"I would hope that you could soon start to work with the material we collected," Tina said.

"Yeah," Arkady said.

There was a sound of worry in his voice. They needed to find a space to do that work first. And money, and the safety and peace of mind to work on a long-term project. They needed a base and funding so that they were no longer forced to conduct their work in makeshift labs.

But all of that was in the back of most people's minds now.

The sound of chatter and relieved laughter was welcome in the mess.

Most of the scientists and their families were unused to the movements of the ship, now that they were going forward and there was just a tiny bit of gravity.

It was very confusing to have to adjust to items falling in a direction you weren't used to.

The kids found it amusing, and the adults laughed with them.

Yes, it would be good to get some sort of permanent base for all these people.

She needed a place for them to work, and a program, and a budget, so that she could offer them contracts. Before they all took off to their families and Tina lost most of her team.

With returning to civilisation also came a slew of news reports relating to what had happened in the intervening months.

She scoured the news for reports from the war. There was a lot less on the subject than on the elections at Olympus.

But she did find some articles.

As Tina had already known, Aurora Station had become the main base for the pirates. None of the news services reported further major conflict, so she carefully concluded there had been none. She couldn't find anything about Cayelle, and she hoped that was good news, too.

The Federacy had forbidden all trade between the Aurora sector and Olympus, and were starting to exert their influence over the Freeranger ships.

This had boiled over into new conflicts with the Freerangers that the Federacy could ill afford.

Apparently, there had been a Federacy Force raid on a Freeranger store, where they were said to have stockpiled pirate produced goods.

The head of the affected Freeranger shipworld Intos was quoted as saying that the pirates at Aurora never produced anything, but since he couldn't tell the Force where he had obtained the items found in the store, it was shut down anyway.

Exactly what sort of things that the Force had found and was upset about was a mystery.

Tina wondered if Clementine's hurry to retreat from Olympus and unwillingness to further cooperate had something to do with this. She wouldn't be surprised.

The ship made its way through the system. Aliz contacted the Federacy headquarters. The scientists worked on their treatment simulations.

Rex and Jens spent most of the time with Clodine on the lowest level of the ship where the docks and weapons were. Tina didn't ask what they did there. She didn't want to know.

Rae investigated how best to sedate the men without putting them in stasis. Once the *Manila* was taken into dock, they would need to remove the men from the ship. Aliz had been asked to provide a list of surviving crew members, and they had decided to leave the men off that list for the time being.

The scientists needed the men. They still hoped to find a

treatment that would improve their condition. It had worked so well with the geese.

Tina received a message from Clementine two days later.

She went up to the bridge to write a return message and found that Clementine had asked for radio contact.

Tina sat in her familiar navigator station while Evelle was at the controls and Aliz asleep in her cubicle near the entrance to the bridge.

Through the grainy screen and in the blue light of the controls at the Freeranger ship, Clementine looked ancient.

"I just wanted to speak to you personally," she said. "And apologise for leaving you on your own. Although you seem to be capable of fending for yourself. I would have loved to see Paulo's face when he realised who he was dealing with."

"I understand why you took the position you did. I understand that your family is your first consideration and that I am not in a position to comment on the safety of your fleet."

"I would have liked the cooperation, but some of the other elders in the shipworld council were against it," Clementine said. "The Federacy has always left us alone, but lately they've become interested in our affairs. Not in a good way."

"I've heard about the Federacy Force's attack on one of the shipworlds," Tina said. "I can understand why you're anxious. You don't need to apologise to me."

"But I do. Because I promised you we would give you a place where you could work, and I had such a place in mind. Unfortunately, I was no longer in a position to offer it to you."

"Because of the Federacy Force raid on one of your stores?"

"There is a lot more behind the scenes, but yes, in a round-about way. I had planned to take you and the team to a place close to the shipworld Intos stores. We can only be lucky that we weren't already there."

"The Federacy Forces would have been happy to find us."

"They would have arrested us for interfering with their ship."

"But you didn't. You just helped us get here."

"That doesn't matter to them. They'll take any reason to arrest us. They don't like us."

Well, the dislike went in both directions. It had morphed into distrust, and while the Freerangers had good reasons to be distrustful, the attitude didn't help. The Federacy was going to assume they'd interfered with the *Manila* because the Freerangers didn't enter the system. If you hid from scrutiny, people were going to assume there was something to hide.

But there was not much point dwelling on age-old attitudes.

"So, what are you going to do? Are you on your way out of the system?"

There was no significant delay on the connection, so the Freerangers couldn't be too far away.

"We're going to continue trading. We need the money, and we need to get out of this area. I am really sorry about the way this has turned out. I would have liked to help you."

"It's all right. I think we will be fine now. But thank you anyway."

Clementine signed off.

Tina wasn't sure how the Freerangers would have been able to help, unwilling as they were to travel to Olympus or get anywhere close to the Federacy's bases.

All she was left with was a feeling of sadness that something that could have worked very well had gone wrong.

The Freerangers seemed nice people, with a lot of care for their community, with a lot of integrity. She would have liked the cooperation.

/ CHAPTER THIRTEEN

TINA SPENT a fair bit of time at the navigation module in the next days. There was a lot to be organised. The ship had contacted the Federacy Force headquarters in secret to let them know they had survived and were on the way back.

According to Aliz, she had sent these types of messages before, but it was a sign of trouble in the Force that they hadn't replied to any of them. The *Manila* was considered lost or too contaminated to deal with.

But the general public hadn't known about the *Manila*'s return. There were two thousand families out there waiting for news from their missing loved ones.

Seated at the communication module and listening to the chatter in space, Tina heard the ripple of rumour go through the news services.

Ghost ship returns from the dead, one service proclaimed.

Apparently people had already held memorial services for the *Manila*'s crew, missing, presumed dead.

General Jolley had been demoted over losing the new and very secret and expensive ship.

And there had been a fair bit of controversy over the *Manila* even before its first flight.

"Hmph, what does sacking Jolley achieve?" Aliz said when Tina told her. "He was a good sort and never had anything to do with our operations. It's the Force's fault, not his, that they never attempted to find us. I'd be surprised if he'd never tried to find us."

"There must have been a change in administration," Evelle said. "I hardly recognise any of these people."

Aliz's shook her head. "Yeah. I didn't think a change of the guard was due."

Tina was pretty sure, in fact, that a change in the top *wasn't* due soon.

Evelle snorted. "They probably got caught up in a scandal."

"Which one?" Tina asked.

"Take you pick," Evelle said. "I've lost count."

"They're all just talking heads," Aliz said. "Being a spokesperson is such a shit job that they get recycled fast. Whatever you say, someone is always unhappy. It's much easier to sack the announcer of bad news than it is to actually do something about it."

Still, no one from the Force attempted to contact the ship directly, so Tina needed to establish those contacts.

What should have been easy—a ship returning from a mission should have had codes for sending important communication—was a bureaucratic struggle. Codes had expired, contact details had changed, command structures no longer existed.

One could be forgiven for thinking that this was deliberate.

Maybe Headquarters were still working out whether the ship's computer systems had been compromised and whether communication could be trusted.

Maybe they were still formulating a policy and response.

Maybe they were just very good at making up excuses while

they were scrambling behind the scenes to figure out what to do with this returned ship.

But a few days later, a message came in without a named sender.

It was written in a plain style with a very formal voice. Tina had seen these messages often enough to recognise the signs: this, finally, came from high up in the Force command.

It said,

Please return to base as soon as possible. Report to Sector General Smith. The recovery and decontamination unit will take care of the ship. You are forthwith stood down from your positions until we can establish the status of the ship.

Tina observed Aliz and Evelle as they absorbed that message. She wasn't familiar with the verbiage, but in her experience, messages from the higher command always had a second meaning. She was disturbed by the words *stood down* and mentioned it when Aliz said nothing about it.

"That's a fairly standard expression for crew of ships that have been in enemy hands," Aliz said. "They like to think that they need to decontaminate the ship before allowing it back into the fleet."

"They do need to do that," Evelle said.

Aliz snorted. "It's a perfunctory process. They can never erase everything from a ship this large, and nor do they want to. These ships and their processing units are a treasure trove for data collectors. They can't legally wipe all of it, because the safety people would have something to say about that. Why, for example, did the air lock open on you while it wasn't supposed to?"

"I thought we agreed that Gerry did that," Tina said.

"If he did, he shouldn't have been able to. That's a design flaw and someone's going to pore over that data to see if they can find out why it happened. There are many companies whose fortunes ride on data like this. They're not going to wipe it. Money is always a more powerful motivator than crew or safety."

"So what are they going to do?"

"Most of the time, compromised hardware gets sold off."

"Ouch. This ship is almost new and worth a huge amount."

"Yup. That's why we're going to face some kind of action."

"But none of it is your fault."

"If it's not ours, whose fault is it? And don't give me this stuff about betrayal by others in the fleet. It's not worth discussing unless we have solid irrefutable proof, and maybe not even then. We're a war ship. Pirates are disorganised rogues. We should have been able to save ourselves. We didn't. It's our fault. Most importantly, it's the command's fault and since they're dead, it's my fault."

"What are they going to do to you?"

Aliz shrugged. "Keep us planetside for a while, is my guess. Maybe people will be 'honourably retired'."

"You're too young for that."

"Most commercial pilots are honourably retired military pilots."

"It seems such a waste. Not just the ship, but all the training. They could surely find something else for you to do?"

"They could, if I asked, but I won't, because their options are not usually very interesting."

"I'm really sorry about this."

"Don't be. It comes with the job. When you're new, people tell you this all the time: have an exit plan because chances are very high that you'll need it. I'm not concerned about that."

"Then what are you concerned about?"

"I am more concerned that they refuse to respond to any of

our messages by simply getting someone to talk to us," Evelle said. "They've had many opportunities to do that. We contacted them after we first came out of Aurora Station. Did you ever hear anything meaningful back from them at that stage?"

"I didn't," Aliz said. "I didn't think that much of it, because we were in enemy territory, and we had just escaped from the enemy, and we might have been contaminated for all they knew."

They left the unspoken truths hanging between them. That the Federacy should have contacted them now that they were in a safe place, but that for some reason they chose not to.

"What do you think the point of their actions is?" Tina asked.

"It's hard to tell."

"I just can't imagine that they would be happy to ditch an expensive ship. I hate to think how much money and effort went into developing this ship and how much they wouldn't want the enemy to get their hands on it."

"Frankly, I'm starting to wonder who the enemy is, and whether anyone knows that for sure," Evelle said.

Well, that, too.

Tina met Aliz's eyes. "You didn't say what *you* are concerned about."

"This General Smith character. Who is he, what's his agenda, and how did he come up in the Force so quickly that I've never heard of him?"

Evelle nodded. "Yeah."

And then no one said anything for a while.

Eventually, Tina asked, "So what do you think is going to happen when we get to this station where you're meant to report?"

Aliz shrugged. "It's hard to guess, but I don't think there is any escaping it. Whichever way we would have turned, we would always have to had come back here. Even if the Force wouldn't come after us for taking off with their ship, we just don't have the crew to operate the ship, and the longer we leave it, the more we are going to be sitting on a ticking bomb. That reactor is not very happy, and it badly needs an overhaul."

So the ship hurtled through system at a much slower speed.

The arrival time would be in weeks, not days. And there was nothing they could do about it.

Aliz and Evelle went back on rotations. Tina spent time in the communication and navigation station, the rest of the crew kept an eye on the ship's health and reconfigured the dock to allow the *Alethia* back out.

The others didn't have assigned tasks.

It was impossible to stop a group of scientists from doing work. They couldn't do any of the protein tracing for the samples that Tina and Finn had collected, but they could prepare the samples as much as possible.

They had unpacked some of their gear and used a meeting room behind the kitchen and mess area as their temporary work space.

Tina also spent some time there.

There had been a hive of activity surrounding the new samples.

Yalinda and Jette had directed their assistants to start the process of analysing the material.

Between the members of this group, they had spent so much time working on a cure for the infection. What they wanted was not a cure exactly, because things were never that simple, but something that would break the chain of events, and would make future generations resistant to the infection.

At least that was the idea.

Tina still remembered how Arkady had stood in front of the gathered section of the scientists on board the ship when they first started and had explained what they knew about the infection and what needed to be done. Everyone had been so hopeful back then. That if only they all got together, they could solve it.

It was kind of embarrassing to see your own DNA floating in a projection, with him pointing out where and how she was unusual.

As they had painstakingly traced during the past few months, the fact that she was unusual had been triggered by that original exposure to the material, and not only that, she had passed it on to Rex.

So this was why they had gone back to collect the original material, because during the time that the infection had proliferated in inhabited space, it had also changed a lot, leading to the weird growth of the cactuses, the changing of geese into something resembling peacocks, and the change in humanity. The infection had adapted, but exposure to the original material could render the person immune.

It had worked with the cactuses and the geese, but it wouldn't work with human subjects.

Tina had looked through the known information about the early cases she had seen: the owner of her shop, Simon Fosnet, and the little girl Molly.

She found that Molly had been born with a degenerative condition that limited her life span, but the condition was unrelated to the infection.

Simon Fosnet was a very secretive person, and Tina only found a handful of reports of hospital visits which didn't mention the reason for his visit. Two of the visits were quite old.

Could she perhaps contact him and ask him how he thought he'd been infected? But no, he would want his money. He probably thought she'd done a runner.

She decided to send a message to him anyway, but didn't expect a reply. If he'd gone the same way that the three men had deteriorated, he'd be a mindless grey monster, or he'd be dead.

Or the whole region would have broken out into war and her message wouldn't even reach him.

She found contact details for Molly's family as well and sent them a message, too.

When had she first started changing? Did they know what was likely to have caused it?

She beat herself on the head for not asking this while she was still at Cayelle, but she'd been preoccupied with other things at the time. She offered for Molly to take part in an extended trial when they had an effective treatment.

Not that she expected a reply to that message, either.

There was a chance that Molly had passed away already. The condition she had been born with—some kind of neural defect—sounded horrible. Sufferers didn't usually live past their teenage years.

CHAPTER FOURTEEN

SLOWLY BUT STEADILY, the *Manila* travelled through the system.

Soon it would be time for the next parting: they had to prepare to take the *Alethia* back out of the *Manila*'s dock. The *Manila* was going to the off-limits military facility at one of the orbital stations at Olympus and Tina didn't want her ship to be stuck there for however long it took for maintenance personnel to check the *Manila*'s systems.

The operation proved less delicate than it had been coming in. Yonta had spent much of her idle time completing training modules for work Gerry used to do.

There were also a couple of scientists—Jette's husband Mattias in particular—who proved to have useful technical skills.

They completed the operation within a day, left the *Alethia* hanging in the *Manila*'s docking arms connected by an access tube that they had scavenged from the Freeranger ship. Tina spent the next day checking the *Alethia*'s reserves, charge levels and communication systems.

Now that she was aware of the problem, that habitat arm

that didn't fold properly really stuck out. She should have it fixed when they got to Olympus—except with what money?

They held a big meeting with everyone who was non-military, scientists, their partners and children, all of them from Aurora Station.

Tina placed herself in front of the group, realising how comfortable they had grown with each other over the journey. Some kids had visibly grown. Others had turned into adults.

These were her people, and she hoped to keep them together.

She outlined the plan.

They would all board the *Alethia* just before they arrived at the orbital station, and make the short trip across in a very cramped fashion. The ship was only licenced to carry sixteen on in-system flights, and eight on long-distance flights. But the water tanks were running low, so mass wasn't an issue and the cargo hold was almost empty. Finn had hung up transport webbing so people who wouldn't have a seat in the cabin could ride safely in the cargo hold and the passage that linked the cargo hold with the cabin. The *Alethia* had enough space, would stock up on air reserves, and the trip would only be for a very short distance.

Once on the station, they needed accommodation, since the *Alethia* was much too small to sleep all of them.

Without payment, that was going to be hard, but someone suggested that they appeal to be classified as refugees—which they were—and get those benefits going.

Next was the question of what to do about the three men and their work and equipment.

Jette said, "We're talking about potentially infectious material, and they could jail any of us for bringing any of these individual items into the orbital station, let alone all of them together."

"We keep the work and samples aboard the *Alethia*," Tina said. There was no way she'd risk her work a second time.

"What about the men?" Jette asked.

The deep silence that followed indicated that there wouldn't be a straightforward solution, or any kind of solution at all.

"Won't they need to go back with the *Manila*, since they're the ship's original crew?" Rex asked.

"Aliz has reported them as missing," Tina said. "She said it was unlikely that once the ship is in dock, the men would be passed to us, nor that they would allow Rae to look after them, and since no one can communicate with them, they're most likely to be executed, unless they die in captivity first."

"We'll have to put them in stasis," Yalinda said after a while.

"Didn't you always say that it would kill them?" Zia asked.

Another silence. Everyone knew that, too.

Yalinda shrugged and spread her hands. "I don't know what else we can do."

She was right, of course, but some part of Tina still hoped that they could arrest or partially revert the condition. It had worked so well with the cactuses and the geese.

But they had run out of time. Giving the men to station authorities would lead to their imprisonment and miserable deaths. Giving them up to the military would be even worse. Better to die painlessly from spending too long in a stasis pod, right?

She told Yalinda to organise to do it. No one protested.

They planned to take as much equipment and as many people as they could. She left it up to Yalinda to decide which projects they could bring and which ones they could live without, recreate or weren't worth pursuing. The cargo hold and other passages of the *Alethia* grew very full.

So now it was up to Tina and her team to complete the work, to find funds for it, and then develop the medicines.

Jette had extensive experience with fundraising for research projects and offered to work on this. Tina was grateful for her help.

She had already contacted a few companies, including Finn's family, and they seemed interested.

Did they know Finn was involved with the project? Tina asked, and Jette said she'd seen no reason to inform them. Finn wasn't doing the research, anyway.

Which was true.

They came closer to Olympus. Through the viewscreen on the bridge, the planet hung as a large blue and green ball in space. At night, you could see the lights of Olympus city. It grew busy in the section of space outside the ship.

Aliz informed the women that traffic control had allocated them docking space on the Orbital Station 3, because it also had a large military base. Station Operations had sent two pilot ships to tow the *Manila* in.

It was time to go to the *Alethia* and detach the last connections between the two ships.

Finn went first while Tina, Rex and Yalinda made sure that everyone else came on board. First came Arkady, Benjamin and Mattias with Jens and Rasa to push the stasis pods with the three men inside. They would be stacked on top of each other in the cargo hold.

Then came a long string of the other people from Aurora Station, from Zia, who looked after the children, to Jette, who was carrying so much electronic equipment that she almost didn't fit in the access tube.

It grew very cosy inside the ship.

But they needed to hurry because they were already close enough to the station to see the larger external structures. And Aliz informed her that the two Federacy Force pilot ships were coming close.

It was with a sense of foreboding that Tina made her way

through the tube. She'd said goodbye to Evelle earlier, but she wanted to do it again.

She knew they would still be on the same station and that Evelle would most likely be granted extended leave before being assigned to another ship.

But she didn't like the insistence from the station that the women speak to this General Smith, because those types of meetings didn't bode well in her experience.

She made her way through the tube, into the cabin, past all the people who sat there, crammed together and who had about three hours of sitting in crowded conditions coming up.

Finn already sat in the copilot seat. Zia was at the navigation post.

Despite all her misgivings, it felt good to fly the ship independently again. It had been far too long.

A short burst of the engine took the craft around the other side to the civilian docking berths. The *Manila* would need to dock at the military side of the station.

"See you inside," she said to Evelle before cutting off communication.

By now, she had to concentrate on getting the ship into the docking queue. She wondered what the *Manila* was going to face and who would be waiting for the ship. She assumed the crew would be debriefed, relieved of their duty and housed somewhere in the station, possibly in the military facility, and that they could meet up somewhere dockside. Then they would decide what to do, depending on what Evelle had been told and how long her leave was going to be.

If Aliz was right and they were going to be honourably retired from the Force, and Tina couldn't see why, they would be free to go wherever. Tina wouldn't mind that, because then she could take both her children home.

It was busy here, and Tina and Finn got busy with the docking procedure.

There was no asking for passenger names, just personal identification numbers. As soon as she had entered Finn's, there was a message for him, and then another one and another one.

"It looks like you're popular," Tina said.

Finn cringed. Not only did he not want to talk to his family, Zia Partlow was sitting in the navigation seat, listening to everything that was happening.

Rex and Rasa we are both looking around eagerly, watching all the craft on the screens. Jens made a running commentary on the makes and models of craft that were coming in and the ones they passed that were already in dock.

The facility was large, and well spaced, unlike that at Kelso Station which had been a mess compared to this, and unlike the facility at Aurora Station, which had been downright hostile with their questions and procedures.

With the docking complete, the artificial gravity from the station took over, and they could collect all the items that had spread throughout the cabin and landed in strange places.

The refugee application had come through a while ago, and with it came the allocation of accommodation in the station.

The scientists got two adjacent apartments, both of them designed for large groups with multiple dorms. It was still a bit cosy, but some people were already planning to travel to the planet as soon as possible.

The breaking up of the group had started, even if the people who were planning to leave were not yet those who were important to the project.

The scientists wanted to continue working.

The two apartments each had a communal room, and they had already planned to convert one of them into a lab.

Tina had been afraid that the researchers wanted to return to their families, and although some did, not all of them were interested in going to the planet or catching commercial flights to elsewhere in settled space.

They were even talking about bringing in the men so that they could start working on the material Tina and Finn had collected at the station.

So that all seemed under control.

Then all they could do was wait until someone from the planet contacted them.

Phew. Administration was not her favourite activity. She wondered how the *Manila* was getting on.

CHAPTER FIFTEEN

BUT OF COURSE THE admin wasn't all done.

After a short and restless night aboard the *Alethia*, everyone was up again early—seriously, why hadn't she noticed how annoying gravity was and why were those foldout beds in the cabin so uncomfortable?

Finn and Thor had managed to rotate the outer arm's central hub, so that the opening faced the cabin and they could now spread out into that part of the habitat as well, despite the fact that the habitat arms were folded and that the furniture was now stuck to the wall.

Finn had established the reason the arm wasn't folding properly, and needed some parts to fix it.

Tina felt cooped up and offered to get these for him. There was no news from the scientists and besides, no one expected a quick reply about work proposals about funding, collaboration or work space.

Tina made her way from the ship to the maintenance shops.

The passages in the station were quite busy in a relaxed way, although she did notice a lot of military personnel. Some were waiting, others were boarding, others still hung around, duffels at their feet. Their chest patches displayed a wide collection of different ships. She guessed that meant that those ships were moored at the station.

She caught snatches of conversation.

Some groups sounded like new recruits: full of enthusiasm and innocence.

And nerves, too.

Were they all being called up for the war? Tina considered asking them, but decided against it. If it was important, she'd find out. It was best not to draw attention to herself.

She glanced at the many notice boards around the hall that displayed the status of various ships. She didn't recognise any of the names.

SF stood for Starfighter, but what did WCS stand for? War Command Ship? That sounded too simplistic. It was not an abbreviation she remembered from her days in the Force.

She didn't see the *Manila* mentioned anywhere.

Was that because their location was supposed to be secret?

It was amazing how easy it was to get around in the station. Tina was only used to having restrictions placed on the civilian population, and it had been a long time since she had been able to move around as freely as this. There were no patrols or check points. People could walk from the surface to orbit shuttles straight into the long-distance docking areas.

Finding the business Finn had indicated was not easy. There were a *lot* of maintenance shops.

Most private ships, whose owners used these shops, were smaller than hers, because in the Olympus system, people had enough stations to travel to that they didn't need larger ships for interstellar travel.

But eventually she found the shop where Finn had ordered the parts, and they had packed them in a transport crate on wheels.

"Are you going to be all right with all that?" the owner asked.

"Should be fine." Tina gave the crate a little push. It was quite heavy, but the wheels rolled easily.

She gave the merchant her credit code.

He entered it, frowned at the screen, and shook his head. "I can't accept this, I'm afraid."

"Eh, what?"

"This account is too far in arrears."

"Oh. I... uh..."

Her heart was thudding. She'd always known her continued non-payment would catch up with her. She stared at the trolley. Finn had specifically ordered this stuff.

"Do you have another one?" the man asked.

"Yeah, just wait a moment."

Tina took a few steps back to the corner of the workshop and sent a message to Finn.

He asked her, *Can you tell them to put it on credit?*

What do you think I've been doing for months? I have no money. There is nothing left in my account and there hasn't been any for months.

He didn't reply immediately. So she added, *I've told you this before. You said you'd pay me back.*

I will *pay you back.*

Now would be a good time. If you want those parts.

Another silence.

OK then. Hang on.

And after another silence, he messaged a code.

Tina passed it to the merchant, and he accepted it without question. Although he paused for a bit while looking at the screen. Was it because the code betrayed that it belonged to the Kaspari family?

"Shopping for the boss, eh?" he asked.

Sure enough.

"This is for my ship."

"Yeah." He flicked his eyebrows, but it was clear he didn't believe her.

Tina took the handle of the trolley, but before she could wheel it out of the shop, he asked, "So, do you think all those people will ever get their money back?"

"I'm sorry, I have no idea what you're talking about."

"You're kidding, right?"

"No. I have no idea."

"Safelink. Finn Kaspari. He obviously has plenty of money."

Tina gave him a blank look. But in the back of her mind, she remembered how Zia had wanted to talk about her relationship with Finn and had mentioned that his family had bailed him out once. Was this about that?

"Sorry, I really don't know. We're refugees from Cayelle."

"Yeah," he said again, but he clearly didn't believe that either.

But the parts had been paid for and Tina pushed her trolley out of the shop. What the hell was she getting involved in?

She made her way out of the maintenance area, and then curiosity forced her to stop. She had to look up this company name. Safelink.

She was hit in the face with a flood of news articles. Holy crap. What was all that about?

The headlines screamed *Safelink default on debt and payments, Safelink trouble for investors.* It wasn't long before Tina came across Finn's name. He'd been the owner of the company that, according to the articles, sold bandwidth packages over a secure network to fund better FTL technology for communication. But the project had run into trouble and investors demanded their money back. These were ordinary citizens, not the usual corporate people.

The Kaspari family had bailed out the worst of it and Finn had slunk away. He'd been thirty.

Holy crap.

Well, that certainly explained a few things. Not even Zia's story had hinted at the true situation.

So when Finn said he had no money, he was probably speaking the truth.

"Excuse me?" a man said.

Tina looked up. The fellow was middle-aged, wearing civilian casual clothing. Short beard, olive skin, friendly eyes.

"I'm sorry. I don't know where anything in this station is either," Tina said. She slid her comm in her pocket and grabbed the handle of the trolley again.

"No, I'd like to ask you a question."

"Me?" Surely he had the wrong person. But a feeling of dread came over her. "And who are you?"

"My name is Farlan Goss, of the Olympus Gazette. You are one of the people who came back with the Starfighter *Manila*, right?"

"Uhm, yeah." She guessed talking about that was better than that he knew her name and started asking about Dexter. Especially a journalist.

"Why do you think that the Federacy is keeping the war victory secret?"

"Uhm..." She frowned at him. *Because there is no victory?* "I... uhm... haven't heard."

"The rumour is that the *Manila* has returned as a result of the victory of the fleet. Is that true?"

"I... don't know."

Hell, what was going on?

"Were you on board the ship?"

"I was, but only on our way back. I'm sorry. I'm not a member of the Force and don't feel qualified to comment on this. You should ask them."

"They're not answering our questions."

"Well, uhm... certainly I can't answer those questions for them. I'm sorry."

Tina picked up the handle and pushed the trolley away.

He ran after after her. "We've been trying for days to get more information. I don't understand why if there is a victory, we don't have a hero's welcome for the crew."

"Sorry, I really can't comment on this. You'll have to excuse me."

Tina walked faster.

But around the corner, a couple more people waited for her.

"Excuse me! Excuse me, can you answer a few questions?"

"No, sorry. I know nothing."

"I am a reporter with the Olympus news," a man called. "We will pay you for the interview."

"I am from the Advance News," a woman yelled.

"I am an investigator for the Federacy News Service," another man said.

Tina kept walking, but the pack followed her. There were at least twenty of them.

"When is there going to be a victory celebration?" a woman asked. "We all want to see our heroes parade through the streets."

A man asked, "Why do you think the Federacy is keeping silent about this?"

And another man called, "Is is because there was much loss of life involved and they want to avoid drawing attention to it?"

A woman added, "Can we even believe anything the Federacy says after all the corruption scandals?"

"Why won't General Smith release their correspondence with the Aurora System?"

"How much did he pay the pirate leader Artan to stay away?"

They surrounded Tina and barred her way. General Smith? That was the same guy the Federacy had wanted the

Manila to report to. Who was not someone either Aliz or Evelle knew.

"It seems you know a lot more about this than I do," she said. "We've been in transit for quite a long time. I was guessing that if the war had ended, the news would have reached us."

She was thinking quickly, because she did not want to mention that they had travelled with Freerangers. Was it possible that Clementine had deliberately withheld the news from her?

But in that case, certainly someone else would have known? Someone like Zia Partlow, who was very much connected and placed a lot of importance on the news.

"We were hoping you could tell us more about the war, since you were in the middle of it."

"I don't know much more. I am not with the Force, and the *Manila* has been taken to the military part of the station."

She also wanted to be careful here, because there might be something else going on, something political that she didn't yet understand and she didn't want to put her foot in it.

"I understand that you returned Finn Kaspari to the system," a woman said.

"I don't want to comment on that."

"Do you at least confirm or deny that?"

"If he wants to speak to you, he will announce his whereabouts himself."

"If you speak to him, can you let me know whether he intends to refund all the citizens who invested money in his company?"

"I am sure he can answer that for himself as well," Tina said. "I am not his secretary."

"But he is with you?"

"If anyone wants to talk to him, and I mean anyone from the authorities, then they will probably know where to find him."

"Are you protecting him?"

"I can't comment on any of that. I have no idea what you're talking about. I came from the world of Cayelle, which is probably the furthest away you can get from Olympus. I have no idea about the politics behind any of these questions, and I prefer not to make any comments that may be taken the wrong way. Excuse me. I have to go."

Tina used the trolley as a kind of battering ram to push her way through the group and walked down the passage. A few voices shouted questions after her, but she ignored them.

Holy crap.

CHAPTER SIXTEEN

WHEN TINA CAME BACK to the *Alethia*, Finn was nowhere to be seen. She sent him a message that she had the parts, and he sent back that he was inside the engine compartment servicing the ion thruster, and was very busy.

Tina wasn't sure if she should be annoyed or glad that he wasn't there. She wasn't looking forward to having this discussion with him.

Maybe not.

She also appreciated that he did this for free, because thruster service was not cheap.

Already, Finn had too many depths that she didn't want to go into. And yet he had never been dishonest with her. He'd told her he didn't have easy access to family money. He hadn't said why, but she wouldn't discuss this type of thing with strangers, either. She had actually disbelieved him.

A lot of strange things about Finn started to fall into place.

Imagine being from a rich family and being pushed into a business that you didn't want nor were suited for, and failing, and everyone baying for your blood.

Sure, these were rich people's problems, but it attested to Finn's honest character that he'd disappeared from the scene and wanted no more to do with the business. He could have so easily swaggered his way out of the tight corner over the backs of his creditors and common people, as many sons of rich families would have done.

He hadn't.

He didn't even want to accept his family's money anymore.

Had those people gotten their money back?

Probably not. That was the way of business.

She sat in the pilot's chair of her ship, watching the maintenance warning lights on the instrument panel come up and wink out again.

They were in such a weird space right now, in this place where people's perception of reality was so skewed that it might as well be alien. Who, for example, had told the civilian population that the war had been won?

They wanted a victory parade?

Really?

Finn eventually emerged from the engine compartment, wearing his overalls and covered in black smears. His hair stood from his head at odd angles where he'd worn his helmet.

"Did you get the parts?" His gaze fell on the trolley. "Oh, good. I better take them down, then."

He seemed nervous.

"Finn?"

"What?" He stopped.

"Thank you for doing this. You don't have to."

"Yes, I do." He looked down. "I guess the workshop guy asked questions, right?"

"He did," Tina said. "In fact, there was a contingent of journalists all asking questions."

"Shit."

He let go of the trolley and leaned against the wall.

"I guess you now know what a pathetic piece of shit I am."

"I can't comment on your history and things I've known about for all of five minutes, but I've known you as an honourable person."

"Are you kidding? I made stupid decisions and when it all got too hard, I walked out and let my family sort out the mess. And the mess was so bad that even they couldn't sort it all out. I've driven people to ruin and trashed the reputation of my family's business."

"Family that you profess to hate."

"I do fucking hate them. The schmoozing, the corruption, the back-scratching. I hate it. All of it. And here you are, asking me to help you get money for your project. You've been good to me, honestly, and you don't deserve a shit friend like me."

"Finn, we've had this discussion before—"

"I know. I haven't forgotten. You told me to start behaving like Finn Kaspari. But that is the problem. I have no idea who the fuck Finn Kaspari is."

"I think I know." She met his eyes and was disturbed to see a tear track over his cheek. "Someone who is eager to be liked and sometimes makes mistakes."

He snorted. "You can say that again."

"But also someone who wants to be honest and do the right thing and can't abide the games that people in power play."

He just looked at her, his dark eyes blinking.

"But because you know these games, we're going to need you when we try to get this project going. We don't want to fall into any traps."

"That's easy. Just promise them everything and sign as little as possible. These people are all about being pally and currying favours."

"Can you help us, please? Can you come with us when we need to meet any potential creditors?"

He breathed in and out noisily. "I guess I'll have to, right?"

"Yes. Do it for me."

Finn changed out of his overalls, and Tina quickly got changed as well. She was back to using her room behind the main cabin with the bunk beds with the straps that stopped you floating away in zero-g. The geese lived across the passage. They were honking their heads off. Must be feeding time.

The next day at breakfast in one of the apartments the others shared, Jette told her she had received two replies to proposals she had sent out.

Tina was surprised. "Two already? That's a good sign, isn't it?"

"I hope so. We have expressions of interest from Olympus Pharmaceuticals and ITG."

"Any further details?" Tina asked. Damn, one of those was Finn's family's business.

"No. They would never share those electronically. We need to go down to the planet to talk."

Yes, Tina had understood that from Finn. These companies didn't discuss business except in person. Schmoozing and currying favour, he called it.

Travel off-station was also expensive and so was accommodation in Olympus City, and they decided they could afford to pay for just three people, and those people would be Jette, Tina and Finn.

Organising this trip to the planet was to be Tina's responsibility. She needed to apply to the appropriate authority for permits.

Of course, her name raised some flags that she dismissed by showing her certificate of resignation from the Force, but she wondered how long that would keep the authorities happy. Only until someone looked and figured the reason for her resignation, she guessed.

The system knew that Jette had been to Olympus, and her

application was met with a long list of *please respond with your actions taken in relation to the following issues*, followed by a list of at least twenty items that appeared to relate to agreements and financial commitments.

Jette's husband Mattias had a few choice words to say about it, but they managed to produce enough responses to make the flags go away.

Finn's application, however, was something different altogether.

After adding his name to the travel application, Tina was presented with a stylish menu that asked whether he would want to book a first-class seat on a shuttle or preferred to arrange a private craft.

Some people were really more equal than others.

Like, what the actual fuck.

Finn wasn't there when she went through this bureaucratic jungle, and she was sure this was by choice. He knew that this would come up, and he hated it.

Meanwhile, over the few days while they waited for their permits, Yalinda finished setting up a makeshift lab where the group could continue their work. They were fortunate that the first set of preparations for the material Tina and Finn had collected at Project Charon didn't require much space. The equipment or samples already took up most of the bench or table space in the apartment.

The rest of the team came in from the other apartment in the morning. This group also included Rasa and Yalinda's daughters. It was good to see Rasa with the younger girls, colouring in images of flowers and fantasy girls with pink hair, if they weren't helping in the lab, or walking the geese. Because apparently the geese were popular with station residents.

One of Yalinda's girls would decorate the poor geese's necks with her hair ribbons.

Rasa had never experienced a real childhood, having to fend for herself at a young age. Rex and Jens were trying to appear older, but Rasa liked doing things she never got to do as little girl.

Walking the geese and helping with the boring lab work was beneath Rex and Jens.

They kept to themselves either in the computer room in the apartment or aboard the *Alethia*.

On an evening that they were doing this, Tina came into the cabin. She first went to the hot water dispenser to make herself some tea.

While she was doing that, the boys were talking and laughing, their voices drifting through the cabin. Well, at least someone was having a good time.

Tina picked up her tea and sat down.

Jens wiped something off the screen. They stopped laughing and fell silent.

"What were you doing? It sounded like fun."

"Just looking around," Rex said.

"What is there to look around? Does the station have such great entertainment?"

Earlier, they had said that the entertainment options were rubbish. Or maybe they had discovered a porn channel?

A sense of discomfort came over her. She should keep a closer eye on what those boys did.

"Tell me, you are not getting us into trouble, aren't you?"

Both of them shook their heads, but Tina didn't like it. They were both old enough to know that they should be careful.

"We are here by the grace of the Federacy Assembly, who are paying for our fees. They don't like us being here, and they will be watching us from every corner. I expect the two of you to behave and not get us into any more trouble than is necessary. Both of you have repeatedly told us that you're old enough for this type of responsibility. Don't make me doubt your words."

They both nodded, but they didn't look her in the eye.

But then Finn came into the room to ask them to help him with something, and the opportunity to demand what they had been looking at was lost.

CHAPTER SEVENTEEN

REX NEVER STOPPED EXPRESSING his disappointment when he heard that he wasn't on the travel list.

"Why can't I come? Is this again about me being too awesome?" he asked.

"It's more about that we don't have money. This is an expensive place. I also want you to make sure that you keep an eye on Jens because I don't know what you're doing in your spare time, but I don't trust it."

"What spare time? We have nothing but spare time."

"Haha, that's funny."

"I'm serious, mum. Do you think that when we're done here, we can go home?"

Tina did a double-take. "That is the first time I've heard you ask about Cayelle. I thought you hated it?"

"It would be fun if we could take Jens and his dad. And Finn. We could start a workshop to fix stuff. Maybe Janusz would like to sell us the farm, and we could build robots to do all the work."

She gave him a serious look. He *had* thought about this. He *didn't* want to sign up?

"That's up to Finn and Thor. But likely, we'll be staying here for a while." If they were successful in securing funds. In truth, Tina wished she could go home. The increasing uncertainty about everything wore on her.

She wasn't even sure there was a war anymore. It seemed like Aurora and Kelso were trivial, unimportant, for the people here. They didn't care about the citizens who lived harsh lives in faraway sections of space.

It was as if, by coming here, the pirate problem had just disappeared. Fought in another part of settled space. It didn't affect Olympus. People didn't seem to think it could ever affect them.

Tina had never felt that the Federacy Assembly was on the same page as the people at Kelso Station or Cayelle or Aurora, but it was abundantly clear now.

They didn't care about the war. They cared about victory parades, regardless of whether a victory had actually happened. They cared about shops and clothing and their comforts. Refined restaurants, comfortable shuttles, modern and airy apartments. They cared about making money. That was how she would have to sell her project: as a way a potential investor could make money.

Never mind the people and their disfigurements. Unless they were rich people, they didn't matter. And they mostly *weren't* rich people. Those who were desperate to sign up for armed forces rarely were.

Tina, Finn and Jette got ready in the evening when the shuttle was due to leave. Tina packed a small bag, made sure that all was well on board the *Alethia*, that Thor, Rex, Jens and Rasa knew where to get help if that was necessary, and that they had enough supplies for at least a couple of weeks.

Rex told her, "Don't worry about us, Mum. We have Jens' dad, Arkady and the others to help us."

"Just make sure that you don't mess with the cargo hold and

its power supply. Really, we do not want those men to get out under any circumstance."

"I know that. Really, Mum, don't worry about us."

"Keep trying to contact your sister while we're gone."

"I will."

Tina handed him all the things he needed to take the *Alethia* out of dock.

She was reasonably sure that he had no idea how to fly the craft, but wouldn't put it beyond Jens. If they had to, they'd manage. They'd spent enough time playing with the simulations. Illegally, of course, but sometimes that was the only way of doing something.

Then, as they were about to leave, Tina remembered something else.

"Rasa, you said you wanted to speak with me?"

Rasa had been watching something on her screen, and she gave Tina a startled look.

"Did I?"

"You asked, a while ago."

"Oh." She frowned and said again, "Oh. It's not really important right now."

Right. Here was another issue that could turn into an unpleasant surprise at any moment.

But finally Tina, Finn and Jette were off.

Just as well, because Tina was getting nervous and having second thoughts about all this. She wanted to hear from Evelle. She wanted to keep Rex safe.

The shuttle port was another airy and modern facility, designed for people who had money. It was quite busy.

Tina wondered where these people had come from. They certainly hadn't been to the war zone, because all of them looked far too refined for that. In fact, they looked like tourists in their pretty outfits.

They acted like they were oblivious to the fact that a war raged in a different part of the inhabited galaxy.

A line had already formed to board the shuttle down to the planet.

Tina, Finn and Jette joined it.

The expression on Finn's face was blank. Tina figured this was not the first time he'd come here. She wondered if anyone recognised him or if he expected trouble.

But their permits checked out, and they were allowed on the craft without question.

Tina was still rather suspicious that something would go wrong, and suspected that this would happen once they got to the planet, at which time it would be impossible for her to leave again.

Was she walking into a trap?

What could anyone possibly want from her?

"Don't worry about it," Finn said to her as they were taking their seats.

"Don't worry about what? I've given up my entire life for this, and I don't want anything to go wrong at the last minute."

"This is a very bureaucratic place. There is always another door out or in."

At this point, the person from the seat next to Tina arrived, and they stopped talking.

The shuttle door closed, and after the usual safety briefings, they were off.

The flight would only be short, less than an hour, and in that time, they would circle the planet almost twice.

Tina looked out the window.

It had been a very long time since she had last been to a planet, and it seemed strange and alien to her. Where she lived on Cayelle was a very dry landscape, even her home world of Tirkala was dry, but Olympus was emerald green and lush, this part at least. Azure blue oceans covered a large proportion of the planet. The continents were small and verdant green.

Both poles were covered in water. One had a permanent ice cap, and the other did not. Something to do with the planet's elliptical orbit and the ocean currents, she'd read. The southern hemisphere was much warmer than the north.

The planet was officially called 2-gamma-1874c. Olympus had been a nickname from the beginning because of the huge extinct volcano that was a clear feature from orbit.

Tina could only imagine how excited those early explorers, hundreds of years ago, must have been at seeing this beautiful green and azure blue world.

The main settlement and seat of the Federacy Assembly lay in a bay surrounded by verdant green hills, the foothills to the volcano. Its summit usually hid in clouds, hence the name Olympus.

The official name of the settlement was Ansell City, but Tina had never met anyone who used that name. This was "Olympus", and it didn't matter that no one knew whether the name referred to the planet, the city or the mountain.

The city was not terribly big, which was surprising seeing the function of the establishment.

People in the shuttle were mostly diplomats returning from elsewhere. The man next to Tina assured her that there were not as many diplomats and bureaucrats as there used to be.

"It's been really quiet recently. Not as many people visit."

"Does that have anything to do with the war?"

He shrugged. "Could be, but I doubt it. We get news about battles and all that, but mostly we only hear about stuff long after it has happened. People are not interested because it's hard to keep track of it all. It's so far away in deep space and these military people are all very secretive about it. That is the good thing about space wars, isn't it? It doesn't affect the population."

Tina wasn't sure that she wanted to enlighten him. On the other hand, *he* didn't seem to think there had been a victory.

He continued, "But did you hear about the ship that came back? It was called *Manila* or something."

Yeah, about that.

No, she said she hadn't heard, and when he asked her about what her reason for coming to Olympus was, she gave him some story about a commercial project.

She wasn't sure whether he believed her. It mattered little.

These people's lives were so different from hers. She could imagine why many people were happy to never come here at all.

When she glanced over her shoulder at Finn, he was hiding behind his info pad, pretending not to be there.

They landed at an airy and well-appointed spaceport, where they went through the disembarking and customs routines without trouble.

There were no multiple checks, no questions and the only uniforms in sight were those of the spaceport staff.

"It's all so surreal," Jette said. "It's like they don't even realise there is a war."

On the other side of the checkpoint, a bus waited to take them to their accommodation. It had rained recently, and puddles dotted the tarmac.

Tina had applied for a diplomatic pass, which gave her access to the Federacy compound. This included both the assembly and the Federacy Force headquarters.

The accommodation complex at the assembly compound was a sprawling, single-storey building. The rooms all looked out into lush courtyards with pools or outdoor dining areas. Tina had seen pictures of places like this but had never been to any of them.

Her thoughts were on the cost of staying here and the mounting bill she'd have to face one day.

CHAPTER EIGHTEEN

IT WAS midday when they got to the accommodation, but there was no time to enjoy the facilities, the pool, the beach or the lush courtyards. They had to start work immediately. Jette had booked a meeting room in the complex and invited a bunch of people from the medical industry to come.

These were not people who wielded huge amounts of power or money, but rather, fellow researchers who might be interested in collaboration.

She had prepared a presentation about the research they had done so far, a huge compilation of work done by Tina, Arkady, Yalinda and her medical team, compared with the existing scientific literature about the subject.

The presentation set out what they planned to do and how, what they hoped to achieve and what they needed.

A few extra appointments resulted from this presentation. Jette said that she would usually hold meetings like this to inform potential research staff that jobs might be coming up.

It was late, and Tina wanted to go to sleep, but they needed to get ready for the next day when they would be visiting the first of their two major contacts. This was Olympus Pharmaceuticals, the company owned by Finn's extended family.

Finn talked to them about the people they were going to visit, their likes and dislikes, and what sort of questions they would be likely to ask.

He spoke at length about their families, their interests and their houses and country estates. Apparently, one of the directors had a liking for sailing.

Jette made a lot of notes.

Tina laughed. "We spend more time stroking their egos and indulging their passions than we will talking about the project."

Finn said, "Believe me, but this is how it goes. The more you impress the person, the more they will be prepared to do for you. You have to make sure that you are someone they can trust and that they like."

"I didn't think anyone trusted or liked each other in this world."

"Trust only goes so far, of course, but personal contact is very important. If you ask these people about business, and you want them to part with substantial amounts of money, you have to please their egos. Most likely, when one of these companies likes us, they will invite us to a social setting and they will give us plenty to drink to see if they can loosen us up."

"There will be no loosening up," Jette said. "That's inappropriate. I've never done that for any of my projects and we've always been successful getting money."

"This is not that world. It's important that we do this, because this is important to these people."

"If you say so."

Tina wasn't looking forward to that part at all. She sided with Jette. "I don't think we should go down that path."

Finn shrugged. "Then you don't get the money."

"You're not going to tell me that your family wouldn't

contribute to a good business proposition if you came to them with it. I may not know that world and all its corrupt processes, but I do know one thing: these people never say no to making more money. You act as if your family would rather that you went to their competitors with his proposal, and I don't believe that at all. We need to sell them on this."

"It's not selling as you know it. It's backstabbing, scheming, even screwing your own family out of money, under the constant threat that so-and-so will cut you out of their will. I do not *care* about my fucking will. Do. Not. Care. I would rather die than use their dirty money. I've told you that many times before, too."

He had.

"We need this money. You know what the scientists can do. You know how close we are to a solution. You know that when they sign, we will have a great facility, and since most of the research is already done and paid for, and we can concentrate on developing ways to get treatment out to the people and sell the stuff. Which pharmaceutical company would not be interested in that?"

"You'll just create another way to be dependent."

"Does true independence exist? I highly doubt it."

"Don't talk so flippantly about this. The level of corruption is astonishing. I may not know what I want. I may be clueless, and idiot—"

"You're not an idiot—"

"Plenty of people would disagree with you. I had the misfortune to be born with a conscience in a family that has none. None at all."

"Yet, we need money and a place to work. And a distribution network, once we find treatment. The Federacy has shown no interest. Companies have. Some private companies have been after that paper I wrote."

That seemed ages ago now.

Finn sighed.

"Then you find out your subject likes sailing. When you visit, you talk about sailing, you go sailing. You let him see that you are a sailor yourself. That is how it goes. There is nothing else to it. You show the plan, and it's just windowdressing. It's not about how good the science is, because they don't know anything about it anyway and these people are pitched so often and all the stuff is fluffed up to the point where it sounds wonderful. It is about how well you can present yourself, and how much they think you're like them. This business, these companies are so corrupt, you don't even understand how bad it is. They're all in the pockets of the Federacy Assembly and Federacy Force. Isn't is handy that all the buildings are so close to each other, and people can meet each other here and dine along the beach in beautiful places. They don't care about what happens in the rest of settled space. They don't care about the war or about anything."

"I don't care what they think about the war. I just want their money. I want to make a case why they should invest. That's the word I'm going to use: invest. Help us build the technology and then make profit from the treatment."

"I don't think it will be that easy. Pirates have no money. Worse, they don't see the need to have the mutation reversed or monitored."

He met her eyes, and Tina knew he was right about this. This was a big flaw in their plan. They might be close to reversing the infection, but who would care and how could these companies make money out of helping people who had none?

"You are still coming with us, tomorrow, right?"

"Sure. I'd hate to see you get screwed even more than necessary."

Wasn't that going to be fun?

Later that evening, Tina tried to contact Rex to see how they were going. But she had trouble getting through and was told that registered residents got priority.

By now, of course, she wasn't tired anymore, so she went in search of a registered communication terminal.

The accommodation had a well-appointed communication room where people could sit and take care of communication that they couldn't access through their devices.

There were screens that allowed the user to log into the Federacy systems—user registration and passcode needed—and also a screen that gave access to the INTAR system, which the attendant said was a bonus for visitors, even if he wasn't sure exactly what it did. Of course, it also required registration.

Off-world communication was limited to residents of Olympus, so it turned out that this beautiful room was of little use to Tina.

Back in their apartment with Jette and Finn, she checked the local news on information about the *Manila*, but didn't find much that she didn't already know. Including talk about the victory parade.

Why were these journalists still harping on about this?

Jette finally put her work away. She said she was tired and went to bed.

Tina went for a walk.

The accommodation lay at the edge of the Federacy compound. Tina walked along the leafy avenues, marvelling at the modern buildings. But inside her, anger burned with an increasing intensity. There was a war being waged in the name of the Federacy, and these people here were just getting on with their lives, eating at restaurants, going back to their houses without being afraid of being arrested or running into pirates. The schools were still going, entertainment was still going. Did these people care?

When she got back, the logjam of communication off-world had subsided and she managed to get onto Rex.

They were doing fine, he said.

No, he'd heard nothing from Evelle, but he had heard rumours that some other crew had been released. Who, he didn't know.

Then he asked, "Do you think I could come down to the planet one day? I'd like to see it."

"Well, we don't have money."

"I know, but once we do."

"Sure."

If they were successful in finding a sponsor, they would probably need to bring most of their equipment down, or they would be allocated a permanent place in a station in which case trips to the planet were a possibility.

"Any reason you're asking about this now?"

"I'd like to talk to some people."

"People?"

She didn't like it when Rex went mysterious. "What kind of people?"

"Apparently, medical procedures have advanced a lot. If I worked and got some money—"

Wait, wait.

"Rex, your father hasn't been talking to you, right?"

"He *is* my father."

Meaning yes.

"Don't believe anything he says."

"I looked it up. It really does say that people can regrow missing body parts. They're advertising treatment."

"Rex, don't contact anyone or sign anything until I can look at it."

"I know, I know, I'm still a child. Everyone keeps reminding me."

Thank the heavens for that.

"Oh, I almost forgot. Some thing came in for you."

"Thing?"

"It's an official-looking document. It says they're going to repossess their claim or something like that."

"Wait, what? Who is it from?"

"It says Federacy Debt Repossession Agency. It has a name here. The claimant is Paulito Distefano."

Oh damn, the junkyard merchant.

"Is he still carrying on about his control module? Can you send that message to me?"

"Now?"

"As soon as you can. I'd like to have a look at it."

She dreaded getting drawn into something else because she wouldn't sleep unless she had replied to it. She needed to be fresh for tomorrow.

Her reader pinged.

It was just as she had feared. The merchant demanded that she pay her guarantee because of "damage inflicted" and he had complained to the Orbital Station authorities who threatened to keep the *Alethia* in dock unless she paid back the bond.

Well, that was nonsense, because one unit couldn't even be worth as much as that. This was starting to look like a way to keep her at the station.

Tina wrote a hasty reply, that she had evidence that there had been another person on the station, that she knew control modules were routinely removed before decommissioning hardware and that if authorities requested, she could provide proof.

She suspected that this wasn't the last she'd heard of this issue.

CHAPTER NINETEEN

OF COURSE TINA worried all night. Mostly about Dexter contacting Rex, where she probably should have worried about the project and meeting influential people like Finn's family that not even he wanted to talk to.

She was sure she'd told Rex what Dexter was capable of, but like with any teenager, he'd probably paid no attention to it, because he didn't know what *betrayed us to the pirates* looked like. He might even feel sympathetic towards his father attempting to keep a project alive by organising their own funding. Be independent. It was what Tina had hammered into him since birth. Don't rely on other people if you don't have to.

Except that this attitude sometimes brought you into contact with the wrong type of people.

Rex was easy picking for Dexter. He missed a father figure, he was curious and desperately wanted to be "like other boys" who didn't have to wear harnesses, no matter how cool.

What had Dexter told Rex? That he could just rock up to a clinic and they'd have arms and legs for him?

Tina didn't allow her mind to go too far down that road. It made her feel sick.

When she had met Dexter, he'd spoken about money. She struggled to recall what else he had said.

Then a thought: where *was* Dexter now? He could have followed them here. It wouldn't have been difficult to get here faster than with the Freeranger fleet.

Would he care that much about disrupting her plans that he would disrupt his own?

Maybe he lived at Olympus these days, close to the source of money and far away from any nasty conflicts. Was he still selling Federacy research to the pirates or had he moved onto different schemes?

Did he care about the chaos he'd unleashed by selling the rift dust?

And if the authorities held her ship in dock at the orbital station, was that part of a scheme to trap her here?

Her mind was going around in circles.

At breakfast the next morning, Finn also looked tired. He'd probably slept as poorly as she had, with the prospect of visiting the family he hated and he'd vowed to never rely on.

Jette, on the other hand, was far too cheerful. She had risen early, gone for a walk along the beach, and prepared a list of things not to forget. It included items of clothing in case of a turn in the weather and important talking points she wanted to make sure were covered.

Breakfast was set up in the accommodation's dining room overlooking the beach.

Like dinner last night, the food was beautifully presented. There was bread and fruit and jams and little savoury pies.

Tina didn't feel hungry but knew from experience that if she didn't eat anything, she'd be cranky later, and they definitely couldn't afford for any of them to function less than perfectly.

So she forced herself to eat some bread and drink some tea. She kept away from the fruit—although it smelled wonderful—but she was afraid that it would give her a stomach ache.

Finn didn't seem to share her objections and piled plate after plate full of food. According to him, it was a good idea to fill one's stomach before the hosts started feeding you alcohol. He was probably right, so Tina went to get some pastries.

While she was choosing a selection of little tartlets from the display, a few people came into the dining room. Tina did a double take, because she recognised one of them.

It was Lisette from the crew of the *Manila*.

She met Tina's eyes.

Her mouth fell open. She spoke briefly to the woman next to her—someone Tina didn't know—and joined Tina at the pastry table.

"I need to speak to you," she said, her voice low.

"You can join us." Tina gestured to the table where Finn and Jette were also staring at Lisette.

Lisette hesitated. Her blue gaze went from the group of women to Finn and Jette and back.

"Just for a short while, then. I really can't stay long."

"I understand."

They made their way to the table, where Lisette sat down opposite Tina.

"How did you make it out?" Tina said. "I thought all of you had to be extensively debriefed. I've been trying to contact Evelle, but I'm not getting anywhere."

"I'm admin staff. I'm only contracted to the military. I haven't signed up for a long-term contract. In fact, my contract had already run out by the time we were captured."

"So they let you go, just like that? Are Aliz and the others still there?"

"As far as I know, yes."

"Is anything going on? You said you wanted to speak with me."

"Yes. It's about your kids."

Tina's heart skipped a beat. "Anything the matter with them?"

She spoke to Rex only yesterday. Damn, she shouldn't have left him up there.

"They've gotten into a secure military system. I came to warn you to tell them to stop, before bad things happen. I went to your accommodation and your ship to warn you."

"You could have told them directly."

"I did. I also wanted to tell you that this is no joking matter."

"I'm sure they already know that."

"Good. Tell them to delete everything they found, because it's only going to cause trouble for them."

She leaned on the table to get up.

"Lisette?"

"Yes?" She seemed nervous.

"When we just met and we were at the *Manila*, you said that people betrayed the ship and the fleet and that there were moles on board the ship. Did you ever find out who they were?"

Lisette took in a sharp breath.

"That was a long time ago that I said that."

"Did you find out?"

"I'm not worried about that anymore. I think we have bigger problems now."

With no further explanation, she rose and left the table.

Tina frowned at Finn.

He voiced the feeling she also had. "What the hell was that about?"

Tina had no idea, but when she returned to her room, she contacted Rex and asked him whether he had spoken to Lisette.

"Lisette? You mean the chick from the *Manila*?"

"Rex, I don't know what sort of people you've been hanging out with, but if you use that word again to describe a woman, I will quit treating you like an adult faster than you can say *travel permit.*"

He took a while to digest that. She could almost hear the gears in his head turn.

Tina continued, "Yes, Lisette from the *Manila*. She says she came to warn you about hacking into military systems. No news really, but it makes me curious what sort of stuff you've been getting into."

"Nothing, really. It's Jens doing it."

"Yes, it's always Jens' fault. But did you see Lisette?"

"No. We saw no one. We did get some strange messages that she may have sent."

"Send them to me."

"If I can. Two already self-destructed. Jens has been trying to resurrect them."

"Don't. This is military stuff you're dealing with."

"The stuff we got was not military. No way."

"Rex. What has been going on?" A cold feeling crept over her.

"Nothing really. I thought we could be useful and found some databases with records from lots of people, and we found a match for the guy you photographed inside the station. That's all."

"*That's all*? You hacked into military and civilian personnel databases and ran image comparison routines on their personnel files? That's all?"

"Jens did it all."

"I. Don't. Care. Stop doing that. We have more than enough trouble already."

"Don't you want to hear about what we found?"

Tina blew out a breath. "Tell me once and then stop doing this kind of stuff. I'm serious."

"It's interesting. The guy works for a secret division in the Federacy Force."

"The Federacy?"

"Yes. It's called the Pegasus Agency or something."

Shit.

Holy shit.

"And you broke into their database?"

"Jens did it."

"You can't keep blaming Jens."

"But he did do it. He's really good."

Evidently. "Was there anything else you got?"

"Mum! You just told me—"

"Was there anything else you got? Because the Pegasus Agency was where we worked. Me more than your father. I was an agent for them for years. They owned the station at Project Charon—"

She stopped, because Jette had come to the doorway.

"Tina, are you ready? Olympus Pharmaceuticals has let us know that our transport is on its way."

"Look, Rex. I have to go. Please promise me that you will do nothing. You *or* Jens. No poking around in databases, military or civilian. Take my card and go to the game centre."

"Those games are for kids."

"Then go and help Yalinda. I'm sure she'd appreciate it. Stay off the computers. Please."

CHAPTER TWENTY

WHILE TINA SCRAMBLED to get her things together, sure that she was forgetting something, she felt like banging her head against the wall. She should have brought Rex. She should probably have brought Jens as well. Just to keep an eye on what they were up to. So they didn't get into any more sensitive databases.

But damn.

The Pegasus Agency?

What was even the agency's business at the junkyard? They could have gotten everything they needed without trouble when the station was decommissioned.

Unless they didn't want the Force to know they were doing it. Double damn. What did that mean? What direction had the agency taken after she left? Were they still on the same page as the Federacy Assembly, or had the two become silent enemies?

So many implications, so little time to consider them.

She dressed in her neatest clothes—which wasn't saying much because she didn't have any business attire, just a simple set of dark trousers and a neat shirt. Dresses were very much a thing of the past for her.

The car arrived at the reception of the resort-style accommodation. Other people in the foyer looked like they were going out for day trips. Mothers with children going to the playground or the beach, all very traditional.

The vehicle that waited outside the main entrance was a dark-coloured, boxy, bus-like thing that came with a driver in a mustard yellow uniform.

The person—Tina couldn't be sure if it was a man or a woman—opened the door for them and did a double-take when Finn walked past. Finn ignored the driver. Tina followed him up the steps into a comfortable cabin. Finn slid the door between the driver and the passengers shut.

The driver clipped on an earpiece and spoke into it.

The vehicle started moving.

Jette said about the driver that *she looked grumpy* and Finn argued that he'd known this person as a member of his family's staff and was pretty sure *his* name was Rocco. He was shocked that Jette suggested "Rocco" was a woman and asked Tina's opinion about it.

"I don't know," she said. "We had people in the Force like that, especially in research. To be honest, I never understood the fuss. We all wore the same uniforms, and they looked baggy on everyone. Officers at the station had their own cabins. I don't care about their gender."

"But what did you call them?" he asked.

"Just by their name."

"That's so awkward."

"No half as awkward as making a fuss."

"Huh."

Tina glanced at Rocco's back.

What a weird discussion to be having on the way to such an important meeting.

A sign that they were all nervous. They didn't want to say anything important.

Finn watched Rocco's conversation through the earpiece with keen eyes. The window did not let through any sound.

The vehicle took them along tree-lined boulevards and through leafy residential areas.

It was quiet on the road.

Gradually, the buildings on the side changed from apartment blocks to single houses, and then single houses with large gardens.

Then they went into the hills and the houses grew increasingly lavish.

The bus turned into a long, tree-lined driveway that climbed gently to the top of a hill.

The house that sat there was huge and white, spread across various wings and two floors with jutting balconies with elaborate metalwork railings. Plants grew in giant pots on those balconies. Tina spotted hoses and tubes of the watering systems. The garden contained a maze-like arrangement of clipped bushes. A man sat on his knees between them. He waved at the van.

Did people live by themselves in big houses like this, or did they have their entire family and a raft of servants living with them?

At the farm where Tina had grown up, farm hands and other contracted staff would stay in a separate wing during harvest season, because they were a distance out of town. During those times, it got very cosy because there would be people camping in the spare rooms and on the veranda.

But her house was nothing like this.

The driveway curved in front of the house so that vehicles could stop under the overhang of an awning.

When the bus stopped, a man came out of the main entrance of the house and opened the door for them. He also wore a mustard uniform.

This person greeted Finn with a polite bow. "We are so glad

that the young master is home again."

Clearly, the driver Rocco had reported Finn's presence to the family.

Finn's expression was hard. Tina pretended not to have heard the remark.

But imagine growing up in a place like this. Bet he'd had a personal driver to take him to school. Maybe he even had his own school.

The man led the three of them into the hallway, and from there, another servant, also in mustard, took them into a large office.

Inside the office stood a couch and several chairs. A man sat in a broad armchair, looking at the door as they came in.

He was round-faced with a bushy moustache. His hair was curly, unruly and more grey than black. He wore a dark blue business suit. His hands were adorned with gold rings, and a glittering bracelet with thick links encircled his wrist.

"There you are," the man said at seeing Finn. "I only heard from Rocco that you were involved with these people. Why didn't you tell me?"

"It's their project."

"And? You're here with them. To tell them what to say. You could have just written the proposal to me. Then we could have discussed it over dinner."

Finn said nothing.

"How is your engineering going, anyway?"

A muscle in Finn's jaw twitched. "Let's keep this businesslike. This is about Jette and Tina's project."

"Yes, let's."

He sat back and folded his hands on the desk. It almost sounded as if he was laughing.

With all the will in the world, even with the fraught relationship she'd had with her own parents, Tina couldn't imagine treating her family like this.

Finn continued, his voice stiff. "Tina, this is my father, Michael Kaspari. Dad, this is Tina Freeman."

The man nodded politely and looked Tina up and down. Finn, she decided, didn't look like his father at all. He was taller, slimmer, less round-faced, his hair was much less curly and his face had a lot more angles.

"Freeman, eh?" Michael Kaspari said.

Tina was wondering whether her reputation had preceded her. She was wondering what the politicians said about her because she might have a bit of a reputation with the establishment. She knew that no one had collected the materials she left in the message box at Kelso Station, but that didn't mean that none of her objections would have come out. Or maybe the reputation of the Freeman name was based on Dexter's antics. Where *did* Dexter live these days?

She started with a polite, "Pleased to meet you."

"My secretary tells me that you have a proposal to make," he said.

"Yes, we sent you a copy."

He *had* to have read it, because otherwise he wouldn't have been so keen to talk to her, right?

But right now, Tina felt certain about absolutely nothing.

These people were playing games over their heads. Maybe he'd only invited her because of her name.

Tina started a brief explanation about the work she and her team of scientists had done so far. Occasionally, she asked Jette to talk about sections of the work. She wasn't sure how much he already knew, and his facial expression remained bland.

She imagined him sitting in front of a business partner, trying to stare down a competitor. It was an uncomfortable feeling.

When she had finished, he nodded and put his hands together and then let another uncomfortable silence lapse while he seemed to be thinking.

Then he said, "We are also working on a cure for this mutant condition as you describe. The last time I was talking with my people about this, they seemed confident that they were close to a solution."

"Maybe our teams could work together so that we could expedite the process?" Tina said.

"That would require extensive negotiations," he said.

"But would you be interested?"

"In principle, yes, but it would be up to my scientific managers to determine the feasibility."

"I think it's important to work quickly. We will save many people from becoming mindless monsters. According to our work, it's not so easy to reverse the process in humans, unless it's caught in the early stages."

"I agree."

Huh. She expected him to tell her how the infection also had useful side effects and that perhaps they could separate those from the harmful ones, but he didn't.

He asked for contact details—even though they were clearly spelled out in the document Jette had sent. He asked if Jette was open to discussing details if his people wanted to talk.

And then, just like that, the conversation was over. They were out in the corridor before Tina realised he hadn't made any commitments and shared any plans.

Or had spoken about sailing.

"Didn't he even want to know how you were?" she asked Finn when they were back in their safe cubicle in the back of the van.

"When he's in a business mind, he talks to me like I'm any other business associate. He doesn't think much of me, anyway." He let that hang between them.

"I don't think we got anything from him."

"No, I think we got the silent treatment. He wants to know what we've been doing, but he doesn't want to share anything about what they have been doing. They're watching us, but not in a good way."

Tina felt doubt and a feeling of despair come over her.

"Don't worry too much about it," Finn said. "This is all part of the process. We'll see a few other people this afternoon. My father will be watching. As soon as someone makes us an offer, and they will, he will pounce. Because he can't stand a competitor getting the better of him."

"Would you want to accept his money?"

"It's not me doing the project. He'd give the money to you. I've told you what I think of this business, and I'm just here to make sure you don't get sucked into signing stuff you shouldn't sign. When it's all settled, I'll just go back to being an aircraft engineer. I've been talking with Thor. Maybe we can set something up together."

So they went back to the accommodation where they grabbed a bite to eat.

Tina told Finn and Jette that Jens had discovered that the person they had disturbed in the station worked for the Pegasus Agency, but didn't think either of them comprehended the seriousness. Finn just shrugged and told Tina the subject was *her department*.

The other two visits they had lined up for the day were to less lavish places, but Tina thought the people were more accessible. One of them showed obvious interest. The problem was that they didn't have work space available immediately. Tina wanted everyone in the project to come down to the planet as soon as possible so that she could keep an eye on Rex and whatever Dexter might be up to.

"I don't think these applications are going to go anywhere in a hurry," Jette said, when seated in the courtyard for dinner after a long day.

"Why not?" Finn said. "We've told everyone. Now we wait until they've finished scoping us and each other out."

"I want to see if we can get a Federacy grant," Jette said. She looked grumpy. "That's a world I understand."

"Are there any applications open?" Tina asked.

"A few."

"But it's going to take ages to get a reply, isn't it?"

"Possibly, but I don't know an alternative."

Tina felt a lot more comfortable applying to the Federacy agencies than trying to out-fox these commercial companies with their hidden agendas and love of sailing and otherwise buttering each other up. Although no one had yet given the impression that social buttering-up would be required.

The Federacy might not give as much money, but at least, it came without strings and the necessity to butter up people who already had over-inflated egos. Or to try to see through their intentions.

On the other hand, the feeling that this was going to be a short visit was evaporating by the minute.

The Federacy Assembly was in sitting, and Tina and Jette found the contact details of a delegate who had openly expressed concerns in the assembly that they needed to fund medical research to combat the spreading infection.

Jette found the grant program in question and she and Tina spent most of the evening retooling their documents to suit the requirements. Jette was really very good at this.

Afterwards, sitting in the courtyard with Jette, they considered how strange it was to be battling the usual bureaucracy while a war was fought in another part of inhabited space. A war the Federacy also denied was happening.

There was still no word from Evelle.

Tina's spidey sense was getting ever louder. She just wished she understood how all the various troublesome facts were connected and hoped that by the time they discovered this, it wasn't too late.

CHAPTER TWENTY-ONE

JETTE MENTIONED at breakfast the next morning that she found out that there was a committee where they could apply for the various grants in person to expedite the process. She had been to the office before, but when they got to the building in question, it was almost deserted. The assembly was in session, they were told by a lone attendant, and the people from the committee were also delegates, so they were occupied with the session.

"They'll be free this afternoon. I can make an appointment if you want to present your case."

Tina said that they would be interested in doing that.

All of this meant they had to hang around for most of the day to wait for that meeting.

They found out that members of the public had access to the public gallery at the assembly. So Tina, Jette and Finn went to the building in the centre of the compound, a familiar round shape that featured in many news reports.

They had to show passes at the door, but were allowed in without question.

When descending into that fabled hall through a door in

the upstairs gallery, it struck Tina that the hall was far larger than it looked in the news coverage.

In those images, the hall looked stately and old-fashioned, but in reality, technology was everywhere.

The news usually showed delegates speaking from the lecterns in front of each delegation's seating, but never showed the admin staff who sat in the box behind the delegate, with all their computers and screens and communication equipment.

It was hard to comprehend just how many people were in this room. A thousand, at least. The hall was big enough to necessitate the use of screens focused on the delegate who was speaking so that everyone could see this person.

Right now, this was a silver-haired man dressed in grey. His voice boomed through the hall, punctuated by jabbing movements with his index finger at the surface of the lectern. He spoke Sinolese, translated on the screen for those who didn't speak it. Even so, Tina didn't understand the discussion. Another screen declared the meeting's agenda, and the assembly was currently discussing the "Joint Ownership Proposal". Whatever that was.

He seemed fired up about it.

Tina recognised Assembly President Jarod Silvers, who sat in the chair in the middle of the hall, his chin leaning on one hand. Frankly, he looked bored.

In real life, his flyaway mane of white hair was more dishevelled than in the broadcast press conferences.

The other people in the observation gallery were mostly reporters. Besides cameras and recording equipment, their supplies also included packets of biscuits and many empty cups.

These people eyed Tina, Finn and Jette as they found three empty seats on the bench, one row back from the railing.

The debate on the floor of the hall raged on.

The old man had finished, and the focus of the screens

went to a woman in late middle age. She had short spiky hair, round cheeks and sharp eyes.

She resembled an older, rounder version of Rae.

"I do not agree." Her voice was clear and sharp.

President Silvers shifted the hand he used to support his chin.

The woman continued, "If we are going to establish a committee to oversee and coordinate Joint Ownership, we cannot have on the same committee people who will benefit from that joint ownership."

A man called out, "Do you want to stack the committee with people's advocates? They will never get anything done!"

The woman gave him an icy stare. "Maybe then it's because they *shouldn't* get anything done, because the proposed deals go against the benefit of the communities and into the pockets of large corporations, like your own. In fact, you just made an excellent point why people like yourself *shouldn't* be on these committees."

"Dream on," the man called. "Why do we waste time discussing this nonsense, when all it does is delay important decisions and cost money?"

Finn looked sideways at Tina. "That's Jonathan Plesk. He's on the board of Trilia."

Tina had learned that was his family company's biggest rival. "Are they allowed to be in the assembly?"

"Yes. Many of the company owners are."

"So that they can take decisions that benefit their bottom lines?"

"That's politics for you."

Tina and Finn's voices had drawn glances from the reporters. Tina continued in a lower voice, "And who is that woman?"

"Greta Ji."

"And she is?"

"Delegate for Valaria. They don't like Olympus very much over there. People say they're jealous because there used to be talk that the Assembly was going to be housed on Valaria."

Tina had heard this rumour, since Cayelle was in an alliance with Valaria. She didn't think the problem was as simple as that.

The woman was still speaking.

"...So, some of you seem to accept that a good section of this assembly peddles alternative truths. Like that the war is over. That the pirate problem has been dealt with. That it's OK to profit massively from someone else's misery. That it's OK for the assembly to abrogate responsibility for this infection that was unleashed upon us by greedy and careless individuals, some of whom are sitting right here in this very assembly..."

She glanced sideways a few rows across to a delegation from the Federacy Force. They stood out in this hall because they were all in military uniform.

"Who are those uniformed monkeys?" Tina asked.

Finn was studying a screen in front of him that displayed the seating arrangement. "It says here the one in the middle is Sector General Hieronimus Smith."

"Wait—wasn't that the guy Aliz and Evelle were supposed to report to?"

Finn shrugged. "They obviously won't be able to meet him in person."

"Do you know anything about him?"

"Besides his name, not really. He hasn't been in the job long, because Jolley used to be in charge."

"And how long did Jolley still have on his contract?"

"Three or four years."

And of course, Finn had just as much information about why this had happened as she did.

While the discussion went on, she couldn't get what Aliz and the other women from the *Manila* had told her out of her head: that this administrative body and the Force command were corrupt to the core.

She scoured the meeting's agenda for topics about the war, but didn't see anything obvious.

From the behaviour of the people in the hall, you would never say that there was a war going on. After Greta Ji had taken her seat again, they just went through their normal bureaucracy. Permit this, permit that. Law this, law that. They looked like peacocks with their coloured garb and jewellery. They didn't want to talk about people who had disappeared, about the war and hardship in other parts of settled space.

Jette pointed at the clock, which indicated that the session was about to end.

A moment later, a bell rang, loud and piercing, and all the delegates rose. It was strange how they abandoned their discussion and chatted and laughed with each other as they made their way out of the hall.

The doors were opened and light streamed in from the foyer outside.

The other people in the observation gallery were also stirring. Journalists packed away their recording equipment and started to talk to each other.

As they walked past, a couple were laughing. Tina asked what was happening now.

A young man replied. "Lunch. Then we'll have a second session this afternoon."

"Are they discussing anything about the war?"

He frowned at her. "The war is finished."

Tina very much felt like telling him the truth, but even she was starting to doubt. If several people here said the war was won, then maybe the war was really won.

Except when Tina was at Aurora Station, there had been no sign of an upcoming battle, or that the Federacy even had enough people in the sector to start a battle. That didn't look like winning a war to her.

Fear clamped around her heart. She needed to speak with Evelle.

They left the observation gallery, and then followed the stream of people back to the offices and the committee's room, where the secretary had already prepared for the agreed meeting.

Apparently, the assembly session in the afternoon was a focus group sitting and not a plenary meeting.

They took their places around the round table.

A tray of snacks had materialised in the room, and people collected their share before sitting down.

Someone offered Tina, Finn and Jette food. Tina accepted a cup of liquid, which turned out to be cloudy and extremely sweet fruit juice.

The committee consisted of nine people, men and women, in pretty garments. Several in the group held an agitated discussion about something that happened in the morning's session. Something about procedures.

When everyone had settled, Jette started the presentation. She was good at this and explained exactly what they had been doing to find out what caused the infection and how to treat it.

She finished with, "We stand on the cusp of a discovery. We need resources to complete it. If you allow us a grant, it will benefit all citizens of the Federacy."

She stopped speaking, and a heavy silence hung in the room.

The first person to reply was the leader of the committee. The woman thanked Jette for her presentation and said that they would consider it.

"I hope you understand that there is an extreme urgency," Tina said.

"Every project where people come to ask us for money is

urgent. We will consider it. Your project has merits, but we will need to consider the benefits."

"I would think that those benefits are pretty clear."

"Of course they are."

"I'm not sure you understand—"

"I understand. Thousands of people are being murdered or turned into monsters. We know. But the pirate army has been defeated. We still have people who were forcefully transformed by these deplorable pirates, and we will deal with those people. But the war has been won. We will consider your proposal, because it will be important."

"Who says the war has been won? Where does that information come from? We've come from the war zone and it didn't look like we were winning at all."

She flicked an eyebrow. "We get our information from official sources. If you believe there is something wrong with their reporting, I invite you to take it up with them."

And with that, the discussion was finished. Just like that.

Everyone got up, people commented it was almost time for dinner, and Tina, Finn and Jette made their way back to the accommodation.

Tina was seething inside. She didn't know what she had expected, but that wasn't it.

"With what army did they win the war?" Tina called out, spreading her hands. "We were there. We know that there weren't any Federacy ships in the vicinity of Aurora. We know the station fell into pirate hands. Aliz showed me the positions of Federacy ships. There is no way that the Federacy had enough ships in the region to win a war. How can they win a war with ships that don't exist?"

Finn shrugged. "Don't ask me."

"I *am* asking you, as an ex-Federacy officer. It's like... someone is pouring people into the pirate armies and then stranding them at Aurora and Kelso, and no one at Olympus is meant to know about it. I mean—there was a military delegation in the assembly. They *know* they didn't win a war."

Finn gave her a mildly disturbed look. "You know you scare me sometimes?"

"Only sometimes? I need to scare you a bit more often. You'll have to agree there is something very strange going on here. If they really cared about people turning into grey-skinned monsters, they'd be all over our proposal, but we're being met with a wall of silence. You know what? Those people and committees are going to take a while thinking about our applications, right?"

Jette said, "Likely. They're bureaucrats."

"Then we can do something else."

Finn said, "Uh oh."

"Yes. Uh oh. I want to speak with Greta Ji. She was the only person in that assembly I saw making any sense at all."

"But we're not from Valaria."

"I don't care. We can find out where she lives, because it's likely to be somewhere in the complex. If you're afraid we'll be judged for it, we'll go to her house outside official business hours."

Back at the accommodation, Tina was going to look up Greta Ji's address, but something in the back of her mind made her hesitate. Who knew how many people were watching her. So she contacted Rex to ask him to find out on her behalf.

"Can't you do that down there?" he asked.

"Yes, but I don't know who's watching. And I wouldn't pass up an opportunity to speak to my awesome son. What have you been up to?"

"Not much. It's boring here."

"Good."

"Why is it, Mum, that you always think that it's good when I'm bored?"

"Because you don't get into mischief. Have you heard from your sister?"

"And why is it you tell me not to get into stuff and in the next breath ask me a question that requires me to get into stuff?"

"It doesn't. I just want to know if you or anyone else has heard from the *Manila*'s crew."

"Mum, they moved the ship."

"Moved?" Her spidey sense started tingling again.

"It went from the receiving dock to another part of the military base."

"For maintenance?"

"I don't know. You can see that the engine is still powered up."

"Wait—what? How do you know that? What have you been getting into? What did I tell you?"

"It's Jens, and we're bored, and his dad said it was OK. We weren't breaking any rules."

"Come on, pull the other one. Jens' dad is just as concerned about you as I am."

"Yes. He's also concerned about the *Manila*'s crew. There is a point where being concerned about breaking rules is less important than being concerned about something else."

"If you're saying that to justify your rule breaking, then you're at the wrong address, young man."

"No. Jens' dad said that he heard technicians talk about moving the *Manila* out. Apparently, that General Smith was involved."

Well, damn. "Then where is the crew?"

"Apparently, they're refusing to leave the ship."

CHAPTER TWENTY-TWO

JENS DIDN'T HAVE much trouble finding out where Greta Ji lived, because every delegate was meant to be reachable for the people they represented.

Tina looked up the address. She lived outside the main gate of the Federacy complex, in a residential quarter close to the ocean.

It was not far from the accommodation.

Tina suggested, "We've been going for walks at night, we can go for another walk after dinner and then visit her."

Neither Finn nor Jette objected.

It was not like they had anything else to do while they waited for additional expressions of interest or questions. Or, for that matter, for a return ticket to the orbital station, because it looked like decisions, if any, were not going to be taken in a hurry and they couldn't afford to stay in this place for much longer.

So they got dressed in casual clothing, and left the accommodation through the door of Tina and Jette's room, because it opened into the garden. They walked along the leafy avenues of the compound.

They came past the assembly building, which was all dark, but light still burned in the Federacy Force building. Tina wondered what was going on in there and whether they believed the war was supposed to be over.

Few things made sense.

While they walked, Finn chatted about the scenery.

Over the treetops, the mountain that bore the name Olympus blazed in light. Even from this distance, the little lights of ski trains going up and down were visible. While the city was subtropical, the mountain was tall enough to be covered in snow year round. Skiing and other snow sports were a big thing. So was sailing, and fishing, apparently, because when the path joined the seaside boulevard, quite a few groups of people waded through the shallows, dragging nets. A few boys shook their catch into a bucket. Tina had a look at the mass of wriggly things they had caught. The creatures glistened in the light from a street lamp on the boulevard.

"They're worms to catch bigger fish," Finn said. "I used to catch them, too."

The air was warm and the night quiet.

There were almost no clouds, and if you looked into the sky, you could see the occasional moving speck which was a station or a ship orbiting.

Once they left the Federacy compound, the road became busier.

At one point, they had to cross the main road, where all traffic had halted to make way for an emergency vehicle.

The sound of the siren echoed over the boulevard. People stopped to watch as the flashing lights cast multi-hued shadows.

The vehicle passed and turned into a side street.

"I haven't heard that for a long time," Finn said.

Tina hadn't, either. Not since going to Peris City, because

Gandama was too small for emergency services to be kitted out with these trucks.

In all, it was quite a relaxing walk, and Tina felt quite guilty about not doing anything about their research proposals.

They arrived at the block of townhouses where Greta Ji lived not much later. The back yards ran into the rustling darkness of the mangroves, from where the sound of bird calls drifted.

Warm light blazed from the windows on the ground floor of the house. Tina went up the veranda and knocked on the door. Footsteps sounded on the wooden floor.

The door opened. A woman looked out, surprise on her face. From close up, Greta Ji looked older than she had in the assembly earlier that day.

She asked, "Can I help you?"

"My name is Tina Freeman." She paused and waited for the *The Tina Freeman?* reaction, but it didn't come. Tina continued.

"I visited the assembly earlier today and watched you mention corruption. I want to talk to you about this."

Greta gave her a frown. "I assume you have been following the news?"

"As far as I can, yes, but we've come from the Aurora system—"

"The Aurora system?"

"Yes. Is anything wrong?" Tina's heart was thudding.

"No, just that few people come out of the Aurora system these days. Not even the delegate from Aurora has made it to the assembly. The commercial flights have stopped and private flights can't get a permit."

"Because of the war that's supposed to be won?"

Greta frowned, glanced over Tina's shoulder, and opened the door further. "You best come in."

She glanced over Tina's shoulder again.

"Is there a problem? We don't want to endanger you."

"You always have to be careful when talking about sensitive issues. The walls really do have ears."

Inside the house, two more women sat at the table in the kitchen. Both wore the grey outfits that marked them as employees of the Assembly.

Greta introduced them as her assistants, Alya and Sherri.

Tina, Finn and Jette sat at the table while Greta went to get tea.

The house was well appointed, although not luxurious. Although Finn had told her that these units were probably worth a bit more than appearances suggested. The position was coveted because of the cool sea breeze and the view of the ocean from the top floor. It was too dark for that now.

Greta brought tea.

First, Tina explained who she was and what she and her companions had been doing for the past few months.

As she spoke, Greta listened and occasionally asked a question.

Tina finished with, "In short, we are highly surprised to hear that, according to the Federacy, the war has already been won. As far as I am concerned, this would have been impossible, because I know for certain that there were no Federacy ships in the Aurora system and that the ships that were in the vicinity combined could not have beaten the pirate fleet. There are serious questions about how the *Manila* fell into the hands of the pirates, but even so, they were outnumbered, and it is likely that even if they weren't betrayed, the pirates would still have captured the ship. We saw nothing in the system that indicated a victory or potential for a victory. Who was the first to mention this victory?"

"The Federacy Force always told us that the war was going well," Greta said. "We have never had a reason to disbelieve what they say, at least not about that subject. I mean—there are enough other questions about General Smith, but not about this subject. Why would he lie?"

"We don't know that he is lying for sure. I was hoping you might know of any independent reports not made by the Force. How did the news reach the assembly?"

Greta frowned. "We get news about the war from the Force headquarters exclusively. I don't know that anyone else could have reported about it."

"Except citizens who happened to have travelled this way via non-official channels."

Greta gave Tina a disturbed look. "I've heard many people say that it's been hard to travel in that direction recently. The commercial flights have stopped, because of the war... but if you're saying there wasn't a war..."

"There was. Still is, according to my own observations. We came from the system. We may have escaped notice because we travelled with Freerangers, who fall outside identity checks. The Starfighter *Manila* came back with us. The crew are currently being held at Orbital Station 3."

The disturbed look on Greta's face deepened.

"I really don't like the implications of those facts."

"No. Me neither. I was wondering if you knew more, or if you're able to make some inquiries. Something doesn't add up. Is the Force reporting honestly? And if not, why not? The crew of the *Manila* has told me that there have been issues with corruption and misappropriation in the upper command."

"Did the Captain come back with the ship?"

"No, but one of the first pilots did, and she told me of the issues in the Force Headquarters."

"This was a reason that Sector General Jolley resigned."

"Resigned or was forced to resign? I understand the troops respected him and I'm getting the vibe that they don't think General Smith is an improvement."

Greta shook her head.

"I'm afraid this is well outside of my influence. The implication that someone in the Federacy or the Force, or both, doesn't want us to know what's really happening at Aurora is extremely serious, and also, I don't understand why anyone would do this. Why would they tell us the war is over when it's not?"

Tina shrugged. "I have no idea. If I understood the ways of the Federacy Assembly, I probably wouldn't be here."

She could speculate. Maybe the Federacy thought to isolate the problem. Not that the tactic would ever work. But then why lie about it? Maybe they wanted the pirates to fight each other. But then, how could they be sure they wouldn't come to Olympus?

"I understand you served in the Force?"

"Yes," Tina said, and she explained in a few sentences how she had left and how the worrying results from her research at Project Charon had sat in a box at Kelso Station for fifteen years.

"You mean—those pirates were a problem even back then?"

"No, but I saw the potential problems and warned the Force Headquarters. I was also working for the Pegasus Agency, precisely to detect such problems. When they didn't listen, I resigned and left everything in the document box, with a message to headquarters where they could pick it up."

"And they never did?"

Tina shook her head.

"Well..." Greta blew out and then said again, "Well..."

"I guess if I gave you the information, you could ask some questions?"

"I could, but it seems to me there is a much bigger apparatus in place to protect whatever is going on. I would almost be hesitant to ask those questions, because that may spur people into closing the cracks in their scheme. Whatever the scheme is. But do give me that information, because I'm interested in making inquiries."

CHAPTER TWENTY-THREE

TINA GAVE Greta all the information she had and promised to keep her up to date with anything new she found.

Greta said she would keep them informed about things that were discussed in the assembly that could be relevant.

After saying goodbye and exchanging contact details, Tina, Finn and Jette walked back along the shore. The air was warm, and the stars were out.

The waves softly lapped on the beach, starlight reflected on the water, and pinpricks of light blinked on the offshore islands across the bay.

"I could live in a place like this," Jette said.

"Really?" Tina said. "Sure, it's pretty, but I've had the feeling we've walked into a giant trap since we set foot on this world, and if anything, the feeling has become stronger."

"It is a trap," Finn said, his voice dark. "Actually, not as much a trap as a morass. A trap suggests intent. Olympus is a morass where you can drown and no one will notice or care."

"I think there is intent."

"Like someone is actually trying to stop us? I think that's placing too much emphasis on ourselves."

"Someone doesn't like the things we say or could potentially say. The *Manila* was not meant to come back. I and my data and my cactuses and my work were not supposed to be heard by anyone except a few bureaucrats who would sweep it all under the carpet."

Jette snorted. "Well, certainly, we're not getting the sort of interest in our work that I would have expected."

All their effort was for nothing. It was becoming a familiar refrain. And it was also increasingly difficult to see that this was not by design.

These people didn't want their comfortable lives questioned or compromised by ugly truths about events elsewhere in the galaxy.

They liked their beautiful lives, their regular salaries, their hallowed institutions like this richly appointed campus that oozed wealth and luxury.

The Federacy Assembly complex lay nestled amongst stands of tall trees. Only the tops of the tallest buildings poked out from above the greenery.

As they walked along the leafy lanes, animals rustled in the branches. An occasional small shadow scampered across the path.

Then Jette said, "What is happening ahead?"

She pointed.

Tina saw it, too: a faint orange glow filtered through a stand of trees. A burning smell mingled with the humid night air.

"There's a fire," Finn said.

"Oh. Remember how we saw emergency vehicles going in this direction?" Tina said.

"Oh, yes. There must be a fire," Jette said.

"It looks like it's on the assembly ground," Finn said.

He was right, but it was difficult to see because of the trees.

They kept walking in that direction because they had to go this way to reach the accommodation.

The noise got louder.

The sound of blaring sirens contrasted with the peaceful, tree-lined lane. Engines hummed. The fire popped. Gusts of embers flew into the air. Quite a serious fire, by the look of things.

As they came closer, Tina was beginning to feel uneasy. This looked very close to where they were staying. No, it was where they were staying.

This became clear as soon as they turned onto the boulevard that led to the resort. A large section of the accommodation building was on fire. Flames reflected in the pond at the entrance. A collection of emergency vehicles stood outside the front gate, and people with hoses surrounded the burning complex.

"Isn't that the part that we were staying in?" Finn said.

And as soon as he said that, he and Tina looked at each other. Finn's face was side-lit by the glow. His mouth was open.

She didn't have to say: are you thinking what I'm thinking?

"Shit."

"We shouldn't be here," Finn said.

"Do you really think it is about us?" Jette asked.

"I don't know, but it looks very much like it," Finn said.

"But who would do something like that?"

"Someone who doesn't like our questioning. Someone who doesn't like our presence here."

And Tina's mind was racing while she contemplated possible connections between the merchant Paulo making unreasonable demands on the ship, between Evelle and the others of the *Manila* being held in dock, between important pharmaceutical companies keeping them at arm's length about their work. Between the untruths being told about a war that was supposed to be over, when in reality, it wasn't. No one here was supposed to know those things.

And they were here, having escaped with the Freeranger fleet, and some people didn't like it.

If that was true, then that meant that Greta and her assistants were also in danger.

Tina grabbed Finn's and Jette's arms and pulled them off the path, across the lawn and into the shadow of the trees.

"We can't allow them to see us," she said.

"What do we do now?" Jette asked.

Tina's head was reeling. Could it really be as bad as that? "I don't know. Getting out of here is the first thing. Make sure that no one is following us."

Tina realised that all her possessions were also in the room, except for the clothes she wore and the few things she had taken. Because they had pretended to go for a leisurely stroll, that was not too much. But at least she had her evidence. But she had no money, and no way to get back to the *Alethia*.

Damn. And she had thought Rex was in the most dangerous place.

"There is only one place where we can go," Finn said.

"Not your family, right?" Tina said.

Jette said, "We should report this to—"

"No," Tina and Finn said at the same time.

Tina continued, "I don't trust any of the authorities."

"I agree," Finn said. "Greta Ji is our best chance."

They turned away from the fire and walked as quickly as they dared without running while sticking to the dark shadow under the trees. Tina was continuously looking over her shoulder, and Finn was doing the same.

If it wasn't for him, Tina would have been thoroughly lost, but he was quite familiar with this part of town, he said, and they found their way back to Greta Ji's townhouse.

The women had since gone to bed and all the lights were off, both in the downstairs and upstairs rooms.

"I guess we'll have to wake them up," Tina said, her hand on the gate.

"Be careful," Finn said.

Tina opened the gate, walked through the small yard, crept up the front steps and knocked on the door.

When it wasn't opened, she felt a sense of despair creeping over her. Would the three of them really have to hide in the woods all night and risk being found?

She knocked again, and glanced over the lawn in front of the unit and the stands of mangroves and beyond that, the glimmering ocean. Finn and Jette at the gate showed up as dark shapes. The sound of wailing sirens drifted on the breeze.

She had another idea. Orbital Station 3 passed overhead. It might still be daytime there. She sent a message to Jens: *Try to re-establish the previous contact and tell them we missed the meeting.* Hopefully, he would understand which contact.

They sat in the dark for another fifteen minutes, which seemed to last forever, and then the door lock clicked and the door opened a sliver.

"Is that you again?" It was Greta Ji.

"Yes. There was an attack."

"I know. Come in. As soon as I heard the news, we locked down and shut all the doors and pretended that we were asleep."

She opened the door further. Tina, Finn and Jette followed her into the hall.

When Greta shut the door, it got extremely dark.

Her voice sounded in the darkness. "You can stay here for the night, but after that we will have to move you to a different location."

"I would really like to go back to my ship and the rest of our group," Tina said.

The hand of fear closed around her heart. She didn't want

to leave Rex behind, and this time, they didn't even have anyone able to fly the ship.

"We have some options. We will see in the morning if we can find a way of getting you to safety."

She took Tina and the others to another room. In the dark, she fumbled with bedding. She took an extra mattress out of the wardrobe. She unfolded something with the squeak of metal.

"I've put a bed on the floor, and this foldout bed is a double. You women might share it. I'm sorry, but it's all we have. I also don't dare make a light. There will be surveillance. They mustn't think anything unusual is going on here. I'll see you in the morning and we will figure out how to help you."

But of course, it wasn't so easy to sleep.

Tina worried about Rex. She worried about Evelle. She tried to remember what she had left behind in the accommodation and what she had lost, or what anyone could find if her possessions didn't burn properly. What incredible luck that she had brought all her notes.

In the distance, she could still hear the humming of pumps sucking up water from the ocean, and the fire trucks driving back to the main road.

They were stuck here, waiting to be picked off by the people who started the fire.

She wanted to call for help from an outside source. Was there perhaps a shuttle on the station that someone could borrow? The *Alethia* didn't have a surface to orbit craft. Not even the *Manila* did. But the Freerangers had one.

CHAPTER TWENTY-FOUR

TINA MUST HAVE FALLEN ASLEEP EVENTUALLY, because the next thing she noticed was that the sun was coming up and a pale glow of light filtered in through the window.

She sat up. Jette next to her was still asleep, but Finn's mattress was empty and the blankets neatly folded at the foot of the bed. The soft sound of voices drifted through the apartment.

Tina was about to go downstairs, but one look at her messages made her think otherwise. Rex had been trying to contact her several times.

The messages read, *Mum, are you there?* And, *Mum, are you okay?* And also, *Someone is stalking us and wants to come into the ship. Do you know this person?* And he sent a picture of a man Tina had never seen.

Rex sounded really groggy when she called him, but when she asked if she should try to call again later, he said no, because he really wanted to talk to her.

"What has been going on?" she asked. "Did you hear about Paulo's claim?"

"No, it's nothing to do with that. There have been people

hanging around in the corridor outside the access tube to the ship. It's like they've been paid to keep an eye on us. If we ask, they don't answer questions, and several times when one of us has walked past, they turn around and take off."

"You haven't asked them anything?"

"They make excuses and won't answer any of our questions. Like yesterday, a guy said he was just waiting for a friend. He walked off and never came back, but later in the evening two women were waiting in exactly the same spot."

"What have you done about it so far?"

"Nothing. That's why I'm asking you. Do I need to report it?"

"No, don't."

"That's what Jens' dad said. Why? These people freak me out."

"They may have been sent by the authorities. Just stay inside. If you need to go out, only go to the shops. Try not to visit the others too often."

"That's another thing: I don't want to stay at the ship. Those freaks in the cargo holds are waking up."

"Ask Yalinda to control them with a stronger sedative."

"We've done that, but it doesn't help at all. She says she doesn't know what to do. Mattias has been here to help us put locks on the cribs."

"How come they're waking up then?"

"She says it might be because of some new treatment she tried."

"I don't know anything about that."

"She says it's based on the stuff you and Finn collected."

"But I thought—"

"She says they worked really quickly because the lab results looked really good and she knew you could use positive news in trying to sell the project."

Tina sighed. She guessed that much was true.

"But now it's become harder to control the men?"

"That's what she says. You can see it. Their faces twitch and their hands move."

"Then... I don't know. Lock them in the hold. Keep yourself safe."

The safety of her ship was paramount. If the science team needed new subjects, they would find them elsewhere. If the men were going to create trouble that Yalinda couldn't solve, they would need to notify the Launch Station authorities, with all the problems that would produce.

She sighed. "Listen, I just wanted to tell you we've hit some trouble here as well. You'll probably hear about it soon. All you need to know is that we're all OK and will try to come back as soon as we can."

Worry in her heart, Tina went down to the living room, wondering what disasters she was going to find there, and found Finn with the three women at the kitchen table.

They turned around when she came in.

"Oh, there you are. We were just talking about our next steps," Greta said.

"Is there any news?" Tina asked.

"The news is full of the attack," Greta said. She dragged her pocketcomm over the table and brought it to life with a touch of her thumb. The screen screamed in big letters, attack at assembly compound. Fifteen people missing. Terrorists suspected.

Tina scrolled through the names, and found her, Finn's and Jette's name on the list of missing persons.

"Are they saying anything about who is to blame?" Tina said.

"No one has claimed responsibility," Finn said.

"Someone has said that they spotted people running through the street," Alya said.

"Have you heard any more news personally?" Tina asked. "Do you think anyone knows that we're here?"

"We are not certain that the attack is because of us," Finn said.

"Really? Why else would they attack this part of the building, when we are supposed to be there? Why else would they attack a tourist and conference resort?"

"These types of attacks are political. They can—and do—happen anywhere at any time. There is a lot of tension in the Assembly and there has been for a while. Greta is not the only one who's been asking questions. We'll only see what the authorities will do once they've cleared all the debris and find out that we weren't in the building."

"I have no intention of waiting that long," Tina said.

That would take a couple of days, at the very least.

Tina asked Greta if she had found out any more information on how they could possibly get back to the launch station.

Greta said that she had contacted a few people to see if they could provide transport.

Tina said, "We'd need a private ship. The official channels require identification."

"Private ships also need to declare who is on board," Finn said.

Greta said, "They do, but there are ways to fudge the details."

Then Tina told Greta about the trouble Rex had struck at the station, and the demands from Paulo, and now, some kind of permanent surveillance.

"I don't understand what the merchant wants. The control units are routinely removed from all military hardware before it's sold on. There was nothing of the sort that he suggests we stole. We only took dust, and there is a lot more of that on the station."

Greta said, "Maybe a third party wants access to the station, if it is as you say and the intruder you interrupted was from the Perseus Agency."

"Then why wouldn't they take it up with the merchant? Anyway, the agency used to own the station. I presume they have copies of all that information already."

"Fair enough."

"It's got to be something that we have that is not available on the station."

Finn said, "Or something that we have that they don't want us to see."

"Good luck to them to destroy all the samples, if that's what they're after."

"We also took some copies of their sample databases."

Oh, yes.

Tina met Finn's eyes. "Do you think that's it? That there is something in there that they don't want us to see?"

From memory, all transactions, origins of samples were recorded in there. It was mostly boring stuff, like where the samples came from, where they were collected, and where they were stored.

Well, damn it.

She blew out a breath. "We're going to have to go through everything you've taken."

"That's going to take a long time. Something is going to blow up before we can look at it all. If it's just a data dump of everything that's been going on in the research base, then there might be so much that we can't find anything. We don't know what we're looking for."

"Did you leave copies on the *Alethia*'s systems?"

"I did."

"Can you get Rex and Jens to do it?"

That was an idea. Except Tina didn't want Rex to do any more risky things.

And Jens would be exceptionally good at this stuff.

"Well..." Tina blew out a breath. "I'll have to ask, right?"

"Yes."

But she would not ask him over any form of electronic communication. First, they needed to get back to the station so she could talk to them in person.

CHAPTER TWENTY-FIVE

JETTE CAME INTO THE KITCHEN, and Greta had to repeat all the news while providing breakfast.

She outlined the things they could do to get back to the station.

"There is a lot of attention on this area," she said. "The eastern wing of the resort has collapsed. I don't know if they realise that you're not in the building. They will realise this at some point, and it will become harder to leave. Time is of the essence."

She said the best option to get back to the station was by private craft, but many of the private operators were well-connected with the levels of government and other institutions of power, and she didn't feel that she could trust all of them.

She said she had invited a small private transport operator who might help.

Not much later, an older couple came to the house. The woman carried a box, and the man wheeled a trolley with a couple of crates stacked on top. Through the gaps at the handles, Tina spotted what she thought were cans and boxes of food supplies.

The weekly grocery deliveries?

But no, Greta invited them to sit at the table and introduced the two as the most hopeful prospect of getting to the station safely.

They introduced themselves as Veronica and Matt Edgar. They owned a company that shipped specialised supplies all over the settled worlds.

"Does that include shopping deliveries?" Tina said, glancing at the boxes the two had delivered.

"Most definitely," Matt said.

"These are supplies we will take out to some of our island communities," Greta said.

Finn met Tina's eyes. "Dissidents. People who don't feel safe living in the city because of political differences."

Oh.

She looked from Finn to Greta and wondered if there was an uneasy dynamic between the two, but the fact that Finn belonged to one of the richest families at Olympus and Greta was politically opposed to the established rule didn't seem to bother either of them.

Damn, this was such a complex place.

Matt and Veronica's transport company owned several vehicles, including a surface-to-orbit shuttle. But Veronica said it was being repaired and wouldn't be available for the next few days.

Did they have a few days?

Tina didn't know. She would prefer to return to the *Alethia* immediately.

"I would prefer to return sooner than that," Tina said.

Jette nodded. Her family was also at the station.

"We might be able to get someone else with a shuttle," Greta said. "I'm still working on that. At the moment, this offer is all we have."

Tina asked, "If you provide supplies for people on islands,

you would have a boat, right?"

"We definitely do," Matt said.

"And you could take us out somewhere on the open ocean?"

"We could, but why?"

"I might have an idea."

Finn looked at her, and she could see in his eyes that he understood what she was thinking. "Do you want me to…"

"Yes, as soon as you can, please."

Finn disappeared from the room.

Jette frowned after him.

"The Kaspari family won't deliver trustworthy assistance," Greta said.

"He is not going to talk to his family."

Her frown deepened.

"We'll just wait until he comes back," Tina said. "You'll hear about it if he is successful."

So they had some time to fill. Greta made tea. They spoke about the weather. Alya went to stand on the veranda a few times to check if the authorities were coming into the street to question people yet. Tina scanned the news. There was nothing about who carried out the attack.

They chatted to Matt and Veronica.

The company had been in Veronica's family for generations and Matt had taken Veronica's last name, Edgar, to be in line with the company's name, Edgar Couriers.

They knew a lot more about the Force than Tina expected, including about the rift dust infection. They had heard of Tina's research.

Matt had served in the Force's Transport division. Those were the people integral to outlying stations, like Project Charon. While officially, the division was only responsible for ships and shuttles, in practice, they would look after a lot of the logistics in remote settlements.

Matt didn't think he and Tina had ever met face to face.

He laughed. "I think I'm of an older generation."

But he definitely knew the reputation of Dexter Freeman.

"He's bankrolling a lot of these other offers you might have gotten," Veronica said.

"Is he?" Tina frowned at Finn. They'd not received any offers yet. "Why would he offer money to stop the very thing he's spread?"

"Because he doesn't want any of the other projects to be successful, and he doesn't want your project to be successful either. I'm sorry if you think my judgement of your ex-husband too harsh, but he will be trying to fend off other people from his grand plan."

"You sound like you know a lot about it."

"Matt was at that meeting where Dexter sold the stuff."

Holy crap. Tina met Matt's eyes.

He nodded. "I was there, as Transport Officer. I flew him and others to the meeting, I set up the venue and organised the communication and record-keeping."

Holy shit. "What do you know about this deal? Who were the people he sold it to?"

"Some rogue company that included people with compromised moral values. They offered him an obscene amount of money. He gave some of that money to the military, but pocketed most of it himself."

"Do you have proof?"

Veronica replied. "We sort of do, although it may not stand up in court. He initially offered Matt a share because Matt could hear everything that was being said and he would know that it wasn't all above the table. Matt was interested initially because we wanted out of the Force for family reasons. You know, the isolation wears on you."

"You don't have to tell me."

"Dexter showed Matt what payments were made to him. We think he was very pleased with himself and was careless.

But Matt only saw it on the screen. There are no records. Believe me, we've looked."

Well, crap.

Matt said, "The company who bought it was called Astral, and it was dissolved soon after the transaction was completed. It was set up for the sole reason to acquire this magical stuff that they call God's putty. They took the loot to some backwater world that was the home of one Jackson Hirsch, member of the Federacy Assembly."

"Artan," Tina said.

"Who?"

"He's changed into a pirate. I met him. He's turning prisoners—civilian and military—into pirates."

"Pirates, aren't they the ones who want to be called Freerangers?"

"No. We need a better name for these people. Mutants. That's what they are. Artan—who used to be called Jackson Hirsch—is one. He says there are health benefits to the transformation."

Matt frowned.

Then he dragged his pocket comm back over the table and looked something up.

He turned the screen to face her. It showed an advertisement for a *health treatment*, especially for people with a long list of serious medical conditions.

The text read, *Make your dream of travel a reality and spend travel time healing from a range of health issues.* The trip's destiny was listed as the magical Aurora Station, Kelso, and Cayelle.

"Wait, they're actually advertising this?"

The document listed a wide range of health benefits and cheerfully mentioned, *Get paid to get better!*

Tina looked into Matt's face and then realised, with a sinking feeling, that it might also be what Rex had seen.

"But why? Just so that they could turn people into pirates?

Is there evidence from people who responded and went on this trip?"

"They never got a huge response," Veronica said. "A lot of people talked about these ads that were springing up everywhere, but I think many people also reported that it's a scam and that the advertisers can't answer legitimate questions about treatments."

No, but Tina realised something else: rather than asking these people to volunteer, the pirates changed course and captured soldiers instead. And someone in the Federacy had been feeding them new recruits, and other elements might now be trying to stop this by spreading a narrative that the war was over.

At that moment, Finn came to the door. "We're on."

CHAPTER TWENTY-SIX

OF COURSE, Tina had to explain.

Greta's eyes widened. "You have contacts with pirates?"

"Not pirates, Freerangers. We came with them to the Olympus system. They are hanging around in the hope to secure a deal or job. The leader of the shipworld family feels that she owes us. We were going to collaborate, but it didn't work out."

"But they're willing to come down to the planet illegally to pick you up?"

"They're very good at quick missions. Boarding abandoned craft and salvage. Their pilots are far better than those who go through the best training courses."

"Pirates," Greta said, in a disbelieving tone, and shook her head.

"Freerangers," Tina corrected her.

But it was their best chance for getting out quickly. And Greta admitted she had an interest in studying the populations in settled space who went unrepresented and lived under the radar, avoiding regulations.

They waited until the evening.

Greta told Tina, Finn and Jette to stay inside. People in uniform were going down the street from house to house. Armoured cars patrolled the streets and even if the occupants didn't get out, there were cameras mounted on the roofs of vehicles and every movement was recorded.

Finn scrolled through the various live camera feeds that were available for the Assembly compound. These were designed for tourists and didn't show any details of buildings, but still, they could see groups of people in uniform move along the leafy boulevards or the beachside walkways. They stopped at each building or corner and took notes.

"They will be talking about who visited where," Finn said. "I am sure that they are now looking for us. They must have noticed that we were still contacting other people after we were supposed to have been killed."

"Just don't make any further outbound calls," Greta said. "There will be a car tonight and we will take you out to the jetty where Matt will come with the boat."

And it was only that once they were out there, they could contact the Freerangers who were going to pick them up.

So for the entire afternoon, they did nothing except wait for it to go dark.

Tina made sure that they copied all the information about their work to safe storage, where it wouldn't be a disaster if devices were damaged or fell overboard. She contemplated leaving hers with Greta, except if the whole situation went bad, she didn't want Greta to be in trouble.

There was much of Greta Ji's professional life that was only marginally legal and Tina didn't want to add to this collection. Or worse, be the reason Greta was investigated and she would be forced to stop helping political dissidents.

Greta took the three of them to a store room in the attic of the house, where she provided each person with a waterproof bodysuit.

"Olympians are obsessed with sailing," Tina said, half-serious.

"A lot of the gear is really handy. Especially if you go outside a lot. You'll be out on the ocean for some time, especially if you can only contact your pickup after you've left the city. The weather forecast is for rain. You'll be glad you have the suit."

"Where do you get all this stuff?"

The room was full of racks where clothing of all sizes and types hung. Some of it was clearly second hand. Other items were still in the original packaging.

"People donate it, often anonymously. They know we support outlying dissident communities. Matt and Veronica take this stuff to the communities, especially when the rainy season comes."

"And people donate money for that? What sort of people are they?"

"Political donations at Olympus often work both ways. A large company will make donations to two or three political causes based on the likelihood of any of them winning influence in the assembly. When the political situation is unstable, dissidents can get a lot of money because companies are hedging their bets."

"That is just ridiculous," Tina said.

"It's the way it works," Finn said.

Greta nodded sagely.

They ate a quick dinner. It had indeed started raining, a steady but persistent drizzle strong enough to make the ground wet but too weak to be audible.

When the word came that the car had arrived, they went out the back door of the house in complete darkness. They walked out a creaky gate into an alley that ran between houses.

The car waited around the corner, a small minibus without any markings on the side.

All the interior lights were off, and there was no one else

inside except the driver, who was speaking to someone via his earpiece and merely gestured for the three of them to come inside.

They did, settling on the benches with Tina and Finn looking forward and Jette facing them, looking back.

The vehicle started moving as soon as Jette shut the door.

They drove along the leafy avenues of the area, where it was deserted. There was definitely not much nightlife out here. It was almost as bad as Gandama.

But then the bus turned into a broader street that led to one of the main roads across the city and found the way barred by a roadblock.

Well, damn it.

The driver was talking on his earpiece again and then he turned around in his seat.

"They have the area closed off," he said.

Tina said, "Then you should do what I already suggested. The boat should come to the beach."

"There is no jetty in the area," the driver said.

"There is a boardwalk along much of the foreshore."

"I'll ask," he said.

After a while, they started moving again.

The driver reported, "Matt says that the tide is out, which makes it harder, because the water is shallow and he won't be able to make much speed. It's also quite a drop from the jetty into the boat."

"He can come up to the beach and we can walk through the water," Tina said.

"I wouldn't recommend doing that, because you would have to wade a fairly long way, and it's very exposed."

The vehicle now picked up speed and zoomed along the leafy avenues at quite an uncomfortable speed. But now it was so late that most of the houses were dark. They didn't see a single other person, although Tina spotted some creatures scurrying away.

She thought of Rasa and Rex on board the station, who would be interested in knowing what these creatures were. In a strange twist of fate, she almost missed those annoying, loud geese.

Then they came to a road that had houses on only one side and an impenetrable thicket of low trees on the other side.

The bus stopped at a spot where a small path lead to a boardwalk that disappeared in the tangle.

"This is as far as I can take you," the driver said. "Walk down the path. There is a viewing platform. The boat will pick you up there."

They clambered out of the van, also in complete darkness.

"Thank you. Give Greta my regards," Tina said before shutting the door.

The night had become quite chilly, and when the van disappeared, it grew very dark.

They started off along the boardwalk where their footsteps sounded loud in the complete darkness, and the only light was that emitted by their pocket comms.

Tangles of branches came past, and things scurried and clicked in the mud underneath the trees.

Then the path opened up to a small viewing platform that looked out over the shimmering surface of the ocean, smooth as a mirror, with the lights of a boat coming towards them. A small light burned inside the low cabin and the engine output was low enough so it produced almost no noise.

It turned in an arc and went along the line of trees before it motored alongside the platform.

Matt stood at the rudder, waving to the shore and peering into the darkness. The minibus driver was right that it was quite a drop down to the water.

Immediately there was a problem, because he couldn't come in close enough.

Veronica came out of the cabin. She climbed onto the roof and tossed a rope. Finn tried to catch it and missed. It fell into the water. Veronica hauled it back and threw it again. This time, Finn caught it. But there was nothing on the platform to tie it to, so Tina held it.

"I got a ladder," Matt called. "I don't think it's going to be long enough."

No, that was clear.

There was only one option.

"We're going to have to jump," Tina said.

"I can't swim," Jette said.

"The problem is that the boat can't come in because it's too shallow, so that doesn't really matter. You'll probably get quite muddy."

Finn was looking at the sky. "Did you hear that?"

Tina hadn't heard anything. She'd been too busy with the boat.

"That must be the Freeranger ship," she said.

"That didn't sound like it. It sounded like a surveillance craft."

"We better hurry up then."

"Yup."

And Finn demonstrated just that by jumping down into the water. He landed with a splash and then a curse.

"It's very muddy down here," he said, his voice muffled.

Tini peered down into the darkness, but could not see a lot.

Finn was talking to Matt and there were some hollow sounds that, after Matt diverted his light, turned out to be Finn clambering into the boat. He left muddy markings on the side.

"Next!" he called out.

Jette was hesitant.

"We'll jump together," Tina said.

She grabbed Jette's hand and, before she protested, pulled her off the platform.

They landed with a splash. Cold and disgusting water seeped into Tina's clothes. The bottom was too soft to walk on, but hard enough to suck at her feet.

Jette gave a squeal.

"Quiet," Matt yelled from the boat. "There are people in the area."

Tina pushed Jette as much as she could, but sank deeper into the mud as she did this. Jette reached out for Matt's hand and he pulled her in. Then it was Tina's turn, but she was too far away, and her boots were now completely stuck in the soft mud.

Finn said, "Wait, you hold on to me while I hang over the side."

Then Matt leaned against the back of Finn's legs as Finn stretched out over the water. He reached for Tina's hands, but from that position, didn't have the strength to pull her out.

Matt couldn't help because as soon as he would shift, Finn would fall into the water. So they consider that dilemma for a while.

And then Finn said, "Let me go. I'll climb back in."

And Matt did that. Finn fell with a splash, spraying muddy water all over Tina.

By now, the sound of an engine came from somewhere behind the trees.

"Quick," Tina said.

Finn grabbed the rope Matt threw him, climbed back to the boat, and Tina hung onto the back of his clothes. First Finn went in, and then Finn and Matt were able to pull Tina up.

She lost one of her shoes.

Then Matt went straight for the boat's controls and set off. He turn off all the lights, told Tina, Jette and Finn to huddle in the cabin, and not say anything.

At first, the boat went far too slow for Tina's liking.

Tina could even hear the footsteps of people on the board-walk and the platform. She could hear shouting, and she could see the glow of a search light track over the water.

"Look," Jette said.

Tina raised herself just enough that she could see out the window. The pursuers were using a searchlight to comb the area near the platform. It also showed who they were: the people who were chasing them wore Federacy Force uniforms.

Tina sat back down.

Here was another sign that there was excessive corruption in the Force and Assembly. That the war was not a simple matter. That the *Manila* had been deliberately led into a trap. That people in power didn't want a cure for the infection.

Her head was reeling.

Gradually, as they moved into deeper water, the boat picked up speed.

On all sides, the ocean was dark. No one followed.

"That is one of the good things about these boats," Matt said. "There are few that are as fast as this one."

A bit later later he added, "That just one of the bad things about this boat, that it's so distinctive that everyone knows who owns it."

Veronica pulled blankets out of a storage box, but it was still very cold, especially when they came out onto the open ocean and the waves were choppy and occasional squalls of rain tracked across the surface.

Tina was extremely glad when Matt shouted, "They're floating ahead."

She came out from under the blanket and unfolded stiff legs to get up from the hard and cold bench.

Water dripped from the blanket. One of her trouser legs was leaking water into her remaining boot.

When the waves and the bobbing movements of the two

vehicles allowed, she spotted the craft as a collection of coloured dots on the water.

Matt turned on the floodlights on top of the cabin.

A door opened in the side of the craft, revealing the warmly lit interior of the cabin.

Ricardo stood in the doorway, hanging onto the doorframe with both hands.

Matt brought the boat alongside. With deftness that belied her age, Veronica jumped onto the craft's wing, and Matt tossed her the rope.

Tina, Jette and Finn clambered across while both craft bobbed independently. The rope slackened and snapped taut and waves washed over the wing.

By now, Tina was so cold that she almost fell.

The Freeranger craft's cabin was impossibly warm.

"Thank you so much for coming," she said to Ricardo. "I don't know how much we owe you."

"You don't owe us anything. We actually picked up a very lucrative project, and we didn't even have to go very far for it. Sit down. Strap in for take-off. Close the door."

For now, they were safe.

CHAPTER TWENTY-SEVEN

RICARDO TOOK THE CONTROLS.

He warned that take-off might be rough, which it was, but Tina had experience in this matter. Her departure from Kelso Station had been rougher than this.

On the way to the station, Ricardo told them about what had transpired since the Freerangers had dropped the scientists and the crew of the *Manila* into orbit and they had parted ways.

"Clementine wanted to stay in the area, because she was unhappy that we had to leave you like that. There was a quite bit of arguing in the Family Mara Council and she never won everyone over. She wanted to help you go to Olympus or do your work, because she said that we need to be involved with people making decisions about us, calling us pirates and blaming us for things that have nothing to do with us. Other people make decisions on our behalf that we have no say over. Of course, the old-fashioned members of the council don't see it that way, and there are too many of them currently on the council so they can outvote the modern members. But she convinced them to stay in the area, because there were business opportunities."

Tina was glad for good old Clementine. She could be prickly, but she was navigating a difficult space in between the old-fashioned Freeranger ways and the new world where hiding was no longer an option.

"I hope she did at least get some business?" Tina said.

"We did. And it was related to this whole situation. We were asked to patrol a certain area and not let anyone through."

"But you're not a military ship? You don't have any military capability."

"No, we don't. I think some people got kind of desperate."

"What people? In what way?" That didn't sound good.

"We are only just finding out. Apparently, there has been a lot of activity on the outer reaches of the system. Some ships have been hiding in the asteroid fields."

"What sort of people are these?" Tina felt cold. People like those from the Perseus Agency trying to steal stuff from hardware that used to be theirs? People who obviously had stuff to hide from the official authorities at Olympus.

"They're not pirates, if that's what you're thinking, but it seems that a section of the Federacy Force is taking matters into their own hands. I'm not sure what they want, but they seem to be fed up with whatever is happening on Olympus."

"You're saying that there has been a mutiny against the upper command?"

"I don't know for certain. We have heard some rumours, but we don't really know what is true. It's not our world. We're not familiar with the politics. We just get paid to report if we see anyone who shouldn't be there."

The fact that whoever had hired the Freerangers no longer trusted electronic reporting also told a story.

"Do these rogue people threaten to come closer into the system?" she asked.

"I can only assume so, from the way they gave us the task of patrolling the area."

"But what are you going to do against a military force?"

"Nothing. We were just supposed to warn people if anyone got through."

For all the good that would do. "Warn who?"

He shrugged. "Clementine knows. Some authority, I guess."

This made Tina even more nervous about returning to the station. And she also knew that she had to, and that she had to make sure that she knew what was going on with the *Manila* and with the people who kept it in dock and were supposedly interrogating the crew.

And they were already almost at the station and there was no more time for talking or deliberating the best route to take in this messy situation that she didn't understand. Ricardo would soon go back to the Freeranger fleet, and the only method of communicating between them would be risky and prone to other people listening in.

Tina was surprised to see how many ships were moored at the station. She didn't think that there were quite as many ships when she had left. She also found it hard to find the *Manila*, but remembered that Rex said it had been moved. She eventually found it at a location on the very end of one of the docking tubes in a part of the station that held other military ships. A *lot* of military ships.

What did all this moving and shuffling mean?

That they needed to make space for an incoming fleet? Did it mean the *Manila* had been offloaded a holding area, or whether it was due to depart soon.

She was pretty sure, though, that if Evelle had contacted Rex, he would have told her about it.

The Freeranger shuttle put into the civilian part of the station not much later. Tina said goodbye to Ricardo and told him to give her regards to Clementine. She also said that she appreciated Clementine's help and any assistance the

Freerangers could offer, although she understood their hands were tied and that they were not a military force.

"Don't worry," Ricardo said. "We're not going anywhere, and the boys know how to contact us."

The boys. Rex and Jens, who had spent time with the Freeranger youths.

Then they were off into the station.

Jette wanted to go to her family, and they resolved to meet up the next day when everyone was rested.

Tina and Finn went straight to the *Alethia*.

But the door was locked and knocking didn't bring anyone from inside to open it.

So she used her key, but the cabin lay deserted.

"I can't even hear the geese," Tina said, looking around the empty cabin.

In fact, the lack of empty cups and electronic devices strewn over the tabletops indicated that no one had been there for quite a while.

While, crap. Finn had spoken to Rex and Jens recently. Where were they?

She went into the passage that led to the cargo hold. The geese were gone, and also one of the stasis cubicles was gone. The other two had been wrapped in silver foil. The sides of the cubicles were warm, so she assumed the occupants were still in there, but what happened to the third one?

The area was very clean and tidy. No evidence remained of the pissing contest Finn and Rex had held in here. In fact, the place reeked of disinfectant.

"What in all the seven hells has happened?" Her voice echoed in the emptiness of the hold. She tried to prise a corner loose of the foil on the bottom pod, but it was solidly stuck down.

Finn was studying markings on the floor. "Someone has

used a trolley with wheels recently. Probably to move the third pod."

So they went to the accommodation where the others were staying.

They found everyone in the living room of one of the units, including Rex, Rasa and Thor.

"Mum," Rex called out. "I knew you were back because of Jette. Why didn't you come with her?"

"Why was there no one at the *Alethia*? What happened to the men? Why didn't you say anything about this?"

"People would listen in," Rex said. "You always tell me that communication isn't secure."

Yes, she did.

"We had some really creepy people hanging around and once someone tried to break into the *Alethia*. We thought it was safer to be together."

Yalinda came in from the other room. "There have been a lot of developments here," she said. "Some of them quite promising. Come and have a look."

She led Tina into the next room, where they had set up a small hospital with three beds. Two were empty, but one of them was occupied by a man who was completely covered in bandages, but was otherwise conscious.

As soon as Tina came in, he met her eyes and she recognised the dark irises. It was Vito.

"You woke him up?"

"We had no choice. Their skin was getting infected something terrible. Big, weeping sores. Vito was the worst. We gave him medication, and we cut off all the infected growths and had to make some skin grafts. But the good news is, we grew the skin from his own cells, and applied accelerant and the new treatment we've been looking at, based on the material you collected. The skin grew back normal. It was a big risk to use it on a live subject so soon, but otherwise, this infection would probably have killed him. We're preparing to get the other two here as soon as possible."

Although Tina didn't miss the double locks on the doors in case something went wrong.

"What do you mean, infection?"

"I spare you all the details, but it wasn't pretty. It's something that can happen with people in stasis. We've had to cut back a lot of his skin and insert new grafts, but now some of the skin is growing back normal, and all three men stopped having aggressive spells."

"Does anyone from the station authorities know that he's here?"

"No, but at some point, there will be a visit from an officer to determine where we will be able to travel or get more benefits as refugees. We'll deal with it then."

Tina didn't have the heart to say that other issues would probably blow up before that time. Having the men awake presented some issues, such as how to explain their presence and their condition. They had officially been listed as part of the *Manila* crew lost in action.

"But what about you, Jette told us that you weren't particularly successful."

"That is to put it mildly."

"But why? Don't they want to cure people?"

"The people who would buy these treatments want to make money from selling them. The pirates don't have money."

"But the families of people who were turned into pirates do."

True. "It might take longer to reach those people. But we need to keep working because I think we are onto something. But the way ahead may be quite hard. We need to make some decisions as a group. There is a lot of trouble coming our way and I don't know that we haven't made it any worse by letting the Assembly know what we're doing. I don't think any of this infection stuff is the way we've seen it so far. Also, Finn and I have a pretty important job for Rex and Jens to do."

Yalinda, good old practical Yalinda, said that her concern was seeing through these new trials, and that she'd move the other two men off the *Alethia* so that they could also be treated.

A bit later, when they all sat in the living room with tea, Tina told Thor, Rex and Jens to go through the files Finn had downloaded from the station.

"What are we looking for?" Jens asked.

"I'm not sure. We need to know what's in this material first. I know it's a huge task, but there is something in this material that either people want or they don't want us to see. I want you to catalogue everything that's there, and make a summary of everything you find."

She had expected Rex to complain that it would be boring, but he looked at Jens and said, "Do you think we could use the sorting program for that?"

"What sorting program?" Tina asked.

"Zia was doing some stuff with us about how to treat data."

Well, that was a new development. "I thought her classes were beneath you."

"We were bored. You told us not to do the other stuff."

"Too right, I did."

So, they *did* see that poking in restricted databases carried risks that the group could ill afford.

Tina also suspected that Rex or Jens couldn't bear the thought that some of the younger, more attentive, kids were learning data processing and search skills they didn't want to admit never having learned.

CHAPTER TWENTY-EIGHT

TINA HAD other reasons to want the two stasis cubicles out of the cargo hold of her ship. She wanted to move the *Alethia* into soft dock, because she didn't think station authorities had officially banned them from leaving, but keeping the ship trapped on the station was much easier in hard dock because all they needed to do was lock the coupling mechanism, while the ship could detach and rip loose a soft docking tube.

Tina wanted the ship to be free to leave the station if that became necessary. Of course, having the men in the cubicles in the cargo hold offered no long-term solution for them either. And to be honest, she felt a rather selfish need to distance her precious ship from these dangerous individuals who, if they accidentally woke up, could inflict a lot of damage that she couldn't afford to fix.

They now had the makeshift hospital room inside one of the apartments, and apparently Arkady was in contact with a medical scientist who worked in the station's hospital, who had shown an interest in the project.

So the group prepared to move the men.

The group had resourced a couple of panels to make a cage.

Having Zia with them continued to be an asset. Because she was in forums and chat groups with station administrators, she had access to all kinds of places to find resources.

They set up the cage and other safety precautions inside the hospital. Vito was awake for most of this, and simply watched with a baleful look, never speaking a word.

Tina asked if he had spoken at all, but no one seemed to have heard him. She wasn't even sure that he understood anything of what was happening or was being said to him.

Tina kept an eye on news from the planet, but after the original outrage about the explosion at the resort died down, officials concluded it was "a terrible accident" and it disappeared from the news soon after.

Greta sent a few disturbingly opaque messages that could be read in a lot of different ways, even when Tina let loose Finn's ability to decipher official assembly speak.

Were people still looking for them?

Did anyone order the attack from higher up?

Did this have something to do with corruption and the split in opinions in the Force?

Those were all things that could be interpreted from Greta's replies, if one was that way inclined.

This was exactly how clever politicians got all sides in a heated debate to accept an explanation. By making it so vague as to be meaningless.

Officially, they were still waiting for word from the planet about the funding proposals—although Tina wasn't so certain anymore if they would come, or if they did, she wanted to proceed. They also still hadn't heard from the *Manila*, although the ship was definitely still at the station. Whenever she came past a map, Tina eyed the sections of the station labelled *restricted* and wondered about the things that were going on in there. She wished she had asked Lisette for more information.

When Yalinda and her people had finished setting up the hospital room, they made a plan.

With Vito, apparently, they'd treated and performed surgery on him in the hold of the *Alethia*, because *it was kind of messy*. Tina didn't fully appreciate what that meant until Arkady described the process of cutting away globs of rotting tentacles and peeling off loose skin like a fruit.

Tina understood why the smell of disinfectant in the hold was so strong.

Yalinda declared that Gerry was the worst of the three and needed to be dealt with first. He'd been in stasis the longest.

So they used the pulley system in the cargo hold to bring his pod down.

Then they secured the pod by slotting the wheels into recesses in the floor, rolled a stretched next to it, and tore the silver foil off the pod.

Its function was to keep in cold air, since Yalinda had lowered the stasis temperature to the lowest level where it would still keep the men alive.

The pod's lid was misty with condensation, but when Yalinda and Arkady opened it, an overpowering stench of decay tumbled out.

Urgh.

Tina tried not to wince. She both wanted to turn away and couldn't stop looking.

Arkady and an assistant lifted Gerry out onto the stretcher.

Threads of dark slime trailed from his skin, where dark patches marked the progress of the infection.

Arkady whipped out the scalpel and cut off the skin that was starting to disintegrate, making slimy heaps of flesh on the floor—hence the smell of disinfectant.

Tina couldn't do much during this process, and was left to try not to feel sick. When the skin was clean, Yalinda applied a white paste to it before they bandaged it up. Then she injected a thumb-length ampoule of clear fluid that was the new treatment.

It would take a few days to do its work—if it was going to work—but with some luck, they might see improvement straight away.

When the vial was empty, everyone retreated to the corridor, except Arkady, who still needed to monitor some signs. He had the stun gun in his pocket.

There was a period of tense waiting until Gerry opened his eyes. They had directed a camera at his head so that they could see what was happening.

He looked around, surprised. Tina wasn't sure how much the men still knew about their circumstances. It had been more than a year since they were first placed in these cribs, and much had happened in that time.

He made an undetermined sound.

Tina looked at Yalinda. The men had not done this before.

"Look at his eyes," Yalinda said.

Tina had noticed that, too. His eyes were not as unfocused as before. That had to be a good sign.

He slowly sat up. Arkady retreated, very carefully, so as not to upset him.

Gerry lifted his hand to his chin, feeling the wad of bandages on the line of his jaw. He had not done that before, either. He was self-conscious.

Definitely a good sign. He just sat there and looked around for a long time. No one said anything.

Then Arkady said, "Gerry, can you hear us?"

Gerry jerked his head around to look at Arkady. He opened his mouth and uttered a mournful wail.

"Gerry, we would like to make you better. Can I come and give you some more treatment?"

He took a step closer, and then another step.

But that was clearly too much for Gerry. He looked

confused and started swinging his arms around him.

"Step back," Yalinda said.

Arkady retreated.

Gerry tried to climb from the stretcher, but didn't have the strength in his legs. Yalinda had already predicted this.

He sat around for a bit before lying back down. It looked like he had gone to sleep, but his eyes blinked.

"I would think that was a success," Arkady said. "I didn't even have to sedate him."

Maybe there was hope yet, if the many developing situations allowed the group the time to refine their treatment.

Bandaged and half-conscious, Gerry didn't object to being manoeuvred into a wheelchair. This was much easier to move around than the crib. Because the crew were all dressed in medical gear, few people questioned them on the way to the accommodation. Some people even deliberately stepped out of the way.

Vito was awake and merely watched, soundlessly, while the team lifted Gerry and installed him in bed. Zia's security panels provided a barrier between them, but Tina had no doubt that if the men really wanted, they could just rip the structure down. She had seen them do worse.

For the time being, things were going well. They could do Stan tomorrow.

Tina went back to the *Alethia* to clean up the cargo hold, and she asked Rex to come with her.

While scrubbing unmentionable goop off the floor with brooms saturated in disinfectant, she asked him what Dexter had sent him.

"Nothing, really."

"But you mentioned you wanted to talk to some people on the planet about having them grow arms and legs for you."

"I never said that."

"You said something like it."

"I was wondering what you thought, because you know, you also say all the time that if it looks too good to be true, then it probably is."

"You have doubts about it." She was actually proud of him to have remembered that line. She was pretty sure her sixteen-year-old self wouldn't have been as cautious.

"Yeah. It's kind of *all shine, no details*." Finn always said that.

"Show me."

The brochure he showed her on his built-in comm on his arm was from a clinic in Olympus City that professed to have the answers to a wide range of medical conditions. It was a pretty document, showing an older couple walking on the beach with grandkids. Underneath, it said, *My grandchildren would have known their grandfather as a cranky old man in a wheelchair*.

"So what made you doubt their claims?"

"Because if it was so easy to just fix problems with people's health, then why are there still people who have these problems?"

"Because it's really expensive and people don't have money?"

"Yeah." He looked at the screen and Tina tried not to see the longing expression on his face. "But we don't have any money."

"Rex, if there was something genuine that would help you, I'd spend any amount of money I don't have, you know that."

"But you don't think they're for real."

"No, and I think you don't believe their claims either."

"Not really."

"If your father gave you this, he obviously wants you to do this."

Rex stared at her. "You think my father wants me to become like Vito and Stan? He wants to kill me?" His eyes were wide.

"I don't know if that's what he wants, but if he does, I want him to be brought to justice."

CHAPTER TWENTY-NINE

TINA HAD no time to help the scientists with Stan. To be honest, she didn't think she was much good at this medical stuff, and she felt guilty about not helping at the same time.

For all its technological advances, the medical profession didn't seem to have made much progress in dealing with the messiness of human bodies.

Instead, she dealt with the claim for compensation by the junkyard merchant, Paulo. After having written the hasty reply when she was on the planet, she knew she wasn't finished with this issue. And she had been right.

The authorities demanded that she showed them her evidence, and because she didn't trust them to handle electronic copies, she went to the office herself because in her experience, that was the fastest way to get things done.

It also gave her an opportunity to poke around the station to see if she could contact Evelle.

Her bad feeling about the lack of responses from the *Manila* was increasing, and the combination with her other recent realisations and the fact that the ship had been moved didn't make for a happy place to be. Up until now, waiting had been the best option. That had changed, but she wasn't sure what a single person could do against a huge military operation. Or what she could do to get the crew released.

Aliz had said debriefing the crew might involve discipline, but how long would that take? How much and for how long could a large force justify punishing crew for something that wasn't their fault?

The Federacy Force had a very long breath. And they could be extremely punitive and petty, if they chose to go down this path.

And her options to act were very limited.

First, she had to get this bureaucratic restriction on movement of the *Alethia* lifted before she could apply for the ship to be moved to a soft dock. So that she could uncouple the ship and leave, without permit, if necessary.

Paulo's claim had to be dismissed. So she collected all her documentation which included copies of the Federacy manuals that dealt with the disposal of superseded assets, and took them over to a very boring office where she handed the lot to a desk clerk who treated it like a routine annual renewal of a permit.

While walking through the station, she noticed it was a lot quieter than it had been before.

She assumed that all the fuss relating to the return of the *Manila* had died down.

There did, however, seem to be a lot of military activity at the station, with groups of uniformed officers hanging around the cafes in groups that were laughing and talking loudly.

When she returned to the *Alethia*, it was to find Thor engaged in an activity he spent a lot of time doing: making tea.

He told her that Finn was assisting Yalinda and Arkady with their work on the men, and that Rex and Jens were using the computers in the control room for the task that Tina had given them. Indeed, she could hear the soft sound of their voices drift from downstairs.

"Jens is very good at this," Tina said.

Thor snorted. "I wish I knew what that boy gets up to. He gets into places he shouldn't be. Those youngsters are getting to the age where the stuff they do is not harmless anymore and if they're discovered, no one is going to laugh it off. He's probably been doing that for years. At Aurora, spying on the pirates was a sport. Everyone knew their system protocols were poor, and they didn't seem to have the knowledge or power to stop these boys. It was cute, you know, these kids getting the better of the pirate-run mess. Here it's going to be different. I've told Jens that if he breaks into any secret systems, he's likely to end up in jail. His eighteenth birthday is coming up, just in time for him to be tried in an adult court."

Yes, that was the thing that worried Tina about Rex as well.

After she finished her tea, Tina went to the scientist's apartment to see whether Yalinda required her help.

By now, the women had finished with Stan. He was out cold in the last of the three beds they had set up in the small hospital room.

Gerry was also awake, but it was Vito who drew Tina's attention. He was sitting in bed.

The women had applied new bandages to him, made of thinner material. Tina could see his skin through the gauze. It still looked very scarred, but the colour had returned to normal.

His expression was also alert.

"He looks much better," Tina said to Jette, who came in carrying a box which she put in a cupboard.

"Yes, he has been talking a bit."

"Is he making sense? Does he know what is going on and what has happened to his fellows?"

Would he realise that he had killed his own girlfriend?

"He asked about the ship," Jette said. "He seemed quite anguished, but it seems a good sign to me."

"Does he actually understand what you say to him?" Tina said.

"It's a bit early to tell," Jette said.

Tina guessed this meant that he hadn't communicated properly, and had simply voiced his concerns without understanding the replies.

As Jette said, it was definitely a step forward, but they weren't there yet.

Jette further said that she had included this new development in the applications for grants, and that she had updated the grant submitted to the Federacy, and had also sent the companies updates.

Tina didn't have energy for the discussion that all this was probably futile, because no one was interested in solving this problem. Jette would know, but she kept going, because she was pigheaded like a scientist.

It seemed easier just to keep on working on a cure and keep busy with things they could do, rather than worry about things they couldn't influence.

They were all in the living room having a break when there was a heavy thump against the door.

People stopped talking and looked at each other.

"What was that?" Mattias said.

Jette grabbed a couple of the children and dragged them further into the unit.

They listened.

Mattias opened the door and looked outside. He came back inside and shook his head. "Can't see anything."

"I don't like this," Tina said.

"When you came back from the ship, did you see anything unusual?" Yalinda asked.

"I thought it was really quiet. I didn't see anything that

alarmed me."

Fear clamped around Tina's heart. Rex was still at the *Alethia*.

Could it be that the pursuers had worked out that Tina and Finn had escaped the attack on the resort?

Tina sent a message to Rex, but he didn't reply.

Mattias had gathered a couple of people in the apartment's hallway.

"We'll investigate," he said.

"I'll come with you," Tina said.

She was still carrying her old Fireseed inside her jacket. She took it out and put it on the table, where it lay amongst the empty cups.

"Do you have any weapons training?" Mattias said.

"A bit. We were required to go through it when I worked at Project Charon, but I have probably more experience than any of you actually using a weapon."

Mattias opened the door and went into the passage outside. Tina followed him, clutching the weapon. There were no people to be seen.

They got to the end of the corridor that held the accommodation quarters.

There was a small reception office, but it was closed.

That was unusual, because there was usually someone behind the desk to check in any guests that turned up without booking.

When they came around the corner, they ran into a Federacy Force patrol. Four uniformed officers stopping people entering the passage.

Mattias jumped back around the corner, dragging Tina with him.

"What are those guys doing?"

Tina knew the signs. "Probably looking for someone."

"Any of us?"

"They know where we are, so I doubt it."

"Let's get out of here," Mattias said. "I don't fancy answering questions."

They turned to go back to the accommodation, but at that moment, there was a sound of a door being opened.

"Wait." A figure staggered into the passage, a slender man wearing a civilian jacket. He ran towards Tina and Mattias, but then he tripped and fell face first on the floor.

"Grab him," Tina called out while sticking the Fireseed in her belt.

Mattias ran, grabbed the man by the back of his jacket, and dragged him over the lino floor around the corner.

"Call Yalinda," Tina said.

Yalinda already came running out of the apartment door. "Don't touch him. Here, put these on." She tossed Tina a pair of gloves.

Between the three of them, they carried the man into the hallway of the unit. There, Yalinda donned a protective gown and face visor before examining him.

"He's probably been poisoned." She pointed to a pinprick of red in his neck.

"Should we take him to the station hospital?" Tina asked.

Mattias shook his head. "If he's just fled the authorities, that would probably be the end of him."

"He doesn't need the hospital," Yalinda said. "I have a test kit and we have ways to treat him. Do you know who he is?"

"I have no idea."

Yalinda collected her first aid trolley and went to work, assisted by a few of the young people who would normally work with her in the lab.

Yalinda might be socially awkward, but necessity had turned her into a very good de facto doctor.

On the ship, they would have had Rae to do this.

Tina hoped Rae was all right.

CHAPTER THIRTY

THEY MADE a space for the young man in the small hospital room. It was cramped enough already, but he was not in a state that he could answer questions, and Tina very much wanted him to answer questions. Like, what was going on in the station and what was he doing here and why did Mattias find a note in his pocket with the location of the *Manila*?

They went through his backpack, which contained a box with fine chocolates and a small box with a gold necklace with a tiny jewel-encrusted heart in it. His ID was in the name Sam Zeller, and Tina had no reason to believe it wasn't his real name. He normally lived on Olympus and worked as a reporter.

Yalinda asked the lab assistants to monitor him and come to see her if anything changed.

The three men from the *Manila* watched silently while all this was going on. All three were restrained to their beds, but Tina had no doubt that if they really wanted, they could get up and create trouble.

"I get the feeling that someone really doesn't like us," Finn said when he met Tina in the hallway.

"Only a feeling?"

Finn gave her a dark look. "None of this stuff is anything like the normal process for funding proposals. Jette is right. My family *should* be all over this proposal, but either they've been told they can't take part by authorities, or someone has made them a better offer. It would absolutely make financial sense for them to get involved, and I would have expected the project to be strong enough to spark a bidding war. But they're not biting. Something is stopping people from collaborating with us."

"I wish I knew why," Tina said. "Clearly, we have information or pose a threat that justifies sending thugs to shut us up. I wish I knew what it was."

And now this young man had turned up who, by the look of things, was also after the *Manila* and its crew. They were missing vital pieces of information.

Rex and Jens had made some progress with the data dump from Project Charon, they said when Tina went to ask them about it, but they said there was a lot of stuff and they hadn't been through it all. Jens had earlier asked her some questions about what she was looking for.

The task she had given them was not easy. Jens might be good, but he was not a miracle worker, and it was hard for him to double-guess what she was looking for. And it was hard to tell him what she was looking for because she didn't know exactly either.

It was one of those *I'll know it when I see it* things.

She should help them.

Jens told her they hadn't yet made any inroads with the correspondence about the project, so she offered to take that off their hands.

The material took her way back to when she used to work for the project. She had forgotten about all those stupid memos and reviews that they would have to send out every day about the work they had achieved that day, even if they had only attended useless meetings.

The data covered a large chunk of the station's existence, from a year or two before she joined until the station was decommissioned.

Tina was tired and found it hard to concentrate.

Most of it was admin stuff and personal correspondence. She couldn't believe the stuff that some of these people sent to their relatives. Station residents were allocated limited time slots for correspondence, and some of them wrote elaborate accounts of their activities, some of which covered what had to be classified material and others were so basic that she wondered why they bothered.

She even found her own messages to her parents and that horrible message that said that they had died.

She briefly wondered how her brothers were going, but she wouldn't know how to contact them.

Then she came across Dexter's correspondence, which included his very embarrassing correspondence with her. Really? Did they send each other that lovey-dovey garbage? That alone was probably worth him coming back to the station to destroy this data.

She couldn't see anything that would be of value to someone else.

But just as she was about to give up because she was hungry and dinner would be ready, she came across another directory in Dexter's large and complicated personal storage area.

What was that? The directory contained documents that detailed retirement plans and investment structures. Not just for him, but other people's names appeared in the documents.

She copied the list of names and tried to find out who they were.

But she ran into problems, because database upgrades had

made it hard to keep track of people, especially when they moved to other worlds.

Well, this was going to take a lot of time to sort out, if it turned out to be important.

But then she spotted a familiar name on the list: Simon Fosnet.

Well, what the...

Her heart thudding, she looked into his file. A month after Tina had left Cayelle, Simon Fosnet had disappeared, leaving a trail of debt. His wife was desperate, and contacted the local authorities, but they didn't have the power or resources to do anything.

The authorities at Cayelle were notoriously inept, so that didn't surprise Tina, but when she looked up his name, she found that Dexter had made a payment to him the week before he disappeared, and that Simon Fosnet's retirement plan was with a company registered in Dexter's name.

According to the file, he had "medical problems".

Yes, indeed.

She was becoming increasingly suspicious.

This was either a coincidence or a con of such incredible proportions as humanity had never seen.

A company offered people with health issues a chance at a cure. Maybe Simon had a heart condition. Definitely limbs for Rex.

The brochures and other information—and Tina had seen this material—gave the sufferers so much hope that they were willing to sign over their finances to Dexter's company.

Then he administered the treatment, and the victims felt great. But after a while, their skin turned grey and warty, and they lost the capability to think properly. Then they disappeared, apparently also so that they could be *cured*. But they were shipped to Aurora Station, where they would join Artan's army and forever fight each other until they died. And because that took a long time, the Federacy made a show of sending ships to the "pirate war" to feed conflict and to help pirate groups effectively kill each other. While the owners of the scheme took the money.

She remembered how rich Dexter had appeared to be. That was not his money.

And he knew that she knew, or suspected, what he was doing. He'd tried to win her over and failed. He had followed her here. He'd sent the merchant Paulo after them.

He had probably sent people to blow up their accommodation, and they had failed to do so because the lackeys hadn't realised that Tina had left the building.

This was why no one had been interested in her cure. This was why no one had retrieved her information from the box at Kelso Station. The area was a war zone by design. They sent the pirates there to die or live miserable lives while these criminals collected their savings and retirement money.

Tina sat staring at the screen when Finn came in. "Are you coming? It's time for dinner—what's going on?"

Tina explained what she had found out and what she suspected.

His eyes grew large as she spoke.

"I'm sorry if this implicates your family, but if I'm right, this is the biggest heist in humanity."

"Yes," he said, his face grim. And then he added, "Nobody could do this without the help of the Assembly."

"Or the military."

Which she had known about, because Aliz had told her about the corruption scandals, even if Aliz didn't know the precise nature of those scandals. But it did have something to do with investment.

Then neither of them said anything for quite a while, while the enormity of the problem sank in. Could they even fight this much evil?

Rex came in. "Mum? Where are you? It's time for dinner."

"Get Jens to come here. Bring all the stuff that I gave you to look at and the work you've done so far."

"But it's dinnertime."

"Go and pick up some food, and then grab Jens and bring him here. Bring all your computers and wherever you've stored the data. And if you've copied it to any station-side computers—"

"Of course we haven't. What do you take us for?"

Tina met his eyes. Thank goodness for her own suspicious behaviour. It had rubbed off on Rex.

Rex left and Tina spent some more time explaining to Finn what she had done and about her relationship with Dexter.

Finn then tried to find more information about Dexter, but he ran into the same problem that Tina already had, that his life was quite secretive, and it was very hard to find out what had happened to him. Did he live at Aurora Station? Could they prove that he was in contact with the pirates or had anything to do with the people who transformed people into pirates at Aurora Station? It seemed that Artan at least knew of his existence, but there were so many questions.

Rex and Jens came back with dinner and their computers.

Now that they knew what they were looking for, Jens went through all the financial records and found evidence of a lot of money being moved into Dexter's account, including a hefty amount from Simon Fosnet.

This was going to require a full sitting of the Federacy Assembly to bring to light. But who in the Assembly was also in the scheme? General Smith? Definitely. Jarod Silvers? Maybe.

First of all, they would need to contact Greta Ji about which people they could trust.

And then the Freeranger fleet patrolling sections of the system.

Were they meant to stop the pirates, or were they meant to stop the people who wanted to expose the corruption?

Tina sent a fairly cryptic message to Greta, and wondered if maybe they should return to the planet, potentially using the Freeranger craft, and simply barge into the Assembly and present them with all the facts.

They hadn't listened to her before. Why should they listen now?

Maybe they needed more evidence. They needed to know where Dexter was and lure him into the open. And they had a way of doing that.

She said, "Rex, I think you should contact your father and tell him that you would like to know more about getting arms and legs."

CHAPTER THIRTY-ONE

TINA TOLD Rex to write a message that she read and approved before he sent it in reply to Dexter's correspondence with him. Rex had shown Tina what his father had sent, and now that she knew what Dexter was up to, the short and rather impersonal message—to his own son!—was sickening. He merely mentioned that Rex could lead "a full and happy life" with reconstructed limbs of flesh and bone, rather than plastic and metal.

The tone made Tina angry. "A full and happy life—does he think you don't have a full life now? Is there anything, like, anything at all, that you can't do that you would be able to do?"

As soon as she said it, she regretted the question.

Rex looked at her.

His face had developed strong angles. His chin hair had thickened. It was getting a bit long.

"No," he said, and then he left a long pause, in which Tina's mind wandered back to Rex tossing fully grown men aside at Kelso Station and his activities in the shower with Rasa, and wished she hadn't gone there.

Then he said, "My arms never get itchy or cold." He started

laughing. "Mum, you know you're so transparent. Yes, it all works down there and no, I never used it on Rasa. She's scared and didn't want to, so I'm not going to force her."

The tension and the feeling of inadequacy all got too much for Tina.

She enclosed Rex in a hard hug of plastic and metal. "You silly. Whatever you do, and however many arguments we will have in the future, never, ever, forget how much I love you."

"I love you too, mum. And Evelle. I love her as well."

"Yes. And Evelle."

So Rex sent the message to his father, asking for more details about the treatment.

Suspiciously, he replied very quickly by sending another brochure, this one for a clinic in Olympus, where *all your medical problems can be taken care of*. The message contained next to no personal information.

To his own son, Dexter only said, "I hope this finds you well", as one would say to a business contact.

"He's got to be in the area if he can reply that quickly," Tina said.

"Do you think he wants to talk to me?" Rex asked.

Tina tried to think back to her life with Dexter. To his credit, he *had* tried to talk to Evelle when Tina could no longer get any sense out of her, but most of the time, Dexter had been absent, "too busy" with work or "not into girly things" like cooking together.

He had sent money when she told him about Rex, and she had sent him a picture of the walking harness that she had bought with that money.

And then he had never contacted her again.

She shook her head. "No. I don't think he cares about you. If he did, he's had plenty of opportunity to show it. He wants you to contact this clinic and he'll have given them goodness knows what instructions when you turn up. I think it would be dangerous to go there. I think he's using you to get back at me."

Or to use Rex as hostage against her releasing information he didn't want her to make public.

"So what do you want me to do about this?"

"Tell him he can meet us when we eventually come to the planet. If he can lead us into a trap, then we can do the same to him."

Not long after that, Yalinda sent a message that the young man in the hospital room had regained consciousness.

Tina rushed over to the apartment, where she met Yalinda in the hallway, taking off her hospital gear.

"He woke up an hour ago, and has been trying to get out of bed," Yalinda said.

"Has he said anything about what happened to him?"

"Nothing that's coherent enough to understand. But you're welcome to question him. We probably can't keep him here much longer. I'm going to grab something to eat. If you need anything, Jette shouldn't be too far away."

Tina pulled a gown from the cupboard near the door that was brimming with protective clothing, the unit's mandatory environment suit liners and breathing masks having been stuffed way down the back.

If a safety inspector saw this, the authorities would have something to say about it.

"Is there anything else I need to know?" she said, while pulling the gown over her head.

"No. Just that he's not allowed to leave. We haven't finished with him. If he's being difficult, call someone."

"What about the three men?"

"They're awake. They're restrained but they've not given us reason to worry about them."

"No more trying to attack anyone?"

"Nothing."

That, at least, was promising.

Yalinda went in the direction of the kitchen, and Tina entered the hospital room.

It was now so crowded in there that barely any room remained between the beds. At least three were normal beds—moved here from other rooms in the apartment. The young man lay on the fourth makeshift bed, which looked like the fold-out couch that had been in the living room.

As soon as he saw Tina come in, he sat up and extended his hand to his backpack, which stood on the floor under the bed that held Gerry, who watched passively from the slit between layers of bandages that surrounded his face.

"Please," the young man said. "I need to go. I need to get out of here."

"Not so fast. You haven't recovered yet, and if I let you go now, it's likely that you will collapse somewhere, and whoever is after you, or whatever you're afraid of, will just pick you up off the floor."

She sat on the edge of his bed.

"Sam Zeller?"

"Yes, that's me." He gave her a wary look. "You've gone through my stuff, right?"

"Would you have done anything else?"

"So you already know why I wanted to see you?"

Wait—did he want to see her?

"You're Tina Freeman, right? Mother of navigator Evelle Freeman of the SF *Manila*."

"Yes." Tina wondered where this was going. She was used to being identified as ex-Force, or ex-researcher at Project Charon. No one had ever identified her as Evelle's mother.

"My girlfriend is Sarina DeLeon. I heard she survived, and that she is on board the ship. I was coming to meet her and take her home. But after the initial message that she was coming home, I've heard nothing more. I tried and tried to contact her.

I am a news reporter and I requested access to the station's arrival and departure data. The ship definitely arrived."

"Yes, it did. We were on it. Weren't you journalists all writing about how there was a need to hold a parade because of the war victory?"

He snorted. "Those are just the dumb fucks who believe everything the Federacy says. We all know the war isn't over and the Federacy definitely didn't win anything. The ship was lured into a trap and wasn't supposed to have come back."

Wait— "You've spoken to Lisette."

He gave her a wary look.

"Lisette is not just an admin officer, isn't she?"

Another wary look. Then he said, "Lisette is a Perseus Agency operative."

Well, crap, she should have guessed that.

"What side is she on?"

"What do you mean?"

"I don't know that the Perseus Agency is clean. We ran into another agent a while ago. I don't think he was either legit or one of the good guys."

"Tombo Fayet."

"Do you know him?"

"He disappeared on the job. Apparently Paulito Distefano got his hands on him, but he would have been disappointed, because Tombo didn't have what Paulito has been paid a lot of money to retrieve."

And now Tina knew what that was. "The database that shows the extent of Dexter's crimes. And Dexter's offering the money."

He stared at her. "Yes. How do you—"

"That's because we have it."

"And? Have you done anything with it?"

"I think we can piece it together like this: He encouraged ill and desperate people to pay a lot of money for treatment that promised to cure them of their diseases. He neglected to mention that it would also turn them into mutants. He made them sign far-reaching contracts that gave him access to their retirement funds. Those funds are paid out to the next of kin or nominated person when the account's owner dies. It was in his interest to get people killed, so he set up his own war games. The Federacy would occasionally sweep in to kill off pirates from a distance. It was all fine for as long as it took place in deep space. Occasionally, he would also let Federacy ships and technology fall in the hands of pirates to keep up the illusion of a real battle and to feed the pirates an ever-increasing number of involuntary recruits, because obviously if the people you 'cure' from diseases disappear, you'll have trouble recruiting many extra people. And all the while, he was draining their savings in various ways, so it was important that no one return from this war. Yet, here we are."

"Yes," he said. "The exact details will probably change after an investigation, but it's something like that."

"You already knew this?"

"Suspected. We wanted to get the information. The Chief Investigator in the Perseus Agency requested the control module of the station, but Dexter had already erased everything from it. Then they realised there might be other evidence."

"Why didn't the operative say anything when we disturbed him?"

Sam shrugged. "He didn't know who you were? He thought you were Paulo's people? I don't know. I speak with people from the agency but I don't know about the details."

Tina considered whether it would have made much difference. Maybe. They could have kept everyone together.

"We need to put pressure on the authorities to release the crew of the *Manila*. I know it's still in dock."

"The ship has been moved."

"Yes, but I've been watching the base, and no one has come out, so they're still inside."

"What about the people who tried to poison you?"

"Lackeys sent by those who don't want me to investigate. It's not the first time this has happened to me. Some people really don't want their secrets brought to light."

"Do you know who is involved?"

"You'd be better off making a list of people who are not involved. It would be a very short list."

"Greta Ji."

"That'd be one of them."

"What about the executive assembly? Jarod Silvers?"

Sam spread his hands. "He's probably afraid to make too many waves, because he knows that the corruption movement holds the balance of power when it comes to voting. Unfortunately, he doesn't have a large majority and depends on different factions to get stuff done in the assembly."

"Would he stand up for the right thing if presented with enough evidence?"

"It's hard to tell. He serves Olympus. I know he is president of the Federacy, but he makes his decisions based on what happens in Olympus. People like money and people dislike scandals. They've seen too many of them recently. The people question the amount of money spent on the war. They tolerate the safety rhetoric, for now. I don't know how many people really believe that spending all that money will keep Olympus free of pirates. Not sure that they even believe in pirates. They just don't want any more scandals."

"I'm thinking they've not seen nearly enough scandals."

Rex's voice sounded. "Uh-oh. It sounds like Mum has an idea."

While she was talking, a few others had come in. Jette, Yalinda, Arkady, Zia, Finn, Rex, Jens and his father, Rasa and the one goose that still squawked like a parrot, because it tended to follow her around.

"Well..." Tina took in a deep breath.

Looking around the group, her heart sank. There was Arkady with his grey hair, Yalinda with her husband and children, Jette, who was a scientist. Even Zia was an administrator, not suited for the job they might need to perform.

They needed more strength than they had already displayed so far.

She told them what she had concluded about the situation.

That the people in power in the Federacy had a money-making scheme. That they didn't want anyone to interfere with it. They had no interest in the science. In fact, they wanted Tina and her group to go away. They didn't want the truth to come out: that the *Manila* had been lured into a trap that would deliver the ship to the pirates, so that, presumably, the pirates could go on destroying each other so that the corrupt elements in the Federacy could force more mutant people into the war, while taking their money.

She finished with, "And there it is, the conspiracy in all its corrupt glory. I hope you will all agree with me that we have to do something."

"Yeah, but what?" Finn said.

This was followed by an intense silence.

"We need people we can trust," Jette said.

She looked defeated.

Jette was a scientist, and doing things properly was her way. She applied for grants in a business-like manner. She didn't schmooze or try to buy favours. Politics was not her game.

"We need people who we trust *and* who can act," Arkady said.

"Do we even know anyone who cares about the truth?" Jette asked, spreading her hands.

"Matt and Veronica do," Tina said. "And Greta Ji."

But while it was great to have them on board, Tina didn't think those people would have the numbers to force authorities into doing something. As far as she knew, almost all the assembly delegates could and probably would choose to keep their mouths shut when it mattered. Because they benefited from the scheme, or because they were afraid of people who wielded power. And these people had shown themselves as being ruthless and murderous, so they would choose to protect themselves. That was only natural.

"Why don't you tell us what your idea is?" Rex said.

"Who says I have to solve the problem?"

"Because that's what mums do. We stuff up and then they put it all right again."

"What about your awesomeness?"

"I can be awesome if you need me to be awesome. But I can also just be your son and let your awesomeness rub off on me."

Rasa rolled her eyes.

Tina started, "My problem is that I can't see an easy way out. Your father has an army of people to do his bidding, so it would be dangerous to engage and challenge him."

"We have an army, too," Rex said.

"I can't ask the Freerangers to fight our battles."

"You won't need to ask if you tell them the right things," Finn said. "They hate being lumped with the pirates. They hate the war and exclusion zones that hamper their way of life."

"We should take this to the assembly," Jette said.

"But there is no guarantee that they have the numbers to do anything," Tina said.

"They will if you make them angry enough," Sam said.

Tina looked from one to the other. "It sounds like you have a better idea than I do."

Sam shrugged. "Not really. But I'm a journalist, and getting information out is what we do. It's why I'm here. It's why they tried to stop me. I know how to get stuff before Silvers, and if we do our work, I'm convinced he will at least table the information in the assembly. If we're smart, we can beat this up into a big story."

Tina looked at Rex and Jens. "I think we might have the people to do just that."

CHAPTER THIRTY-TWO

BUT FIRST, they decided, they needed a few things: to get everyone together. To have transport or other means to get everyone to safety.

It was not so much a plan, but it was a hare-brained gamble. It was about pulling together the groups of people they could trust and the material they had. About saving the family and making a last-ditch attempt to reveal the truth to whomever would listen.

There was no plan B.

First part of the plan: get Evelle and the others out of the military base. Only they could provide evidence of how the *Manila* had been set up, and more than two thousand lives had been sacrificed for the sole reason of feeding the futile war. Was it too much to hope that some military leaders would be appalled and would choose to support honesty and integrity?

Part two, arrange transport to the planet, probably using the Freerangers.

Part three, use Sam and Greta with the help of Rex and Jens to hack into means of communication to broadcast their message to as many people as possible, while making a big show of talking to the assembly. Send them enough detail to make them curious, but not everything, because if she sent the data from Project Charon, the data that Dexter was looking for, it might fall into the wrong hands and might accidentally go missing.

Then the assembly was forced to meet with her so that she could give them the important data in person.

Whatever happened after that... she preferred not to think about it. That would depend on the level of success they had. Anything ranging from staying at Olympus to fleeing back to Cayelle and digging herself in.

Hopefully, people would come down on the side of honesty. Hopefully.

Jens had collected detailed maps of the station. He understood what Tina wanted because they had done all this type of stuff before.

He had really become a most useful young man. Still lanky and mousey, with elfin-like blond hair, he looked young, but he was about to become an adult.

He knew where the *Manila* was. He had established that there was an emergency airlock in the section of the station that wasn't too far from the military base.

They would have to walk across the outside of the station for a bit, but there were railings with handholds, and they could use the tethers from the *Alethia*. They had done this before and it was easy, compared to the process of shooting lines between ships and abseiling between them that they used to do with the Freerangers.

The distance they needed to cover was further than Tina would have hoped, but Jens said that shouldn't present a problem. The station was well laid-out, quite new, and hadn't yet acquired rambling extensions that made navigating these types of structures hard.

Station builders used symmetrical designs, which meant

that the airlock on the civilian side corresponded with another airlock in the military base. It was labelled as *Emergency Only* and hadn't recorded a single instance of use in the last ten years —which was the furthest back Jens could scroll in the maintenance database. His concern was not being discovered but the operational status of the airlock. How well had it been maintained?

While Tina was working out these details with Jens, Finn contacted Clementine.

One of the things that had surprised Tina that it had been Finn who had initially made contact with the Freerangers and throughout their period together, it had been Finn whom Clementine had trusted the most. Almost as if Freerangers grew intensely suspicious when authorities did something, but accepted the same action from someone with a commercial motivation without question. It was strange.

Tina got Jette and Sam to write to several publicity channels both on the station and on the planet. Their messages promised big reveals about the root of corruption and that the Federacy had a chance to stamp it out, without offering too much detail.

"We want to create a situation where they will have to meet with us," Tina said.

And then she went back to planning to free the *Manila's* crew.

Moving around the military section of the station would be risky. They didn't know what they would find once they entered the Emergency Only airlock and the maps of the station were not terribly helpful. One needed military clearance to get this information. Tina debated using her alternate IDs, but Jens said that not only would military authorities be aware that she owned those IDs, their use would spark interest.

"I think we should be able to move freely. I'm reasonably

sure that these are storage and machinery areas. It would go well with us pretending to be maintenance crew."

Tina chuckled. The good old maintenance crew disguise. "One day, someone will figure out this gap in their security."

"They're trying, but until they pay their maintenance crew better, there will always be those who will accept payment for others to borrow their gear and passes, or for them to turn off surveillance equipment at nominated times."

The solution was easy, and Tina had been involved with this at Cayelle. "They should make individuals responsible for submitting complete surveillance records."

"That won't happen. You can do that for small businesses. Not for big organisations like this. Employee groups would ban it."

He was probably right.

They gathered the EVA equipment from the *Alethia*, because the gear in the appartment's emergency cupboard was civilian, not military grade, and it would stand out when they wanted to enter a military sector. Some of the stuff on board the *Alethia* still displayed fifteen-year-old military insignia from second-hand gear that Tina had bought when kitting out the ship at Pegasus Station. She was strangely proud of having chosen quality material that had stood the test of time.

They decided that it was Tina's mission and that she, Rex, Jens and Sam would go.

Thor, Finn and Rasa would stay at the *Alethia*.

Finn would stay on board in case they needed to get out quickly when things went wrong. He could fly the *Alethia*.

"When I get discovered or drift off into space, you can have my ship," Tina said.

Finn met her eyes in a sincere moment.

"But you're not going to get lost. I can be your annoying pretend-nephew for the rest of your life. You are the first real friend I've ever had."

"Watch out what you're saying."

Tina was trying to be light-hearted, but she was unsettled by the moment. She had found Finn impenetrable and quite frustrating to deal with, but somewhere in that stubborn brain of his, some of her words had initiated a change in him. He wanted to do the right thing, even if he was awkward and not the most popular employee material. His engineering skills were good. He was all right, really, and she had no right to tell him how to lead his life.

She grabbed and held his hand. "Yes, you can be my annoying nephew. You've been a loyal friend, and I hope that this won't be the end of our cooperation."

"We need to go, mum," Rex said from the door. "Jens says that there are a couple of military ships coming into the station. Flight control will be busy and not looking so much in our direction."

They got ready, putting on overalls and stuffing all their vacuum gear in a crate. Since there were four of them, packing everything was a challenge.

In his work as a reporter, Sam had undertaken all kinds of training. He had been stationed with some of the larger mining operations, and knew how to move in space. He had also undertaken first aid and EVA courses. He even knew how to handle and use weapons, so Tina gave him the spare Fireseed.

They went to the airlock in question and then had to wait until the shift change, when it would get quiet and they could sneak into the maintenance rooms to "borrow" some air tanks.

The tanks were heavy and awkward and needed to go into the crate, but after Rex had gone into the workshop twice and came back with the four tanks they needed, the lid to the crate wouldn't shut anymore. It was now or never.

The airlock was near the end of a quiet passage. Tina wheeled the crate into the space next to it, through a set of double doors that said *Maintenance Only*. It was very dark inside this room.

The four of them got into their suits by the light of Jens' pocket comm. Sam was pleasantly capable and even helped Rex do up his tanks.

Then they parked the crate in a corner against a shelving unit, and went back to the door.

The corridors were likely to be monitored, especially close to an airlock, so they all put on their helmets, clipped on the tanks, and covered the distance to the airlock as quickly as possible. These suits were too heavy and cumbersome for running.

The airlock would only let in two people at a time, so Sam and Jens went first. Tina and Rex waited in the passage, quietly, nervous, knowing that were were highly exposed, probably monitored and, if discovered, had nowhere to go. Tina desperately didn't want to use the Fireseed yet. Not before they had rejoined with the women from the *Manila*.

Sam and Jens were safely outside, and Tina and Rex went into the airlock.

But as the door closed and the air pumps started working, an alarm went off.

"What does that mean?" Rex asked. His voice sounded weird in her helmet.

"I guess we've been discovered. Hang on. I'm going to vent the space. When the door opens, get out of here."

CHAPTER THIRTY-THREE

TINA CHECKED her and Rex's tethers. When she was sure that they were both attached, she turned the large manual handle and opened the outer airlock door. The remaining pressure inside the airlock still made this hard to do.

The atmosphere in the cubicle vented with a pop followed by a soft hiss, which faded away to nothing.

She could see into the darkness of space punctuated by stars, and the glow from the planet below bouncing off the spokes of the station overhead.

As the station rotated, shadows crawled over the outside of the hull. Even if the airlock was in shadow, the glare was blinding.

Sam and Jens showed up as sharp silhouettes, both of them hanging onto the railing that led from the airlock to the nearest trail of dots that marked a path over the outside of the station.

Against the glare from the planet, Tina could see the huge shapes of ships that hung on the outside of the hull. This was where there they would have to go, although she wasn't sure which one was the *Manila*.

"What was that noise?" Sam asked in Tina's helmet.

"There is some alarm going off," Tina said. "I'm not sure what it means, but it can't be anything good for us."

"Probably some kind of alarm that's related to us opening the door."

"We better hurry before someone turns up," Tina said.

They set off, following the path of dots that led over the outside of the station.

When Tina looked over her shoulder, the door to the airlock had closed automatically.

It was almost certain that someone knew that they were outside.

They walked in single file, with Jens at the front with his map, directing them over the various paths, still in the shadow of the station.

Tina was the last one in the row and followed Rex's back.

After a while, Jens turned to the left. They needed to climb down the side of the station, first down a gentle slope and then more steeply. It became harder to move quickly.

Tina kept looking over her shoulder and was expecting someone to come out of hiding any moment.

Sam was still listening to the channels inside the station, and he said that he couldn't pick up anything unusual.

They stopped at a small maintenance platform on the side of the habitat ring. The planet hung huge and blue below. The glow made all the reflective surfaces on the outside of the station and the many ships that hung on docking structures glitter.

The military section, marked by large painted letters that were impossible to read from this angle, was less well-occupied than the civilian section. A few lights blinked along the path and at various control boxes. There was little sign of life. There was no sound. All Tina could hear was the sound of her own breathing reflected back at her.

Jens started climbing again.

The protrusion on the hull that held the emergency airlock had come into view. The path that led to it went over a metal walkway suspended along the side of the station. Through the grate underfoot, Tina could see the constantly moving surface of the planet. It made her dizzy. She wanted to get out of here. This place was too exposed.

"There," Jens said, and he pointed ahead.

At first, Tina wasn't sure what he was pointing at. She expected to see something on the hull of the station that indicated the airlock where they had to go, but his finger moved.

Then she saw it too: a small ship was hovering over the outside of the station, not at all near the docking bays.

"Who are they?"

"Their identification says that they belong to the Station Inspection Authority," Jens said.

Well, crap. "What can we do?"

She checked the gauge on the tank. They had plenty of air, but there was no way that she wanted to get stuck out here.

Jens said, "We have to make a run for it."

"It's exposed," Sam said.

"But not far," Rex said. "I can go first to open the hatch."

"Better be quick."

Rex undid his tether and clipped it onto the railing. Then he did the same for the others.

"Go," Sam said.

Rex set off along the walkway at a crazy pace, followed more slowly by Jens. Then Sam and Tina bringing up the rear. Since even Sam was about half her age and—let's be frank— less burdened with middle-age spread, they were all much faster.

And Tina tried to keep up as best as she could, but the station kept turning and the patch of bright sunlight hit her in the face when she was a short distance away from the emergency hatch.

The brightness flooded her helmet, turned insignificant scratches on the cover into brilliantly reflecting mist that made it impossible to see.

One of her companions—she couldn't discern who it was—shouted garbled words and she mis-stepped, tripping over an uneven spot in the walkway. She went flat on her stomach. The loop of her tether swung around the walkway and slapped against the underside of the metal grate.

Oof.

Ouch, her knee.

"Are you all right, Mum?"

"I think so."

Tina checked her gear that she hadn't lost anything that hadn't already fallen, and would drop on someone's head in Olympus City below.

"Hurry up. The patrol is coming this way."

It had been Jens speaking when she fell.

Tina pushed herself up to cover the remaining few steps to the emergency hatch, but something yanked her from behind. She fell again, backwards, hitting the railing and tumbling awkwardly on her backside.

What the hell was that? There was no one behind her.

"Your tether is caught," Sam said.

Yes, it was true. The rope that should lead to the clip around the railing disappeared under the walkway instead. Tina pulled at it.

"Hurry up," Jens said.

"I'm stuck."

She pulled harder. When that didn't free the rope, she crawled over the walkway and found that the rope had wound itself around a metal structure underneath the walkway. She poked through the gaps in the grate with her gloved fingers, but they were far too short. She unclipped the gun, but the barrel was too fat to fit through the holes.

"It's stuck. I need something long."

"Mum!" Rex called out.

He pointed over her shoulder.

Tina turned around.

Saw the patrol craft flying low over the surface of the station.

Oh shit.

"Unclip the tether and run!" Sam called.

But something in Tina's mind refused to do that. It had been drilled into her during her training. You never—ever—unclipped your tether. Never.

So she did something else she had learned in training and hadn't realised her body still remembered. She rolled onto her back while pulling the Fireseed from her belt. The voice of her military instructor still sounded in her head as if it was yesterday, and not twenty-five years ago that she'd reluctantly submitted to this training, arguing that "war games" were for people who wanted to play them. Not for researchers.

The instructor's voice said, *If the threat is in the air, you have one shot. Aim for the place where the craft is most vulnerable and where you're most likely to do enough damage that it will have to abandon the chase.*

Tina knew where that was. She had flown these little workhorse shuttles herself. The navigation and engine control module was under a panel on the side of the nose of the craft. Tina aimed and fired.

The effect was most unspectacular. There were no fireballs in space.

Did she even hit anything? It was impossible to see. The craft disappeared over the curve of the station. Jens ran to her and climbed over the railing. Rex held onto his tether while he balanced at the bottom of the walkway, and kicked Tina's tether loose with his feet.

"Pull it in!"

Tina did.

Rex hauled his friend back over the railing.

The craft had not come back. That was a good sign, right?

They all ran for the emergency hatch.

The light came on as soon as Sam shut the door. The glow was impossibly bright. Tina's helmet was fogging up on the outside and she couldn't see anything.

As air, and with it, sound, returned, warning sirens blared through a speaker in the ceiling of the cubicle.

Warning, emergency in sector seven. Repeat, we have a hull breach in sector seven.

That *could* be because a wayward shuttle had slammed into some part of the station's structure, right?

One could hope.

Jens took off his helmet and suit before the green light had come on.

"Come on, take everything off. We need to run."

They stripped off their suits, no mean feat in that cramped space.

Jens had grabbed the door handle and pushed against the door. It opened the moment the green light came on.

They scrambled over the mess of suits.

Tina accidentally kicked one of the the helmets while running into the passage. It rolled like a football before coming to rest against the wall.

They had come out into a grey corridor with closed doors along its length.

Jens led the group, holding his map. It wasn't far to the ship, but they had no time to get changed and pretend to look like maintenance personnel.

All plans were off.

They were in a passage underneath the one that led to the ship. The upstairs passage would be busier, because it led past all the ship entrances.

They went into a stairwell and then up. Jens stopped at the door.

"The ship is across from here," he said. "There will be people in this corridor, and there may be patrols."

He opened the door a crack and looked out.

"Yes. There are two guards outside the entrance to the ship."

"Let me have a look," Sam said.

Jens stepped aside. Sam also opened the door a tiny sliver and looked out with one eye.

Then he pulled his pad out of his pocket, opened the door completely, and walked out. Before Tina could say anything, he'd struck up a conversation with one of the guards.

Tina realised: he was playing reporter.

She gestured. "Come."

They left the stairwell and crossed the passage, a fairly busy thoroughfare that led past the entrances of many ships.

Sam still stood with the guards. He was asking the men whether he could have an interview with the ship's captain. He sounded genuine, too.

While Sam spoke with the guards, Tina led the two boys past the guards' backs into the entry tube to the *Manila*.

Phew.

CHAPTER THIRTY-FOUR

THEY WAITED for a while inside the entrance. A screen displayed the area outside the entry tube and showed Sam still talking to the guards. No one appeared to have noticed that three people had gone into the ship.

The dockside activity involved maintenance and emergency personnel rushing past with equipment and trolleys.

The screen also displayed the *Manila*'s ship parameters, including readiness at ninety-five percent, probably a result of the ship having been moved recently. But Tina knew the ship could move with a readiness of as little at thirty percent. There were just functions that wouldn't work.

She knew the ship better than even some of its regular crew who hadn't gone through the same ordeal as she had.

Even the smell of the interior was familiar.

Then the screen showed one of the two guards speaking to Sam talking on his comm. The two ended the discussion and walked off. Sam went in the other direction.

A moment later, the sound of quick footsteps preceded Sam who came came running through the tube.

"Quick, close the door."

Tina did.

"Did they see you go into the ship?" Rex asked.

"They must have seen something. I can't believe that they really wouldn't have any surveillance. Probably they're not expecting us to have penetrated into the base. The guys outside were pretty frank. You know, I used to work as a journalist embedded in the crew. I'm sure they thought I was one of those."

"Did you find out anything about the ship?" Tina asked. Like, why it had been moved, what was happening to the crew or why details had been kept secret.

"I thought it best not to ask. I asked them about the current emergency. They knew no more than we heard, hull breach in sector seven. Let's have a look to see if we can find the crew."

That was dicey enough, because the ship looked deserted.

What would they do if there was no one left on board? In Tina's experience, when ships were moored at a station, the crew would normally stay on board. But because of the unusual situation, they might have been removed and could be detained elsewhere.

They walked through the empty corridors, from the entrance to the mess, and found all the rooms and passages deserted. Even the cabins looked like they hadn't been used for a long time.

And Jens said he was intercepting signals from station authorities about an emergency and there was talk about military assistance.

"It sounds like everyone is nervous," he said.

"If the crew were still on board, where would they be?" Sam asked.

"I think they would only be in one place," Jens said. "We haven't looked at the bridge, but that is where I would go if I were them."

That was a smart thought, so, rather than comb through the entire crew section, they set off in that direction.

Even before they had entered the bridge room and climbed all the ladders, they could already hear voices.

Tina's heart jumped.

A group of women was gathered around the central command module. Aliz sat at the controls. Evelle next to her. Sarina, Zafira, Clodine, Yonta, Rae, Margot and Giselle all balanced on the bars in the middle of the room, on top of the ladder that now had a purpose because the ship took gravity from the station.

They all looked at the entrance when Tina, Sam, Rex and Jens came in.

"Mum," Evelle called out.

She half-climbed, half-jumped down the ladder and closed Tina in a hug.

"You came." Tina was disturbed by how emotional Evelle sounded.

"Of course we came. Did you think we'd abandon you?"

"We thought they would forbid you from seeing us."

"Of course they did, but has that ever stopped us before?"

Evelle laughed, but it was a kind of uncomfortable laugh. The women all knew that there was a point where disobedience became desertion or mutiny, and that they would probably soon have to step across that line.

Sam had also joined up with his girlfriend.

"Where are all the others?" Aliz asked.

Tina explained as quickly as she could what had happened. But there was just so much that they didn't know. Firstly, because while they were with the Freeranger fleet, the military women had never been terribly involved with the science, but also because so much had changed.

Tina had to stop several times, when someone called out, *Wait, what, they actually wanted us to go missing in the war?*

And Tina explained that most of what she said was a theory, but then they'd arrive at the next point, and when Tina spoke of people's retirement savings accounts, Rae said, pale-faced, that she had tried to see how much money was in there, because she was sick of the military and wanted to see if she could retire, and could not find out. A private company had taken over the account and in order to get access, she would need to prove that she was a close relative. As if they assumed she was dead already.

The expressions on the women's faces changed from shock and disbelief to anger.

"So, what next?" Aliz said.

"We can't just walk out of the ship," Evelle said. "Since we arrived here, and they questioned us and we chose to stay on board, we have been locked up here as prisoners. They never told us we weren't allowed to leave, but we haven't been able to, and we've heard nothing from the extra crew that was supposed to join us here. They moved us out of a prime position, because they said they needed to fix the ship. They did some fixes, but are just letting us hang around here, supposedly waiting for replacement crew that hasn't arrived. Maybe they figured that we're in the military and we're used to waiting and won't question it."

"What did they ask at your interrogation?"

"Just usual stuff," Aliz said. "They were less forceful about it than I expected."

"They had already decided they were going to ignore you," Tina said.

"Yeah," Aliz said, her voice dark. "Let us sit here and then quickly ship us off to a less glamorous location where everyone will forget about us."

Tina added, "But they have also discovered that a percentage of people on the planet regards you as heroes, and want a victory parade, because apparently some people have been spreading the rumour that the war has been won."

"Who came up with that garbage?" Yonta said.

"I don't know. Sounds like they were a victim of their own lies."

"The Olympus media have been keen to report on the war," Sam said. "General Smith in the assembly dropped a hint that the war was 'less of a concern', that's the words he used, and sections of the media ran with this and called it a victory."

"And because it's being fought in another system, no one can easily check," Aliz said. "Because the military controls the communication channels."

And that was the ultimate problem.

"And what can we do about that?" Margot asked.

Tina said, "The reason I'm here: because we're going to tell them the truth. One way or another, we are going to have to get you out of here. We can either go through space, or we can go out the main door, the same way we came in."

Yonta spread her hands. "Are you kidding? They will stop us any way they can. We don't even know who we can trust."

"Isn't it good, then, that we have one of the most advanced warships ever built, and that it's at ninety-five percent readiness? And that we have found something that will halt the infection, and we have proof of what the corrupt forces have done, and we even have a fleet of small ships that can take us to the assembly. And if they don't listen, then I want to say we've tried."

Aliz met her eyes. She opened her mouth to say something, but shut it again. And then, after another long silence, she said, "That's mutiny. I wish you were kidding, but you're not, right?"

"Nope. I have a reasonably successful business selling security equipment at Cayelle. I also have two children out of work, and a cactus collection that I'd love to attend to. I have some friends with pets and useful skills I'd like to help, and I hate politics. I'd like to get back to my peaceful life that involves bickering with my neighbour over the back fence. I intend to get out of here alive and with my integrity intact. I assume this is the same for you."

"Well, if that community of yours needs a doctor, I'm all ears," Rae said.

"Or a cook," Margot said.

"If you open a bar, I will sing," Yonta said.

There were nods all around.

"Let's do it."

Mutiny, it was. Tina should have done this fifteen years ago.

CHAPTER THIRTY-FIVE

OF COURSE, they now had even fewer people than before.

But they knew what to do because they had flown the ship with less than minimum crew levels before. And there was help.

Jens managed to get access to a schematic of the station that showed which areas were affected by the "emergency", which Tina took to be the crash of the shuttle she had shot into a section of the station.

He also managed to get onto Yalinda, and told her to evacuate and create another emergency, if she could. Yalinda, being Yalinda, she asked if a chemical spill would do the job. *Anything, Yalinda, as long as it causes the station's population to be evacuated to the safest core.* The men could walk now, Yalinda said, and Tina wondered how the scientists were going to cope with guiding three live mummies through the station, but the group would have to solve that. She trusted Zia, Arkady and Jette to deal with it. Although the stories would be funny to hear, and she hoped she'd have the chance to hear them.

Tina messaged Finn and told him to take the *Alethia* out of dock.

The Freeranger fleet waited in higher orbit. Finn was talking to them, apparently, telling them that the *Manila* was on its way. Another thing she had to delegate. Tina wanted to speak with Clementine to explain that there might be danger, but there was no time. She hoped Clementine understood what she was getting herself into.

She couldn't keep up with what all these people were doing.

A lowly ranked medical officer came to the entrance of the *Manila* and wondered why he couldn't come in, because he needed to collect regular samples. Apparently, the women had been subjected to blood tests. What for, not even Rae could tell.

He left again after Rae had told him a story about having an infectious disease on board, but of course he'd be back soon with more people, maybe even people with weapons. This meant that they now had a very limited time frame to get away from the station.

Tina, Aliz and Evelle considered the best strategy to get out of dock.

The ship had been locked into place from dockside, and they needed someone to unlock it, or risk damaging the station's structure.

Aliz didn't know anyone on duty in military traffic control, and said that even if she knew them, it would only be in a professional capacity. She had never considered that so many of her colleagues might be compromised, if not directly, working under the orders of superiors who were.

"We really can't trust anyone, can we?" Her expression was haunted.

"No," Tina said. "I've done two unauthorised departures now and I know we can do it, but it won't make us any friends stationside."

"What about Jens?"

So they asked Jens to look at the hacking into the locking mechanism. Meanwhile, time was ticking away.

Rex commented on the activity in the dockside passage. Some officers had gathered there. They stood in a circle, presumably talking about what to do about the *Manila*'s closed hatch.

Aliz and Evelle prepared to engage the engines.

But leaving without disengaging the lock would tear apart that section of corridor and toss those people into open space. It could destabilise the station's rotation. At Aurora Station, they hadn't worried about it because staying at the station would have been so much worse.

"I don't feel good about causing damage," Aliz said. "At Aurora, it was about immediate danger. Now it's about... politics."

"Not good politics," Evelle said.

"No, but still, those people out there don't deserve to die for our escape."

A light at Evelle's elbow flipped from red to green.

"What's that?" Tina asked and pointed.

Evelle turned around. "What... Jens, did you just disengage the lock?"

"No. I can't figure out how to get in. I could, but... not in so little time. I know you think I'm a wonder kid, but really, I'm not."

"It must be someone at the station."

But who? Finn? Thor?

"I'm going to try it." Aliz slipped on her earpiece and tapped some buttons on the controls.

With each touch, a bigger part of the control panel lit up. She whispered, "Yes, yes, yes."

And then she turned around. "I hope you are all strapped in. We're ready to go."

Tina clambered up the ladder to the navigator station and swung into the seat. Evelle was already strapping herself into the second pilot station. Clodine left for the weapons control room. She took Yonta, Rex and Jens.

Lines of orange lights blinked on the panel.

"What are those?" Tina asked.

"Warnings about unoccupied positions," Aliz said, while turning the lights off.

A moment later, the structure of the ship shuddered.

An alarm starting blaring, but again Aliz turned it off. The ship lurched to the side, pushing Tina into the harness.

"Everyone all right?" Evelle called.

Yonta said over the comm that they were.

From where she sat, Tina could only see Margot and part of Rae's leg, both of them strapped into a control station seat.

Gravity faded.

Tina looked over Evelle's and Aliz's shoulders. One of their many screens displayed the visual camera feed, showing the station's structures receding.

The screen in front of Tina lit up with messages and communication requests.

Base Control to Manila, please state your intention

Base Control to Manila, you do not have permission to leave

Base Control to Manila, repeat, you do not have permission to leave

Tina watched the messages track over the screen and prepared to send the statement that she had written.

The crew of the Manila has acquired important information that we will be presenting to the assembly. We will remain in the system but will take any action to intercept us as hostile. I'm sending you, and all news services across the Federacy, a summary of our statement. It deals with corruption on a scale you won't have seen in your lifetime.

Then she pressed *send* and again *send*.

There.

Down in the weapons control room of the ship, Clodine would uncap the ship's large guns and rotate them, so they pointed at the station. Rex and Jens were there with Clodine, and Tina desperately hoped no one was going to do anything stupid that would lead to the use of those weapons.

The message board in front of Tina lit up with communication from Station Operations, still requesting the *Manila*'s intentions and demanding that they return to the station.

Tina didn't reply to any of them.

Slowly, the ship backed away from the station. There were signs of activity at the many military ships moored at the station, but none of them would have the capacity to move immediately, not even if they urgently recalled the crew's leave. It took at least a few hours to ramp up a ship.

Tina hoped that cooler heads would prevail and the commanders would be happy to wait and see what the *Manila* had to say.

Or, heaven forbid, those commanders would know that things weren't right and hadn't been for some time.

She rotated the receiver and sent a message to the Freeranger fleet.

We expect to join you soon.

And added another message, broadcast to the channels Sam had given her.

If you're involved with this scheme, your game is over. The day of reckoning has come.

That was for Dexter. Because he was sure to be listening. Thanks to the message Rex had sent him, he might even be close.

The ship slowly moved away from the station.

Aliz pointed out the many ships waiting in orbit. Were they silent observers, friends, or would they descend like a swarm of angry bees? How deeply rooted was this scheme and to what lengths would people be prepared to go to hide their involvement?

Tina listened to broadcast communication.

There was a lot of panic on the publicly accessible airwaves, a cacophony of voices speaking to each other and wondering what was going on. Ships asked if they could still approach any of the other orbital stations, since Number 3 was out. People at the station wondered why there was a hull breach warning and what the Force was going to do about supposed rogues. Some people even suggested that the pirates had come to the station—well, maybe those people had spotted Vito, Gerry or Stan.

But the Force could do nothing that wouldn't endanger the citizens of the station.

They arrived at the Freeranger fleet not much later. A shuttle came to the ship and Aliz parked the *Manila* in orbit, so that the Federacy Force could eventually collect it.

"A charge of mutiny is much reduced as long as you don't misappropriate Federacy property," Aliz said.

She was probably joking. They were all in trouble over their ears.

The women collected their duffels with their meagre possessions. The group was smaller than it had ever been. Faces were grim. This would be the last time any of them did anything for the military.

Aliz and Evelle would be the last off the ship, and Clodine kept Yonta, Rex and Jens in the weapons stations to protect the shuttle while it went down to the planet.

Clementine was waiting for the group in the main living area of the Shipworld Mara main vessel *Endeavour of the Deepest Night*.

She was wearing an environment suit liner instead of her usual flowing robe.

Tina asked what this was about.

"I'm coming down to the planet with you. I have a thing or two to say about how you have been treated and while we're at it, we might talk about how we have been treated."

Tina said it might be risky and there might be armed

conflict, but Clementine said, "Is there ever a trip that doesn't include risk?"

Tina heard in her voice that there were additional reasons for wanting to come, and there was no time for explanations.

They all piled into the orbit to surface shuttle flown by Riccardo, and cast off from the ship not much later.

While the Freeranger fleet receded, Clementine told Tina that they had found that the Federacy-based system where they reported movements of ships in the sector they were monitoring on behalf of the Federacy Force, also read the contents of the ship's core data, which included communication between it and other ships, including other shipworlds.

"I know they don't care much about rules, but *we* do, and *we* would prefer our communication and travel details to remain private. This is a very serious breach of the rules and our rights."

She might have been about to go on a rant about how Freeranger families always fell outside the Federacy's definition of a citizen, but Ricardo said, "There."

CHAPTER THIRTY-SIX

TINA LOOKED where Ricardo was pointing. He enlarged the projection on the screen. Now she saw them too, several small specks were coming in their direction. When he enlarged them even further, the shapes of fighter craft became clear.

"So they really are going to play space invaders," Tina said.

She meant this to be a light-hearted remark, but she was deeply worried.

The *Manila* was still shadowing them, but they couldn't come all the way to the planet, especially when the shuttle entered the atmosphere. They were too far away from the unknown ships to see if they were capable of entering the atmosphere.

"What are they doing?" Tina asked.

In reply, Ricardo enlarged the projection even further and added historical data to the positions of the craft. The software plotted the course and future course.

The ships were clearly coming in their direction.

"Who are they?" Tina asked.

"They're not registered," Ricardo said.

This wasn't saying very much, because the shuttle was also not registered. None of the Freeranger ships were.

"Have you tried to contact them?"

"They're not replying."

"Do you recognise any of them?" Tina asked.

Ricardo shrugged. "If they were Freerangers, they would have already identified themselves."

So there was only one option. These were hostile craft, pirates or others who were lackeys for those who wanted to protect their exploitative scheme, and they were going to try to stop the shuttle from reaching the planet. Or die trying.

Ricardo was making some calculations and displaying the results on the screen.

"All we can do is try to get down as quickly as possible. There will be a short period where we're not covered by the *Manila* before we reach the atmosphere, and then potentially beyond that as well. I don't know what sort of weapons they have. Our capability is limited to being highly manoeuvrable and being able to land on water. We have very limited defensive capabilities. This shuttle is old and won't have all the new stuff."

"Look," Clementine said.

She pointed out two additional craft that had suddenly entered the projection. Behind the shuttle. On a trajectory from the Freeranger fleet on a path that would intersect with their course in about half an hour.

Tina felt sick.

She recognised the registration numbers displayed next to craft from the *Manila*.

"These are the *Manila*'s fighters, aren't they?"

"It's likely," Ricardo said

"Can you check who's on board?"

Each craft had two occupants. Each of them listed a military number and a code.

She guessed that these were Clodine and Yonta, with either Rex or Jens.

This was what she had feared all along, that Rex would become involved in a space battle.

A tense period went past when they still moved under the cover of the Manila.

Then Ricardo said, "I'm getting an incoming message."

"What is it?"

"He wants to talk to you."

Tina knew who it was before she had taken the earpiece from Ricardo.

"Dexter."

"What do you think you are doing?"

"I'm revealing all your workings to the Federacy. All your advertising for victims, accounts of what happened to them, the money you stole, everything."

"I would very much caution you against doing that."

"It's already done. Whether we reach the planet doesn't matter. I have already sent all the information to the news services. I'm going to answer the assembly's questions."

It was bluff but he might believe it.

"Oh no, you're not going to. We will bring the welcoming committee, and you will disappear never to be heard from again. To be honest, I'm sorry that I let you live, all because I had the illusion that you might come around to my point of view."

Ricardo was making some hand signals, which Tina interpreted as to keep him talking while he prepared for a quick dive to the planet.

The transmission stuttered when the shuttle bumped through the outer atmosphere.

"Sorry Dexter, I have no interest in what you have to offer."

"I wouldn't think you were smart enough to know what's

good for you, but your cyborg son will probably want a better life."

"I'll let him decide that for himself."

"I'm sure he will do just that."

The screen at the controls showed that two pursuing craft had followed the shuttle into the atmosphere, but they in turn were followed by the two fighters from the *Manila*. Dragon fighters, Jens had said. These two teenagers knew everything about these dangerous ships. They had spent months and months playing with the simulations.

Ricardo skimmed low over the clouds. "I can't shake them. We're not fast enough."

Then Rex said, "Go mum. We'll distract them."

Ricardo called out, "Hang on, we're going down."

And the shuttle turned upside down in a tight curve and dropped in between the clouds.

For a few heart-stopping moments, the world turned dark grey. Ricardo swung the craft around again, flying purely on instruments.

Then they shot out of the clouds.

The ocean beckoned before them, dark and brooding. It was late afternoon and under the cloud cover, the water appeared black.

Tina searched the radar screen for the two fighters, but they must have lured the attackers out of range, because the screen showed no activity other than their own.

They descended towards the ocean.

Little specks of light indicated the position of boats. The weather was calm.

As the ship landed on the water, Tina could already see the familiar boat close by. Matt was at the controls. Both Veronica and Greta were also on board.

Veronica jumped onto the craft's wing and waded through a breaking wave with the rope to tie the two vehicles together.

Tina opened the door to the craft.

"You go first," she said to Clementine.

The humid breeze came into the cabin. Only the real ocean could smell like that.

"Be quick," Ricardo said. "I don't have a landing permit and need to get out."

"Are you going back to the fleet?" Tina asked.

"If I can. I don't like the communication coming out of the station, so I may need to collect our scientist friends."

Tina stepped into the gathering darkness.

A stiff breeze made the water choppy, and stepping from the craft's wing to the boat was quite dicey. Matt had already helped Clementine across, but she was wet from the waist down, so that manoeuvre hadn't gone to plan.

Veronica handed out blankets.

Tina sat next to Clementine and pulled the crinkly foil-coated sheet over her own and Clementine's knees.

"Are you all right?" she asked.

"I've experienced better things," Clementine said, her face stoic. "But I've also experienced worse."

Tina guessed she was freezing. As added annoyance, it started raining.

Greta sat down on her other side.

While the boat raced towards the mainland, she filled in Tina on what had happened since they had left.

The investigation into the explosion at the resort had revealed that the people who had placed the explosives were hired contractors. There were suspicions about who had hired them, but the investigation had been kept secret, and many people were angry about this.

Protesters in the public gallery had disrupted assembly meetings.

When the authorities closed the public gallery, angry people recruited formal delegates to ask questions on their behalf: about the investigation into the explosion but also about the war and about transparency of war spending and reporting, especially since certain journalists had reported that the war was not over, and that the crew of the *Manila* were in detention for reasons unknown.

Others were still demanding that damned parade, even if the reasons for holding it had shifted from a war victory to defiance against a bureaucracy that obfuscated reality.

By the time Greta finished talking, frequently interrupted by loud thumps of waves slapping against the hull of the ship, the lights of Olympus City blazed on the horizon.

It was now raining in earnest.

The radar at Matt's control panel showed the presence of a number of other vehicles in the area. Some of them were other boats, moving slowly, but others moved much more quickly.

"Air search vehicles?" Tina asked.

"Probably," Matt said, his voice dark.

Tina wondered if he was going to drop them at that jetty again, and they would have to clamber through the muddy water and up the wooden poles. Clementine would have trouble with that.

But Matt steered the boat towards the lights.

They had now come so close that the roofs of the assembly buildings were discernible. The entire Assembly complex blazed in light.

Greta, Veronica and Matt all peered over the bay. The water was not as choppy here, but the intensifying rain made for reduced visibility.

A voice crackled over the radio.

"Ah, there they are." Matt steered the boat straight towards the beach.

Another boat was coming out from the shore to meet them. The thing was flat and wide and resembled a floating pontoon. Two people stood at one end.

One called out to Matt.

He brought the boat alongside. Veronica threw the two men a rope and then helped everyone clamber across.

"Sit down in the middle and grab the handholds," one of the men called out.

Except everything was cold and wet. Tina held one half of her jacket over Clementine, who was shivering.

Fortunately, the platform-boat had a powerful engine. It went right up the beach, where a van waited, all its lights off.

After a scramble through the sand, Tina followed Clementine up the steps into its impossibly warm interior.

Phew.

When everyone was inside, the van started moving. Greta sat just behind the driver, looking over his shoulder. Both kept pointing at a screen that blazed bright light in the darkness of the van's interior. Tina picked up shards of their speech and gathered Greta was afraid that they were being followed.

The bus made its way through leafy back streets.

"Where are we going?" Tina asked.

"A number of members of the assembly are waiting to see us," Greta said. "The president has been warned and is waiting for us."

The rain had stopped. When gaps appeared between the clouds, moonlight glittered off the ocean and the wet streets.

Tina peered into the sky. They'd shaken off their pursuers in orbit, but Tina doubted Dexter and his cronies would give up so easily.

The van came to the entrance of the Assembly precinct. Ahead, a line of guards with guns blocked access into the leafy avenue.

The van stopped. The driver turned to Greta and asked what he should do.

"It's not that far to the assembly hall," Greta said. "There is a back way that goes between the buildings. I know the way well. If we can get out of the bus without anyone noticing, you can wait here and try to negotiate a way in while pretending we're still inside."

The bus backed away around the corner.

Tina, Greta and Clementine got out of the bus on the grassy road verge. The bus took off again immediately.

Greta led them over a dark path that led between dark and tall buildings.

The path opened up ahead, in what looked like the lawn in front of the Federacy Assembly building. The bright glow from the streetlights and the lights directed at the facade of the building created a yellow glow.

Greta stopped at the point where the path ended. There was no more tree cover between here and the steps leading into the building's entrance. And that entrance was open. Armed guards stood on the steps and under the overhang of the entrance porch.

"Are those guys friendly to us?" Tina asked.

Greta said, "I doubt they know what's going on."

For a while, all was quiet. One of the guards walked around the perimeter of the lawn.

But suddenly he looked over his shoulder, in the direction of the boulevard. A vehicle came roaring up the road, swerved around a two guards, ploughed into a flower bed and tore through the middle of the lawn.

Every guard ran after them. One of them fired at the truck.

"Let's go," Greta said.

They ran along the perimeter of the lawn, sticking as much as possible to the shadows. A fight had broken out in the middle of the lawn.

Tina, Clementine and Greta ran up the stairs to the entrance of the building, but as they were about to reach the open door, the truck that has caused the mayhem in the forecourt broke loose from the guards trying to stop it. The vehicle tore across the grass, through another garden bed, and bumped straight up the steps to the building. Guards fired at it, but Tina could see from where she stood that there was no one behind the wheel. The front window shattered, but the truck kept going, coming to a halt against a pillar on the porch.

The entire side of the vehicle ripped open, and a figure jumped out. A pirate.

No. It was Vito, still covered in bandages, but his expression was clear.

And angry.

He grabbed a guard by his clothes and tossed him aside as if he was a rag doll. He flew sideways into a group of colleagues, and the lot of them fell backwards down the stairs.

Meanwhile, other people clambered out. Gerry, Stan, and then smaller people.

Arkady, Thor, Jette, Yalinda, the familiar faces just kept coming.

"What are you all doing here?" Tina asked.

"You didn't think we'd let you go alone?" Arkady said. "That's not why we followed you all this time, to fail at the last moment."

There were so many people, that Tina wondered how they had all crammed into that truck. And she wondered how the group had come here.

But those were tales that would be shared later.

She called out, "Come on, let's go."

A few surprised guards came out of the building but were overwhelmed as the group surged in.

They crossed a richly appointed foyer and then went up a broad staircase. Greta knew where to go.

They came out onto a landing where a couple of doors stood open. Armed guards stood at the entrance of each door, many of them with slightly alarmed expressions on their faces, as more and more people streamed onto the landing.

"President Silvers is waiting for us," Greta said.

"You applied for a group of three. Only three people can go in."

"The rest can wait out here," Greta said. She looked at Tina and Clementine. "Our turn."

Tina followed Greta into a spacious room with soft carpet underfoot and rich furniture.

Some people already sat in the room.

She recognised Federacy Assembly president Jarod Silvers in one of the chairs. Across from him sat someone else, surrounded by four guards.

Dexter.

He glared at Tina as she came in and sat down on a couch opposite the president.

Clementine sat next to her. Greta remained standing.

"I hope this will be worth my time. I don't make a habit of mediating in disputes between married couples," the president began.

And that was enough for Tina.

She understood what sort of man he was.

Jarod Silvers was a man hungry for power and he would accept support from whoever could give it. He wasn't interested in doing what was right. He did things because he was forced to. Tina was through with people like that.

"This is not funny, and it's not a time to make smart remarks. We are here because of the corruption we have uncovered, because of the disregard for basic decency, because of the lies perpetuated by people in the assembly and the military, and because of the blatant and rampant fraud. I sent you the documents that show a fraction of what has been going on."

"Your husband has a different story. He says that he has been helping people who are ill recover."

"While stealing their savings and retirement money," Tina said.

As she said this, Dexter gave her a wide-eyed look. He knew that she knew that she had the files that showed his misconduct. The files he had been desperate to retrieve. Not just since she visited Project Charon, but probably even when she was still at Cayelle. Why else would he have sent Simon Fosnet to give her ultimatums?

Dexter inserted his hand in the pocket of his jacket—

And the guards in the room all ran for him—

And crashed into him as he pulled out the gun—

And fired into the ceiling—

While his chair toppled backwards, with him at the bottom and a pile of guards at the top.

Tina got up and put her reader on the president's desk. She turned it on and pushed it so that he could read the text on the screen, a summary of her conclusions.

Dexter screamed obscenities as the guards held him down.

The president flapped his hand at the guards, who carried Dexter out of the room, tied to his chair.

The president read. He flicked through the data. A few times, his eyes widened.

Then he looked up, said nothing for a while, and then he nodded at the reader.

"Can I have that data?"

"Of course. That's why we're here."

CHAPTER THIRTY-SEVEN

THE PRESIDENT KNEW the game was up.

Tina didn't think he was directly involved, but be had probably known that something wasn't right and had ignored it and tolerated it for as long as this was politically the right thing to do for him.

But now he could no longer avoid the subject.

He asked a lot of questions: who Tina and her group were, why they cared, who else was involved, how they'd found out.

He called in advisers to listen and ask further questions.

Clementine spoke about how the Freerangers had initially helped groups of mutants, but how they had hijacked the term pirates that Freerangers had proudly used for many years.

Tina found it hard to believe that the president was as ignorant of the goings-on as he claimed to be, but even if this was a convenient lie, he couldn't avoid the subject anymore.

He called in a string of people in uniform and shared Tina's document at least six times. Important people came in, took their orders, asked Tina questions, and left again.

By the time the last officials had come and gone, it was starting to get light.

The president invited everyone to breakfast.

As they walked out of the room and went down the stairs, people started cheering.

The entire entrance hall had filled up with people. Many were locals who started chanting Greta's name, but Tina also recognised Freerangers. Young people, who would see who made the decisions about settled space, in a place that was far removed from their lives in deep space. Hopefully, the Freeranger youth would learn that engaging with officials was important.

They made a path to let the group through on the way to breakfast. Tina couldn't see Dexter anywhere.

The Federacy put up Tina and her group in a wing of the accommodation complex that had not been destroyed.

Tina, Finn, Greta and the scientists spent several days answering questions. Arkady did this in between his visits to the hospital, where Vito, Stan and Gerry were taken and where Yalinda and Jette had an eager audience learning about the infection. Tina heard that Jette received several grant offers.

Rex, Jens and Rasa spent most of the time on the beach.

Dexter was in jail and legal people worked on getting him charged while identifying those in the assembly and the Force who had been working with him. Sector General Smith solved the problem for himself by disappearing from his base with one of the Federacy Force's Surface-to-Orbit shuttles. A random patrol later discovered the shuttle adrift, but the General himself remained elusive. Since further investigation brought to light that the airlock had been opened and no suits were missing, one could only assume that the planet of Olympus had acquired a small, human-shaped satellite.

Of course, the process of investigation and charging everyone would take forever.

When Tina heard that her part of the investigation had

concluded, she asked if she could return to the *Alethia* and Cayelle.

Finn wanted to come, and so did Thor and Jens.

Several women had been officially released from duty at the *Manila* and had chosen to step out of the Force. Yonta, Evelle and Margot took up the remaining spots in the *Alethia*.

Tina was surprised that Rasa didn't want to come.

"I want to stay here," Rasa told her. "This is what I wanted to tell you before. When Jens was looking at the pictures of the guy you disturbed in the station, he found a list with people who worked at the Pegasus Agency. My brother is on it. He doesn't go by his real name when he goes out into the world, so that's why I never found him."

"Have you been in contact with him?"

"Yes. He's going to take leave and come here, and then he says he'll put me in a boarding school and then I can learn to be what I want. I think I want to be a teacher."

Tina had to smile at that. She doubted that an urchin like Rasa was going to learn easily, but she told Rasa to keep in contact.

When the *Alethia* left the Orbital Station 3, Tina was glad to go home, but sad to leave many of her new friends.

Clementine and the Freerangers were in their own negotiations with the Federacy. A number of other shipworld family fleets had turned up, much to the consternation of the Olympus locals.

Most of the scientists chose to stay at Olympus, where they had set up a hospital to help affected people recover as much as they could from the infection.

One of the things Tina had secured from the Federacy was money for the development of Gandama that had been promised many times over, but had never eventuated in the fifteen years she'd lived there.

She found the area in disarray.

Pirates had been through the town of Gandama, and the outlying community Dickson's Creek, and had destroyed all the buildings of her shop. The house was uninhabitable. Janusz still lived nextdoor, but the neighbours on the other side had packed up and left Dickson's Creek.

Tina bought the land for a ridiculously low price, and the group camped in their house while rebuilding Tina's house, the shop, a workshop, and restaurant. Work was scarce in Gandama, and young people lined up to help.

Margot's eatery opened to the public not much later. It was a simple place, where people sat on mismatched chairs looking over Janusz's fields sipping tea and eating cactus chips while Yonta entertained them, where they could buy wonderful cactuses while Finn and Thor fixed their vehicles. They came from all over the district and even Peris City.

The day Tina heard that Dexter was jailed for forty years, they all had a big party.

Aurora Station returned to Federacy control. The Force swept through Artan's labs, publishing horrifying images of rows of stasis cubicles, abandoned labs with dead mutants and lists of thousands and thousands of names, mostly of Federacy recruits, who had passed through the facility, and vanished without a trace.

The Force had discovered Artan in his private quarters, unable to move because his tentacles had grown through the fabric and structure of his chair. He was, the report said, in excellent health, even if the state of squalor suggested that he'd been trapped in this position for months.

Ew.

Since the publicly available report only stated that "he had passed away", Tina found a military report about how the Force had tried—and failed—to shoot him, and that an officer with a knife had ended his life "after considerable struggle".

Double ew.

Even while hungry, unable to move freely, and having sat in his own shit for months, he was dangerous.

Vito, Stan and Gerry were doing much better. They secured jobs driving trucks and collecting rubbish at the Federacy complex.

Evelle returned to space, but instead of the military, she signed up with a volunteer organisation that helped stricken ships, marooned crew abused by their captains, and mutant pirates wanting to get treatment. She would sometimes send Tina orphaned kids to help with the workshop, the restaurant, the cactuses, or just to recover and find time to locate their families or move to a permanent foster family. The kids often remained in Gandama or even Dickson's Creek, working for the farms, now that the planet was in a cool cycle and the rivers flowed again.

Rex and Jens eventually signed up for the Federacy Force, but both secured planet-based positions, mapping the desert of Cayelle and its resources. Margot became interested in politics and entered the Gandama council, while Finn became interested in Yonta and produced three children in impossibly close succession.

And Tina ran her shop and grew her cactuses, and made sure that everyone who came to her community was made to feel welcome.

———

Thanks for Reading

THANK you for reading *Project Charon 4: Swarm*. As the author of this book, I would hugely appreciate it if you could return to where you purchased it and write a short review. Thanks so much!

Never again miss a new release and get four books free if you sign up for my newsletter.

ABOUT THE AUTHOR

Patty Jansen lives in Sydney, Australia, where she spends most of her time writing Science Fiction and Fantasy.

Her story *This Peaceful State of War* placed first in the second quarter of the Writers of the Future contest and was published in their 27th anthology. She has also sold fiction to genre magazines such as Analog Science Fiction and Fact, Redstone SF and Aurealis.

Patty has written over thirty novels in both Science Fiction and Fantasy, including the *Icefire Trilogy* and the *Ambassador* series.

pattyjansen.com

BOOKS BY PATTY JANSEN

MORE INFORMATION:

PATTYJANSEN.COM

For a complete list of books, scan the image below with your phone.

www.ingramcontent.com/pod-product-compliance
Lightning Source LLC
Chambersburg PA
CBHW060802190726
48285CB00002B/517